Slamba... Com...

A new day had dawned over the wild wastes of the Arndale Centre and Arnold was on his way to school. He was doing well today. He had remembered his sports gear. But not well enough. Today it was swimming. He felt great and he had just thought of a new adventure on Klaptonia. His bride to be, Roshan, had vanished on the eve of their wedding and he had to choose: did he ride off to rescue her, or did he hang back just in case it was a plot by the dreaded Purple People to capture him? Life was difficult for heroes. And when you were a coward in real life, it was twice as difficult.

What Arnold did not know was that right at that moment, in real life, a cunning, dastardly and utterly ruthless enemy was lying in wait to destroy him . . .

Robert Leeson

Slambash Wangs of a Compo Gormer

LIONS · TEEN TRACKS

First published in Great Britain 1987 by William Collins Sons & Co. Ltd
Published in Lions Teen Tracks 1988
Second impression November 1988

Lions Teen Tracks is an imprint of
the Children's Division, part of
the Collins Publishing Group,
8 Grafton Street, London W1X 3LA

Printed and bound in Great Britain by
William Collins Sons & Co. Ltd, Glasgow

For all compo bonzot kojers

KLAPTONIAN YURBUL

Important yurbs to know in Klaptonia

YACCA   or   GREETING

Brecca Yacca	Good Morning	Pacca Yacca	Bon Voyage
Snacca Yacca	Bon Appetit	Shacca Yacca	Bless This House
Nacca Yacca	Good Evening	Lucca Yacca	Congratulations
Sacca Yacca	Good Night	Wacca Yacca	Hi, Friend!
Cracca Yacca	Merry Christmas	Fracca Yacca	Come Outside
Licca Yacca	Good Health		

(You can invent more. But be careful. Klaptonians are touchy)

DAJIS OF THE WEEG   or   DAYS OF THE WEEK

Sizda	Sunday	There are:
Soggerda	Rainday	Sef dajis in a weeg
Murda	Mist-day	Flor weegs in a monz
Blizda	Snow-day	Wonti-tree monzes in a yex
Wafda	Winday	
Verda	Greenday	
Gloda	Warm-day	

DIDJERS   or   NUMBERS

Won	One	Wonti-won	Eleven
Too	Two	Wonti-too	Twelve
Tree	Three	Wonti-tree	Thirteen
Flor	Four	and so on	
Fry	Five	Tooti	Twenty
Sox	Six	Treeti	Thirty
Sef	Seven	Florti	Forty
Yate	Eight	Fryti	Fifty
Nan	Nine	and so on	
Wonti	Ten	Wunter	Hundred
		Wumper	Thousand

So a Wumpa or a Thousand Pats or
paces is a Klaptonian mile.

(For fuller vocabulary turn to p.282)

Chapter
1

KEEN-BLADED SWORD in one hand, wicked needle sharp dagger in the other, he sprang lightly down the curving stone steps that spiralled into the depths of the castle. Below lay the dungeons, their dark corners full of horror, behind him his pursuers, baffled, furious and deadly. He paused for a moment to gather strength for his next move, his mind concentrating on the task ahead.

Suddenly a voice broke into his thoughts.

"Arnold, put that book away and eat up your Crunchy Snibbles."

He stared blankly in front of him. There across the table sat Mum and Dad. She was smiling, he was frowning. Arnold protested:

"Aw no, Mum. I've just got to the exciting bit. I have to decide whether to be taken down to the dungeon to be tortured or leap off the battlement into the shark infested moat."

Dad spoke. He always looked big. But when he used this voice he looked even bigger.

"It's nothing to what'll happen to you if you don't get ready for school."

Arnold stared:

"School? What for? It's Saturday, isn't it?"

Mum shook her head.

"No, love. That was last week. It's Monday now."

It all came back.

"Oh, no," said Arnold desperately. "It's Games today and I've . . ."

He sprang up, snatching his razor sharp sword from its scabbard and leapt lightly towards the door. His chair crashed over.

"Don't panic," soothed Mum. "I've packed your bag. It's . . ."

"Great, thanks, Mum. Where is it?"

". . . on the floor, love, just . . ."

Arnold found it, with his foot. He fell across the kitchen floor.

". . . by your feet," Mum finished the sentence calmly.

Arnold's head rose above the kitchen table.

"What did you put it there for, Mum?"

"So you wouldn't miss it, love. Now go and brush your teeth before you . . ."

"Can I take my book with . . .?"

"Don't be silly. You can't read a book and clean your teeth at the same time."

There were some things that even his Mum didn't know.

"Aw, Mum . . ."

She shook her head and Arnold left the kitchen. He surged up the stairs, keen-bladed sword in one hand, tripped over his pyjama leg and sprawled over the top landing, just as he heard Dad's voice from the kitchen:

"Just look at this load of old rubbish 'The Castle of Doom'. You know, that lad worries me."

Mum smiled. "Oh, he's all right. Just a bit absent minded."

"Absent minded," snorted Dad. "He doesn't know whether he's coming or going."

"Oh, I wouldn't say that," Mum looked up at the ceiling and called.

"Hurry up love. You'll just make it if you run."

There was a clatter as Arnold crashed down the stairs and burst into the kitchen.

"Where's my sports gear, Mum?"

"On the floor, love . . ."

Arnold fell over it.

"Just under your feet."

He picked himself up.

"Thanks, Mum."

He looked across the table.

"Can I have my book please?"

Dad shook his head.

"No, I'm reading it. Anyway, you've got it wrong."

Arnold brightened up.

"You mean it's not sports today?"

Dad made a face.

"No, there's another way out, through the torture chamber."

He turned the page and said no more. Mum picked up the breakfast dishes and left the kitchen. Arnold left the house.

With one bound he vaulted on to the back of the thoroughbred horse that stood outside, metalled harness gleaming in the spring sunlight. With a scramble of hooves he set the beast in a wild gallop along the edge of the cliff, while below the wild sea surged.

"Hello Arnie."

Arnold wobbled on the edge of the pavement, traffic noise in his ear. A slim dark girl in school uniform was grinning at him.

He blushed. "Oh, hi, Sandra."

"It's Sharon, actually. Listen, Arnold, why have you got your windcheater on back to front?"

" 'Cos the wind blows through the zip holes." He gazed thoughtfully at her. "Got to hurry, be late for school."

"You're going the wrong way, Arnie."

He wasn't listening. "See you, Sandra . . ."

She watched him go, shaking her head. Why did she have to fall for the Wally of the Year at School? It was a fact. He'd won it three years running. There wasn't any real competition when Arnold was around. But, she thought, he's really quite nice, quite intelligent. Just disorganised. She shouted after him:

"''Shall I walk with you – see you over the road?''

He called back from the middle of the High Street.

''You're putting me on. Bye.''

Next instant there was a grinding shriek from the brakes of a twenty-ton lorry as it loomed up over him. From high in the cab, the driver, who had aged ten years in the last two seconds, looked down, speechless.

Arnold looked up blankly, then bowed low towards the driver.

''Stacca grovels, O Nurbul Topwon,'' he called.

The driver's mouth fell open. He gawped as Arnold made a whipping gesture with his right hand and galloped up on to the farther pavement. Shaking his head, he slid in the clutch and the truck moved on.

How was the driver to know that he had just missed running down, not an insignificant and totally disorientated third year, but Himsir Dornal, Replic of the Yondo Mondo of Tanji Klaptonia, distant world that spins through the cosmos a million light years from Earth. Dornal, no older than Arnold, was the popular prince of this world, heroic, capable, impetuous, undisputed leader, Hodbung Slammer of the Bashi Rangles. The inhabitants of Klaptonia ranged the plains, swamps and mountains of the Orange Planet, speaking their own exotic language, engaged in never ending battle to the death, which only the boldest, most skilful, reckless and decisive, could survive.

Each day as Arnold wandered to and from school, usually the wrong way, the fantastic planet came to life in his head, the weird landscape, mighty warriors, ferocious foes, human and monster. There, whenever he could escape in his dreams, he lived and fought, master of his destiny, bold young leader of a world he had shaped himself.

It was an incredible place, known only to Arnold. Even Sharon, listening sympathetically, as they walked home from school in the afternoon, could not share in all its mysteries. For Klaptonia was full of secrets.

And there was one secret which even Arnold did not know. Life on Klaptonia went on, even when he wasn't thinking about it.

Chapter 2

THERE ARE FOUR roads from Tipalac, chief city of Klaptonia. To the north and south they lead to the vast level plains where humble clodders toil amid the endless fields of wallock plants. To the East lies the great tideless sea of Necoa, source of Klaptonia's mysteries. And in the distant west rise the brooding blue-shadowed mountains, the Prussy Peakers.

Across the westward road lies a hugh stretch of wild country, swamps and tangled forests, bottomless ravines, infested by creatures of unspeakable evil. Here are the Killing Swamps, the Bashi Rangles, where the warriors in their five moblots or divisions, Bladers, Slammers, Crushers, Skullers and Shredders find glory or renown. The way to the west is only for the brave or for the insane.

Here, in the Bashi Rangles, as the sun swept up into the dazzling sky, Himsir Dornal, Prince of Klaptonia, swung down lightly from his long-necked, six-legged nedder and took his stand on the rank grass of a forest clearing. Today he was to face his greatest combat test, to win the rank of Hodbung Shredder. In the distance, Klaptonians crowded to the city walls, orange faces alight with excitement as they gazed down on the wasting wilderness. Above them, from the high tower sounded the booming voice of the Slamboss, Controller of the Killing Games.

"Oh, Tanji Klaptonians, your Slamboss yurbles. Today is a slam to the morb in the Wonzo Moblot, a wango rumble to the last glob of gora. On this side, Himsir Dornal, Replic of our Nurbul Topwon..."

A storm of cheering burst from the crowd at the name of their prince.

"... soon to be ringed with Hermiss Roshan, Replica of the Topwon of Necoa — whose glinti blusher he has never iballed..."

The mention of Dornal's unknown bride-to-be brought a gust of sighs from the women and girls in the crowd.

At this moment, Dornal struck the rump of his nedder which lumbered away into the trees. He drew his long two-handed Misti Sticcer, his Magic Sword, and let it sweep in a glittering circle through the silent air. The crowd drew a deep breath all together. Dornal was ready to fight to the death, not to run or retreat. Again the voice of Slamboss boomed:

"On the yondo side, no less than flor hostos..."

Four opponents? Four against one. There was a sudden, deathly silence from the walls of the city. Slamboss went on:

12

"Flor hostos. The Loomgru shroudi and lurci ..."

As he spoke, swirling in menace, the Night Monster appeared in the clearing.

"The Hulko Vaster, with his morbi reechers ..."

Grunting, the Long Armed Giant lumbered forward from the trees.

"The Sef Bonced Coiler."

Out of the sweltering undergrowth, slid the Seven Headed Snake, its hissing tongues darting towards the unmoving face of Himsir Dornal.

"Last," bellowed Slamboss, "the won you gruj to siccers, the one you love to hate ..."

The voice paused as the crowd broke into a storm of disgusted booing.

"SLURD SLUG."

The oozing white bulk of the Slime Slug welled out of the rank grass.

"Since Himsir Dornal is the rajist, the bravest slammer in Klaptonia, to chex that he is fit to be ringed with Hermiss Roshan, that he is fit for the Rank of Hodbung Shredder, he must slam, and champ these flor hostos – at wonz."

At one go? "Aaaaah," breathed the crowd.

"They will attack him at wonz."

"Cor," murmured a thousand voices.

"And Himsir Dornal will be allowed only won dong of his Misti Sticcer."

One blow? Dornal turned and looked up at the tower. There was amazement in his voice.

"I yurb! I say! Flor hostos, at wonz, with won dong?"

"Hissers!" cried the spectators.

The Slamboss roared again, this time with an unpleasant tone.

"Is anyone winkling that the rules of this slam are hoko?"

There was a fearful silence. No one but no one challenged the rules.

"Let the slam begin."

The crowd watched in frozen horror as the attackers strode, sprang, slurred, skidded, slithered and slobbered upon the young prince. He stood stock still, not a move of his limbs as his devious, dastardly foes closed in their foul breath clouding the morning air around him.

"Won dong, Himsir Dornal," bellowed Slamboss for the last time.

Dornal shrugged.

"Acco, acco," he assented. He breathed in and began the count down: 'Tree, too, won." Then he flexed his young muscles and made the blade spin in a singing arc of light around him, and with a cry of,

"DONGO!"

He struck once and once only in a tremendous swing of mortal doom which seared through the ranks of his enemies.

"Aaaargh. Yaaah. Oooooh." The howls of triumph changed in an instant to shrieks of agony. Ghastly bodies collapsed in a welter of spurting gore. The perfect circle of light formed by the Magic Sword vanished. The long blade dropped to Dornal's side swinging on his wrist-thong. In the silence that followed Slamboss's voice cut short any cheers.

"Himsir Dornal has champed tree at won dong. A reppi doo, never before iballed in the Bashi Rangles. But not enough. Won hosto remains: the Sef Bonced Coiler."

The crowd, mute with horror, saw the writhing Snake with Seven Heads, eyes glittering with malice, rise seemingly unharmed above the carnage.

Slamboss spoke: "By our doolis, our rules, the Sef

Bonced Coiler must now have the hando dong, the next blow."

Cries of distress resounded from the city walls. Handkerchiefs were pressed to weeping eyes. Strong bladers turned their backs unable to watch the horrible fate of their young prince who now stood still, sword at his side.

The Snake hissed in fearful glee, its sleek scaly body swaying above Himsir Dornal.

"Breezed me. Now it's my dong."

"Oh, yum?" replied Dornal calmly. "Breezed you did I? Kindly nod your bonces — all of them."

Without thinking the Seven Headed Snake nodded.

"Ooooo — aaah —." His howl was cut short as the seven deadly heads thudded as one to the ground and the twisting coils shrank into a lifeless heap, amid a torrent of cheering from the city walls.

Dornal whistled to his nedder, sprang into the saddle and rode towards the city walls.

From his tower the voice of Slamboss was silent.

Chapter
3

DORNAL URGED HIS trusty nedder through the admiring crowds that swarmed around the gilded palace gate. Then, throwing the reins over the beast's neck and leaving it to the care of a groom, he moved swiftly up the marble steps and down the broad passage way into the ornate throne room.

As he burst in, dripping sword swinging carelessly at his wrist his mother Topma raised eyebrows and shoulders:

"Darlo Dornal, how many toccas have I asked you not to glob gora on the wall hangings. We can't have a re-dec every tocc you champ the slams."

"Oh, don't be narco, Topma," replied Dornal brusquely. "I must yurb with the Nurbul Topwon — at wonz."

"Why, Replic, you look quite siccers."

"Yum, Mawon, I have a finkle that the Grand Slams are being rigged."

Topma shook her head.

"That must wait. Your Fawon, the Slamboss and Necro the Hoker, are waiting in the Yurbi Cham. They have a far more doobic matter."

Dornal turned towards the Council Chamber with a grimace, but without another word to his mother. As he entered three men bent over maps on the table looked up — the Topwon, an older, fatter copy of Dornal, Necro the Court Hoker or Magician, stringy, short-sighted with straggly white hair, and Slamboss, huge, richly dressed, bald head above the brutal face covered with three strands of green tinted hair, plastered down. They bowed and greeted him:

"Stacca Yaccas, O Nurbul Replic."

Dornal nodded: "Fawon, I must yurb with you — but singo."

The Topwon looked across at Slamboss, then shook his head: "Not now, Dornal this matter is more nojo."

"Zitto," interrupted Slamboss, "Nurbul Replic, we have scanned a scim."

Dornal's eyebrows rose. Slamboss was always discovering plots.

"Well, what is it this time – an inslam, a snaff or a morb?"

There was a sudden quiet sound of chuckling, which vanished as Slamboss snarled at Necro, whose hand was held in front of his mouth.

"WHAT ARE YOU CHIMPLING FOR?"

Necro wagged his white head and answered, face now quite straight.

"I'm not chimpling, Shrefful Slamboss. It's just my aji flutt, my nervous twitch."

Dornal went on: "All these scims. Nothing ever occas does it?"

"Zitto," answered Slamboss swiftly. "My Lurci Flunkaj spokes all hokes, trims all scims and baffs all snaffs."

Dornal stared. Secret Service? What was this? "I've never iballed a Lurci Flunkaj round here," he said.

"Nibbic," replied Slamboss triumphantly. "It is so lurci. That's why it's so champi."

The Topwon coughed and pointed to the table.

"This tocca, O Dornal, the scim is more rixi. It is an inslam, and a snaff, and a morb."

Dornal's eyebrows rose. Invasion, kidnapping and murder all at once!

"Who is it this tocca?"

The Slamboss came round the table and stood over Dornal. He was twice as big as him and knew it.

"The Gloami Kojers, from across the Prussy Peakers, plot to inslam our Topwondom. They are scimming to snaff and morb you. They know this is the only way an inslam could succeed."

"What chex do you have of this?"

The Topwon turned from looking at the map.

"The froobli Hermiss Roshan has shivanned, gone without trace, just before your ringing. She must be in the shredd of the Gloami Kojers."

Dornal leapt to his feet pushing back his chair.

"Then I atta mount my shreddi nedder and gallop to div her."

"That's my wipper," said the Topwon admiringly. Slamboss raised his hand.

"Numdo, that is what the Gloami Kojers hank. You will jacc right into their piccers. I have a better scim."

"What?" asked Dornal. "Inslam the Gloami Kojers?"

The Topwon looked shocked.

"That is grooso rixi. No one has inslammed the Topwondom of the Gloami Kojers."

"Well, they have nocca inslammed us," retorted Dornal.

The Slamboss raised a finger.

"Nibbic. We have been too triggo for them."

"So, what are we fratching for?"

"Have you forgotten, Nurbul Replic? Hermiss Roshan is in their piccers perhaps suffering torture. I command you, Himsir, to go to a secure place, and jacco ..."

"Just a nimmot," interrupted the Topwon indignantly. "Who's freebing the doosos round here? Sonwon, I doos you to todd to a shelto loc and ..."

His voice trailed away foolishly. Slamboss began again.

"... and ding there until we wig it is shelto to return. Unless they can get their piccers on you, they can nocca inslam."

"Ding a nimmot," said Dornal, baffled. "If I'm not here, they'll inslam won't they?"

"This wipper's no gormer," said his father admiringly.

18

"Ah ha," replied Slamboss. "Not if they do not know you are gone."

"You mean," Dornal's face was a study of bewilderment. "I'll know I'm bego, but they won't?"

"Nibbic," said Topwon.

Dornal shook his head: "Sinters, brilliant."

The Slamboss turned savagely on the Court Magician.

"What are you chimpling for, you seeni Hoker?"

Necro covered his mouth with his hand.

"I'm not chimpling, Shrefful Slamboss. It's just my aji flutt."

Necro raised a thin arm in his long, black robes.

"Nurbul Replic," he said to Dornal. "If you will kindly todd with me to the Hoki Cham, I will explain our wizzi scim to you."

Chapter
4

DORNAL WRINKLED HIS nose as he followed Necro through the heavy studded door into the Hoki Cham, the Spell Chamber. The air was thick with smoke and steam and the smell was atrocious. Amid the haze came the sound of bubbling cauldrons and retorts. The slim, dark figure of a girl in dirty brown tunic stood near the circular table, Necro saw her and spoke sharply.

"Zoff!"

The girl slipped past Dornal, eyes downcast, and went out.

"That flunker-dima is always hanging about. Always moling," grumbled Necro. Dornal shrugged. All servants looked alike to him. Necro pointed to the table with its polished mirror top.

"Scan the Misti Crist, O Nurbul Replic," he invited.

As Dornal approached the table a sinuous shape uncoiled itself on the chair, eyes glittering, deadly tongue flickering. Dornal raised his foot and booted the snake away. Sitting down, he gazed into the smooth polished surface of the Magic Mirror. The image was covered in clouds. Necro made a pass with his hand across it.

"The murgs are cristing. What do you ibe, O Nurbul?"

Dornal peered at the picture.. He could see the crowded streets of a strange city. Great buildings reared up, throngs of people hurried by. What seemed to be carriages without nedders to pull them, hurried along. It looked like a madhouse to him. He turned to Necro.

"What is this wangi place?" he demanded.

"That is another mondo, another planet, which we know as Dirt. But the kojers there are so snobbot that they call it 'Earth'. This is the mondo from where the first Klaptonians came, a thousand yexes ago. Scan hander. What do you ibe?"

Dornal looked at the hurrying people in the picture, first at the weird flapping clothing on arms and legs, next — he stared at their faces, mostly a kind of dirty-pink in colour. That was even weirder. He turned to Necro.

"Well, you could yurb that these are kojers, like we are. But their cloot and tinjer are just nuffi."

"Yumda," answered Necro, "blanco, white is a yonco tinjer."

"Blanco? You must be chimpling. Their tinjer isn't blanco, it's rosi-dirt. And," Dornal pointed, "those kojers over there are carbi, black."

"Yes, I know," said Necro hastily. "But remember that the toppo tinjer, the official colour on Dirt, is blanco and they think it is a glinti tinjer."

Dornal's lip curled: "Blanco, rosi-dirt, those are not tinjers. Now, tanji, like we are, that is a crozmi tinjer. Or gloami even, like our hostos, the Gloami Kojers...

"Yumda," went on Dornal. "Gloami, I can imagine gloami." He turned suddenly to Necro. "Tell me, have you ever hanked to shanx across the Prussy Peakers and ibe the Gloami Kojers?"

Necro looked round nervously.

"Well, yum, I have, but I've nocca yurbed it. After all the Gloami Kojers are our hostos, our yarbon hostos."

Dornal shrugged, then he laughed.

"But, rosi-dirt. How can anyone hank to be rosi-dirt?"

Necro looked embarrassed.

"I fear, O Nurbul, you will have to wonz to lux it."

"What is this burbul yurbul?" asked Dornal astonished.

Necro coughed.

"Our wizzi scim, O Replic, is to slyp you down the Misti Slypa to Dirt, and shuff you with a Dirt wipper who scans like you."

"Like me?" The Prince's voice rose.

"Ibe that young kojer, who stands by the road, there."

Dornal followed Necro's pointing finger.

"Him, that gormer? Can't even wig to cross the

road. You must be ex your misti bonce."

Necro slowly shook his head.

"Numda, O Nurbul. That wipper is as like you as a duplic, apart from his nuffi rosi-dirt tinjer."

Dornal felt his head begin to swim.

"You mean, I'll take his loc on Dirt, while he cops my loc up here?"

"That is the scim."

"Num!"

"Nurbul Replic. It must be so if our scim is to work."

"But he ... I ... How will it all ...?"

Necro rose and bowed.

"Ma-da, tomorrow, I shall scroll you more."

He bowed once more and ushered the Prince to the door. As it swung open, Dornal heard the scurry of footsteps outside. He thought he saw the ragged figure of the servant girl disappearing down the dark passage.

Chapter
5

MEANWHILE, DOWN ON Dirt, a new day had dawned over the wild wastes of the Arndale Centre. Arnold was on his way to school. He waved vaguely to Sharon as he hurried along the pavement. He was going the right way for a change, but Sharon kept an eye on him, just in case.

He was doing well today. He had remembered his sports gear. But not well enough. Today it was swimming. He wasn't late, as it happened, but he thought he was, so it didn't make any difference. Because this morning, as he struggled out of bed, he suddenly thought of a new adventure for Himsir Dornal.

His bride to be, Roshan, had vanished on the eve of their wedding and Dornal had to choose. Did he ride off to rescue her, or did he hang back just in case it was a plot by the dreaded Gloami Kojers, the Purple People, to get their hands on him? Life was difficult for heroes. And when you were a coward in real life, it was twice as difficult.

What Arnold did not know was that right at that moment, in real life, a cunning, dastardly and utterly ruthless enemy was lying in wait to destroy him. Not him Dornal, but him Arnold.

It was a firm called the Yobs. There were four of them. They each had names and two of them had birth certificates. But they were known as Eenie — he was No. 1, Meanie — because he wasn't very nice, Mynie — because things that belonged to other people mysteriously became his, and Mo — because he was an under achiever. He was as planky as they come, in fact. But provided Eenie pointed him in the right direction, he could be a real dangeroo.

Their real mission in life was providing alternative entertainment for the crowds at Denfield Rovers, on Saturday afternoons, when the home team wasn't doing very well. Unlike the home team, the Yobs always won their fixtures. But, during the week, they had to keep their hand in, and since they didn't want to go on camera with marks on them, they picked soft targets.

Arnold was one of them. Arnold was No. 1 soft target. There wasn't much to duffing him up, it was the prelims that made it worthwhile.

So, there they were, on their way, happy as sandbags, heading through the Arndale. As they tripped along, they sang, and shopkeepers hearing them in the distance, made haste to put up their shutters.

If you go down on the Street today
You'd better go in disguise
If you go down on the Street today
We'll give you a bunch of fives
It's no good telling the Fuzz — me Dad's
A police inspector and he's just as bad
Today's the day the Teddy Boys have their picnic.
Nick, nick time for Teddy Boys
They romp along all full of horrible joys.
At six o'clock, their Mummies and Daddies
Will come and bail them out,
Because they're all tired Teddy Boys.

Ms Heathcote, Head of Denfield Comprehensive, was waiting in her car by the junction on High Street when she saw the Yobs standing menacingly near the traffic lights. She rolled down the window.

"Hello, boys."

"Hello, Miss," they chorused cheerfully, shuffling their feet.

"I don't think you should be hanging about here. You'll be late."

"Oh, you're OK, Miss," said Meanie. "We're just hanging about for Arnold."

He grinned evilly.

"We're going to . . . aaargh!"

Eenie's boot caught him a crack on the ankle bone. Eenie finished the sentence:

". . . to see him across the road."

"Yer, when the lights are green," muttered Mynie.

"That is nice," said the Head, beaming at them. "But, don't be late, yourselves."

She rolled up the window and drove off, leaving the Yobs staring at one another.

"She's a right wimp," said Mynie.

"Don't be dimmo," said Meanie. "Birds can't be wimps."

"She's a nice bit of crumpet," said Mo, his eyes glistening.

Eenie turned and thumped Mo.

"What do you know about crumpet? You can't even spell it."

"Yeah I can," said Mo. "K ..."

"Hang about," interrupted Meanie. "Our lovely boy's coming."

"Right," said Eenie. "Get in the 'phone box. When he comes past, get him to step in, and take a call from Madagascar."

"Nah, he won't believe you."

"Him, he'll believe anything."

"He's nearly here now ..."

They slid into hiding, as the victim, sports gear under his arm, came into view.

Chapter
6

THE CLOUDS COVERING Necro's magic mirror cleared and once again, Dornal saw the distant planet, Dirt, unfold. Gradually the image grew larger and he saw once more the street scene with its crowds, its huge buildings and moving carriages. He shook his head.

"Do I crozmi have to todd to that wangi loc?" he asked.

Necro tut-tutted: "Nurbul Replic. We must now yurb Dirt-way."

Dornal began again, hesitantly: "Do I truly have to go to that crazy place?"

"Do not fratch, O Nurbul. Life will be different there, but you will get accustomed to it. No need to be timpi."

"I am not timpi," yelled Dornal. He, the hero of a hundred gora slams in the Bashi Rangles, afraid? Still, he was feeling rather strange in his inside.

"It's this wangi way they yurble," he said, then went on slowly. "How can anyone who isn't totally out of their bonce, yurb at-way."

"It is the way everyone used to talk, Nurbul," said Necro helpfully, "until our ancestors discovered the way along the Slypa to Klaptonia."

"Ah, yes, the Beam. I've never quite understood the Beam."

"The Slypa," proclaimed Necro pompously, "is one of the wonders of Nature. By means of the Beam, one can pass from Klaptonia to Dirt in twenty seconds."

"But you said it was millions of wumpas, of miles away."

"I know. It is like a slide down a bannister. One moment you are up here, next moment you are down there."

Dornal brooded on this a moment then,

"Wait a minute. If I slide down, how do I slide back?"

He rose and took Necro by the front of his robe.

"I am not STAYING down there."

"Oh, no, Nurbul. When the time comes you will be able to slide back."

"How?"

"Well, you won't be sliding up. It'll be down. Because then you'll be up there and we'll be down here."

Dornal frowned. "Suppose two people slide from either end at the same time."

"That never happens," said Necro hastily. "These days the Beam is only used in a dopa, an emergency. Nobody at the other end knows about it, anyway."

"What do you mean, these days?"

Necro hesitated: "Well, a long time ago, in my Pawon's day, there used to be regular trips. Pawon scrolled me all about Dirt and going to school and all that." His voice was wistful. "But that all stopped."

"Why?"

Necro looked over his shoulder: "Slamboss decided that it was a security rix. Imagine what would happen if the Gloami Kojers knew about it."

"I can't. But never mind. Tell me about School. What is it?"

Necro began to speak, but after a while, Dornal interrupted him.

"You mean, people in their right minds, sit in this house all day and make marks on bits of paper."

He looked despairingly at the magician.

"I'll never get used to it. I mean, I keep wyping — forgetting those yurbs you taught me."

"Sluff, sluff. Calm, O Replic. There are not only lessons in School. There are Games on the playing field."

"Ah, Slams," the Prince's eyes shone.

Necro shook his head quickly.

"Do not get the wrong idea. There is no morbing, no killing. But — er — you may frac reechers and

standers — break arms or legs," he added comfortingly.

"That's better than nothing," mused Dornal.

"But, only by accident. Otherwise it is poggi slam,
and no fair play."

"By accident. What does that mean?"

"The Games Master must be looking the other
way."

Dornal smiled suddenly. "Ah ..." he began.

Necro's head wagged.

"No dongers are allowed, no weapons."

"What no cutter, no sticcer."

"No."

"No twanger, no gasher?"

"No, no."

"Not even a little razor-edged jabber."

"Numda. Abso numda, Nurbul. All injuries must be
caused with fist or boot in fair play."

"Yonco ... strange ..." said Dornal. Then he
frowned again.

"This tinjer, this colour business worries me."

The Magician rose and waved his hand.

"When you pass down the Slypa, your tinjer will
shuff, your colour will change little by little. When
you reach Dirt, you will be white — well, dirty-pink,
like the rest of them — or most of them.

"But," continued Necro, "certain parts of you, vital
parts will remain the true colour. Under great stress
or excitement, the true tanji colour will return to all
parts. So remember," Necro grew solemn, "do not get
excited, do not attract attention. Do as you are told,
even when you are badly treated or punished."

"Wiccot? Punished? Me?"

"Yum, Nurbul. On Dirt juvis are reggo wiccot.
Being punished regularly makes them grow up Nice
People."

"It would just make me siccers."

"Oh, no Nurbul. That will never do. If you are furious you will turn tanji again and that will make you yonco, different from the others, and that will be a disaster."

"You mean I'll have to creep around like a hovel clodder, all the time. I'll go mad. I'll burst. I'm NOT GOING."

Necro shook his head.

"Num. No, no, no. That will not do. Look on the bright side. There is lots of fun at school. At midnight in the dormitory, there are feasts, buttered muffins and cream cake. And pillow fights."

"What are those?"

Necro shrugged: "I am not sure. I have only read about them in Dirti-Scrolls."

He smiled and went on dreamily. "In the end, you will fight the school bully behind the gymnasium, and thanks to your skills and bravery, the school will win the vital rugger match."

"What is rugger?"

"Ah, a slam with thirty players and an egg-shaped lobber. One player grabs the ball and ..."

"What do the other twenty-nine do?"

"Ah, they leap on each other with many violent oaths and hurl each other to the ground."

Dornal was becoming more cheerful. Necro looked at him with relief. He waved towards the door.

"Nurbul Replic, you must soon be triggo to bego, ready to depart. You'll be escorted, for you must travel unarmed. Even now Slamboss is giving orders to the Secret Service. Go to your room and wait. So secret is the mission that our agents will be hooded and unknown to you."

"I'd better say pacca yaccas to Topma. Bit of a narc."

"I fear not. Only we must know that you are being exchanged for the Dirt Wipper. Otherwise the Gloami Kojers may find out."

He looked guiltily at Dornal.

"Pacca Yaccas O Nurbul Himsir. Todd slecc."

"Yaccas, Occul Necro."

As the Prince left the Spell Chamber, Necro sank down by the Magic Mirror and looked once more at it before waving a hand to clear it.

In the passage outside, Dornal almost fell over the crouching figure of the dark-haired servant girl. She leapt up and stood in his path. For a second she gazed at him, then grovelled. "Nurbul Replic, a yurb with you."

Dornal stared at her, in distaste. "Zoff! Back to your graf, dima. I have nojo doofers to doo, than eerol a graftona."

He shoved her aside and strode away down the passage.

Chapter 7

IN HIS FUR-LINED chamber at the heart of the palace, the Slamboss sat alone, eating fresh grilled chunks of flork, shot on the wing that day and washing it down with large gulps of yoot wine. A deep frown ran lines from the top of his nose on to the ridged plateau of his bald head. Dornal was not turning out the way his father, the Topwon had.

There was something unpredictable about him, like thinking now and then. Still, you could get treatment for that.

A discreet knock at the door behind him made the Slamboss cock his ear.

"Inco," he grunted.

The door half opened and two figures slid in, closing it behind them. They made a low grovel and stood in front of him. One was huge, ape-shouldered with a blank expression. The other was small, far more intelligent and wicked looking. They were Hitman and Nobbin, father and son, most trusted members of the Lurci Flunkaj, the Secret Service. In fact they *were* the Secret Service. Keeping it small, kept it secret. And since Hitman was too thick to do anything he wasn't told, and Nobbin was so ratty he always split on his father, the Secret Service was totally under Slamboss's control. Knowing this helped him sleep at night. He loved those boys.

"Eerol," he said. They listened respectfully. "Here are your doosos. You will shanx with the Replic Dornal down to the yondo mondo of Dirt."

"Sinters," said Nobbin. "And morb a stacca Dirties."

Hitman lifted his son up in the air by his hair and dropped him to the floor, stunning him.

"Grovels! O Shrefful Slamboss," he said.

Slamboss continued: "On Dirt you must find a juvi Dirtwon, who scans like the Replic Dornal. You will shuff them, and their cloot. You will bring the Dirtwon to Klaptonia, and you will leave Replic Dornal on Dirt. Himsir Dornal will cop the loc of the Dirtwon, and ding there until it is shelto for him to meho to Klaptonia."

Fat little Nobbin looked up from the floor where his father had dropped him: "Why?" he asked.

His father reached down automatically to grab hold of him, but the Slamboss raised a hand.

"There is a scim by the Gloami Kojers, to snaff and morb Himsir Dornal."

Hitman looked perplexed.

"How do we know?"

"The Lurci Flunkaj reported it to me." Slamboss said distinctly.

Hitman looked baffled: "We nocca . . ." he began, but broke off with a wince of pain.

His son, who had noticed the look of irritation on Slamboss's face, quickly bit his father on the ankle.

"Oh yes, a snaff hatch and an inslam scim." Hitman smiled as the idea sank into his mind.

Slamboss mastered his fury and continued slowly.

"This atta be done in zalti lurc. Himsir Dornal must travel in the yorni brecc. No one must see him bego."

Hitman's face saddened.

"Num Topma. Num his Mawon?"

Slamboss clenched his fist.

"Especially not his Nurbul Topma. She will only hank to recc where he is todding. She does not know about the shuff, and her finkles must not be aroused."

"So, she has to wing he is here, when he's not."

"Zitto. Until we scroll her that he is not. If he shivanned before the morb attempt, she would finkle foul play."

"But," Hitman's eyes swivelled in his skull. "There isn't going to be a morbi dib."

Despite the signal from his son, Hitman went on.

"The Lurci Flunkaj scanned the hatch and hitched it."

Slamboss ground his teeth. "Nibbic. But the Gloami Kojers do not know that. That is lurco."

"Yumda," nodded Hitman. But he was still baffled. Slamboss went on:

"Before they try to morb the kojer who they believe is the Replic Dornal, we shall make our move."

"Oh, how?"

Little Nobbin jumped up and down.

"Can't you wing it, Dadwon? *We* morb the Dirtwon first."

Slamboss smiled a benign smile.

"Now," he said brutally. "Fring the Dirtwon to Klaptonia, in Dornal's cloot. No one must see you arrive. Scroll him that he must gallop to the Bashi Rangles to div the Hermiss Roshan."

Hitman's face took on a look of heroic stupidity.

"How will the Dirtwon recc he's supposed to be Himsir Dornal? He may not hank to plog to the Bashi Rangles."

The Slamboss put out a hand and raised Hitman up and down.

"Zitto. He will not hank to plog to the Bashi Rangles. He will be so scared he will be sogging his cloot. You will persuade him."

Nobbin looked up.

"We will?"

Slamboss looked down at fat little Nobbin and nodded.

"Hurry to the Bashi Rangles with the Dirtwon and morb him. Fring his gora-stained chooner back and we shall scroll the Nurbul Topwon and Topma that the Replic morbed in a raji dib, a brave attempt to rescue the froobli Hermiss Roshan."

He paused. "Acco?"

"Acco, acco, Shrefful Slamboss," Hitman and Nobbin answered in chorus.

Chapter
8

AS DORNAL, HITMAN and Nobbin began the long slide down the Beam to Dirt, Arnold wandered along the pavement towards the crossing by the Arndale. He was feeling great. He'd discovered he was early for school. He had his games kit with him. He didn't realise it was swimming today, but that was way in the future. There was plenty of time to have this adventure in which he fought his way through the ambush in the ravines of the Bashi Rangles, slaying eight of his opponents and rescuing Hermiss Roshan from an awful fate.

"Arnie, hello."

Sharon called from the other pavement, teeth gleaming in her dark, handsome face.

"Oh, hi — er — Sharon."

"You're going the wrong way, Arnie."

He looked embarrassed.

"I'm going the long way round. Plenty of time."

He moved off diagonally across the broad pavement. His mind quickly filled with the thrilling pictures of dark forests, flashing swords and jingling harness. Then he heard his name called, again. Someone was speaking from the half open door of the kiosk. An arm held out the 'phone. The figure was familiar, but his confused mind could not place it.

"Psst, Arnie. Long distance call from Mars."

Without thinking, he stepped closer. The 'phone was

drawn back a foot. He followed, was suddenly grabbed and pulled inside. The kiosk was packed scrum full of bodies. They were all around him, bullet heads and bad breath. Oh, no, they were ... They couldn't! He tried desperately to work out what was happening and stop it. He couldn't do either.

"Here," grunted Meanie, "hold his legs."

"How can we get his strides off if we do that? Hold his arms. Keep still you little dozer will you – it won't take long."

Now they had his windcheater off. Then his shirt. His head banged on the 'phone ledge and he felt sick.Oh no, now they were peeling his pants off. A sudden gust of cold air swept into the booth. The awful truth dawned on Arnold. He was stripped to his Y-fronts.

"Right," grunted Eenie. "Let's have his knickers, now."

Arnold felt rough hands grope round his legs and a surge of strength sent him into an onslaught on his tormentors.

"Ooh, the little ... He hit me. That hurt," said Mo. "Let me give him the old ..."

"Nergo, mate. Don't mark him. Just get those briefs off, quick, before somebody comes."

Arnold, almost naked, made one last frantic effort to escape. He lashed out again. Now, amazingly, his blows took effect. He heard the others groan in pain. He heard the crunch as blows landed, the thud of bodies falling around him. What was going on?

Then he heard voices. Was he dreaming?

"Jacco, Dadwon. Use your gorner. Grid these clodders. We only hank es-won."

Clunk. Clunk. The space around him had cleared. Someone hoarsed in his ear.

"Dirtwon. Cop es cloot."

In a dream, he took the clothes pressed into his hand. A long pair of hose, a tunic, a belt with scabbard, but no sword.

35

"Jacco," the voice blasted in his ear.

Dazed he dressed himself. His arm was seized. He felt his body launch forward out and down as though he were on a big dipper at the fair. 'Phone box and buildings vanished. He was in free fall. His unseen rescuers held him still, but their grip was less fierce. His eyes closed in a mixture of bewilderment, excitement and fear. He was launched into a great white dazzling nothing, sliding, swooping into infinity.

Just as suddenly the slide ended. His feet jarred on solid ground. He rocked to and fro. Hands steadied him and slowly the sick feeling drained from his stomach and he dared open his eyes.

"Eerol, Dirtwon," said a voice.

Arnold looked round. Next to him were two figures, faces hidden in masks. One was enormous, the other small and fat. Both of them, and this was weird, had bare arms and legs, and their skin was bright orange. The tunics and jerkins they wore were dull brown. Each carried in their belt a short bladed sword.

Now Arnold looked down at his own body. His astonishment increased. He was wearing a tunic, but his was rich blue and edged with fur. Around his waist was a carved leather belt, its scabbard studded with precious stones. But his eyes opened wider when he saw that his skin was the same colour as theirs — he was like a tangerine.

Now he looked beyond his companions. He could see flower beds with strange plants, dazzling blue and green. Then high, white stone walls, turrets, towers with narrow windows, gleaming against a golden sky, in which flamed a crimson sun. He drew in a deep breath, his lungs filling with a heady scent. His mind spun like a top. Never in all his imagination, day or night, had he had a fantasy as clear as this. His fingers touched the rich, satin-like fabric.

But wait. Where was his horse? Where was his sword? And who were these two herberts? He'd never imagined anyone like them.

"Heelo, Dirtwon."

Arnold stared. What was this Dirtwon business? He'd never heard that word before. They stared back, eyes peering from the mask holes. The little fat one nudged his big partner, then tapped the side of his own head.

"Dadwon. He doesn't bonz."

The larger one nodded then bent close to Arnold, foul breath galing into his face. A finger like a pork sausage poked into his chest. Then the huge thumb jerked back over his shoulder.

"Heelo. Todd with us. Jacco."

Arnold, excited, drew himself up, the words he had invented tumbling out of his mouth.

"What yurbul is this. I am your Nurbul Himsir. Where is my shreddi nedder? Where is my Misti Sticcer? I must plog to rescue — to div Hermiss Roshan."

At the sound of his voice, their jaws dropped below the masks. The little one nudged the big one.

"Jacco, Dadwon. Grovel, grovel."

And grovel they did. They sank to their knees then to their bellies on the gravelled garden path. The larger one reverently took Arnold's foot and placed it on top of his head. Then he squinted sideways at the little one and whispered:

"Pogsers! What's occot?"

Horror in his voice, the little one whispered back.

"We've frang the blunt won back. This isn't the Dirtwon. It can't be. It is Himsir Dornal!"

Chapter
9

FROM ACROSS THE road, Sharon saw Arnold dragged into the 'phone kiosk. She swore to herself. She ought to have spotted the Yobs hanging about and warned him. He wasn't safe out on his own. She didn't hesitate but rushed to the crossing. Just as she stepped on to it, two enormous container trucks thundered by and nearly flattened her. She leapt back; waited until they had passed, then started across to the other side, shoving her way through the crowd.

She skidded to a halt a few yards from the 'phone box. That didn't make sense. It was empty. About a couple of yards away, the Yobs, all four of them, sat on a bench holding their heads. One had a black eye, another a lump as big as an onion over his ear. The third was trying to fit two teeth back into his mouth. The fourth looked unconscious, but there was nothing special about that.

Her eyes travelled back. Oh, no! Scattered over the pavement were Arnold's towel, sports gear, windcheater, pants, shirt, Y-fronts. But where was Arnold?

She picked up the gear and as she did so the 'phone box door opened and at knee height, Arnold's face peered out, looking baffled and furious.

"Quick, Arnie," she thrust his clothes at him. "Get these on before those animals recover."

She waited impatiently, one eye on the convalescent

Yobs. She gripped her bag strap and swung it. The booth door opened again. Arnold stepped out. He had his shirt on over his windcheater and his pants weren't zipped up properly but otherwise he was all there. She grabbed his arm. He seemed dazed.

"We are late, but late, mate," she said. "Come on before those woodentops wake up."

He stared blankly.

"Arnie," she put a hand on his sleeve. "Are you OK?" He seemed in shock.

He squared his shoulders. Suddenly his face glowed, orange.

"I am Himsir Dornal. Grovel O graftona."

She bit her lip. On impulse she brought up both arms and clapped him smartly on both cheeks. Like magic his colour came back to normal. She took his arm and dragged him to the pavement. He glared at her again and threw off her arm in a gesture which was both brutal and strong. That wasn't like Arnold. He must have freaked out completely.

Now Dornal looked across the road, his brain slowly clearing. Around, the great grey buildings towered into a hard blue sky. In front of him, roaring, grinding and wheezing, moved an endless parade of lurching monsters, with eyes that shone like windows, while blue smoke belched behind. Inside each eye, the pale, grublike face of a Dirtwon gazed ahead. Gone were the slender turrets, the round domes of the Topwon's Palace, the flower beds, the golden sky, the sweet smell of the air. Instead his nostrils filled with the pungent odour which burst out in waves after each of the metal monsters as it lumbered past.

His arm was taken again. This time he was too bewildered to shake it off. The tall, dark girl spoke again.

"Come on Arnie."

Arnie?

"I am Himsir Dornal," he muttered.

"Yes, Arnie," she murmured soothingly. "We know you

are most of the time but just now you have to come out of orbit and get to school.''

She stepped forward and raised her arm. Before Dornal's stupefied gaze the giant creatures in the road lumbered to a stop. Beneath them there suddenly appeared a path marked out in black and white bands. She pulled him on to it and he followed wonderingly. Above, behind the monster-eyes, the Dirtwons looked down on him. Now the girl and he were across the road, but behind them came the crash as the procession began again.

This must be magic. He studied his companion with new respect. Now she hurried him along the other side of the road. They turned sharply. She began to run. He followed. Again they turned. More roads, more metal shapes, but smaller with groups of Dirtwons inside. More buildings, walls. This city was endless. Royal Tipacal could be put down here and lost. What ghastly place had Slamboss and Necro sent him to? Worse than the hellish caves beneath the Prussy Peakers.

Now they were in the middle of a hurrying crowd, dressed like them, young males and females mixed together, pushing, shoving. He tried to remember the words of the Dirt Yurb he had learnt so carefully.

Ahead an iron gate, half open, set in a long brick wall, loomed up. There stood a tall man in dark jacket, pale face half hidden by a beard. His eyes glinted, his voice full of menace.

''Let's be having you now, thirty seconds to go,'' he roared.

The girl at his side muttered.

''All the same, little boys, big boys. All got to be boss.''
She smiled sweetly up at the man as they ran past.
''Good morning Mr Harris.''

''Good morning, Sharon,'' he rumbled. ''Got young Arnold with you? Just as well. He wouldn't make it otherwise.''

40

There was a burst of laughter from the crowd. Dornal sensed they were laughing at him and a flash of anger went through him. But he suppressed it. Now they hurried across a stone yard. Ahead of them was a brick building, with walls like a sheet of glass that flashed in the morning sun. It was bigger than a palace, and towards it hurried yet more males and females. There must be — thousands. The girl Sharon had grasped another boy by the arm. The Dirt-dimas had no modesty at all.

"Hey, do us a favour. Show Arnold where his locker is and get him into class. He's a bit funny today."

"So, what's new?" said the boy. "What have you been doing to him over the weekend, Sharon? He's like a zombie."

"Doing nothing. The Yobs duffed him up."

"Like that? Well, he does buy it. He's a right wally."

"Never mind that. Just point him the right way, will you?"

"Arnie," she shook his arm. "You'll be all right now."

Dornal fixed his eyes carefully on the tall dark girl. Her face was amazing. He had never seen anyone like her. He looked round at the hurrying people around him, then up at the red brick and glass and the hard blue of the sky. His mind ticked over frantically. He looked at the boy next to him, and then he looked at his own hands. They were the same absurd dirty-pink colour. His face must be like that too.

It was as Necro had shown him in the Misti Crist. These were the Dirtwons and he was now one of them. He felt sick. He looked for a sight of the girl's friendly face, but she had gone.

Chapter 10

ARNOLD WAS BEWILDERED now. Who were these characters? What were they muttering about? Why were they using the Klaptonian language he had made up, but with words that he hadn't? He wished he knew what was happening. This fantasy was too real.

He'd started it on the pavement just by the Arndale. Usually he would have a dream in his head while he kept an eye on the outside world. But now he seemed to be totally inside the dream. He couldn't see the Arndale. He could only see the palace, the walled gardens. He could smell the flowers, too. He stretched out his hand and touched the arched wall on his left. It was rough, like sandstone. He touched his tunic, a velvety texture. And he looked again at the two charlies on the ground. A grovel, the little one had said. And grovel they did. Excitement rushed through him. He was in it now and he'd have to play the fantasy for all it was worth.

He snapped his fingers. The little one squinted up at him.

"On your pats," he commanded.

Reluctantly they rose.

"My sticcer, my nedder, we atta plog to the Bashi Rangles."

The big one shook his head stupidly.

"Numda. Slamboss yurbled ..."

The little one kicked him on the ankle and edged closer, his voice oily.

"No tocc to lose, Nurbul Himsir. Hermiss Roshan dings in the Bashi Rangles. We can rescue her if we jacc. You can cop a sticcer from us. Es-way."

He pointed to a narrow arched doorway in the corner of the wall. Arnold hesitated. He knew that Replic Dornal would have dashed off without a thought, ready to kill two hundred monsters with a toothpick. But this was real, and he was really Arnold and Arnold had more sense than that. Suddenly the two of them looked round in alarm. From somewhere beyond the garden wall a voice called.

"Dornie, O Dornie."

A small gate in the farther end of the garden, opened. A lady in rich silver robes appeared, hand outstretched. She was carrying a sword, its blade and jewelled hilt flashing in the sun.

"Dornal, there you are. Wicci wipper. Todding off to morb kojers without your Misti Sticcer."

She swept along the path. The haughty nosed orange features were lined, the hair gleamed with grey streaks. She must be the Topma. He looked round. They were alone. The others had vanished, like smoke.

He thought rapidly. Should he grovel? If so, how much?

"A stacca grovels, O Topma," he said.

He dropped on one knee, reaching out both hands to take the sword. He'd seen it done in Disney films often enough. For a second the proud face was full of astonishment. Then, she smiled and the face softened, a warm, relieved smile. He rose, she slid the sword into the scabbard, stretched out her hands and touched his cheeks, his shoulders, then his elbows.

Looking out from their hiding place beneath the arches, Hitman and Nobbin were bewildered.

"Nobbin," gulped the father. "We're gravved. That *is* Dornal."

"What do we do? We can't hoke him to the Bashi Rangles, nimmo."

"We atta. Slamboss ..."

"But Dornal'll morb us. He's got his shreddi sticcer."

"But if we don't Slamboss'll morb us."

"So, what's the difference?"

"Dornal'll morb us jacco. Slamboss'll morb us doddo."

A slight scuffling noise came from the dark reaches of the passage.

"What was that?"

"A pog. They run loose, sometimes."

"No, it wasn't." Nobbin rushed to the corner. In the gloom he saw the brown wisp of skirt and the quick flash of bare knees.

"It's that Norsha dima, nebbing."

"Heel her."

The two charged off into the depths of the passage.

Out in the garden, Arnold made his farewells to Topma. He'd done well. Not said too much. He hadn't understood everything she said, which was weird considering he'd made up the language. But she seemed pleased with him.

Now, what next? Where were those two dimmo faders? He skirted the garden wall, looking in each opening. The depths beyond were gloomy. Should he call? But what should he call them? Dongo and Pongo? Little and Large? He had an inspiration —

why not Hitman and Nobbin? The thought made him laugh.

He gripped the sword and plunged into the passage, just as Hitman and Nobbin came out into the garden from the opposite side. They found it empty. Frustrated they looked at each other.

"What do we do now, Sonwon?"

Nobbin shook his head. "Dadwon. We have to scroll Slamboss."

"He'll flake us."

Nobbin shrugged. "Can't be liffed. I can't piccle this. Eerol, Dadwon, if that is Dornal, why has he come back to Klaptonia? Slamboss atta recc, and he won't lux it."

Hitman nodded. As usual, Nobbin was right. It would be bad if they told Slamboss, but worse if they didn't.

Fearfully the two headed towards the garden wall and the passages that led to Slamboss's chamber.

Chapter 11

SWORD IN HAND, Arnold plunged into the cool gloom of the passage, that led from the scented heat of the palace gardens. In fact, he didn't plunge. He would have done if this had been one of his fantasies, but this time it was for real. The rich tunic was real, the light, bright sword was real. The edge was like a razor. He'd touched it with his real finger and a

trickle of blood ran down. It stang like a nettle. He
was real, this world was real, even though he'd
invented it. And if he really was Himsir Dornal
Replic of Klaptonia, Hodbung Shredder of the Premi
Moblot, then Arnold Radleigh from Denfield was a
fantasy.

The trouble was, he didn't feel like Dornal. He was
scared. He'd been scared ever since that rat pack had
jumped him in the Arndale. Then those two herberts
had whipped him up here.Where had they gone to?
The light from the garden vanished round the corner. Now he was in near darkness and he reached
out to guide himself along the walls. He jerked his
hand back. It was clammy and something was using
his middle finger as a slow motion ski run. He
gasped, jerked his hand and whatever it was flew off
and hit the wall with a squishy sound. He stumbled
on. He had to find Hitman and Nobbin, though he
didn't trust them. They looked as straight as a spiral
staircase. But he needed them.

If they were telling the truth, if Hermiss Roshan
had been kidnapped he ought to do something about
it. After all he'd rescued her often enough in his
dreams. He ought to be able to get it right. After that,
he was supposed to marry her. He'd never gone as
far as that in his dream and wasn't all that sure
about it. Still maybe he'd wake up before he got that
far. Or maybe he'd get destroyed. He always won
when he dreamt it, but this was for real. Was this
sword really magic, would it beat anything? He had
a sneaking feeling that it was only magic when the
real Dornal used it. He stopped in the darkness. He
wasn't the real Dornal.

The thoughts choked in his throat, as something
tugged at his sleeve. Mockers, another crawlie. He
brushed violently with his free hand and felt firm

flesh. Whatever, whoever was touching him was no insect. He jerked again but the grip on his elbow tightened and he was drawn into a side passage.

"Slep me," he snorted. He tried in Dirtyurb. "Leggo." But another hand came out of the darkness and closed his mouth. He was drawn up against another body in the darkness, soft and warm. He could smell sweat and flesh. A girl's voice spoke.

"Replic Dornal. It is Norsha, the graftona. Todd with me. Your bree is in rix."

Well, yes, he knew his life was in danger. But Norsha didn't seem dangerous. She didn't feel dangerous. He started to blush in the dark as they stood pressed against one another.

He gulped: "String on." She moved away pulling him with her. They twisted and turned through the tunnels, Arnold stumbling after her. By some nimble footwork, he managed to change step and slide the sword back into its scabbard so that he could use his free hand to keep himself from banging into the rough stonework.

They came free of the tunnel and through a narrow doorway into a passage lit by the sun's rays, through high round windows. Now he could see Norsha. The simple dark dress was stained with dirt and kitchen grease. The face was orange, heart-shaped, the eyes deep green and bold. For a second she looked at him, as if astonished, then looked down. She let go of his hand and ran lightly ahead of him. He followed her to a low arched doorway. She struck the studded timber with her fist and a thin, high old voice called from inside.

"Inco."

Arnold waited for Norsha to go first. She stared at him, the same puzzled glance, but stood back. He shrugged and went first. He fell down two stone steps into a dimly lit room with heavy draped walls and deep curtained window. The only light came from a brazier of coals that stood in the centre of the floor with a foul smelling cauldron bubbling over it. In the shadows stood a tall skeleton-thin man, whose straggling white hair stood out against the black of the cloak that covered him from shoulder to feet. The old man bent so low his hair almost swept the ground.

"A civil grovel O Nurbul Replic."

Who was it? Arnold tried wildly to remember. This was the Court Magician, he guessed, but what had he named him? Why hadn't he taken more trouble with his fantasies and kept a filing system? But the old man wasn't even looking at him now. He glared past Arnold.

"Exo, garber."

Arnold stared. The old devil was talking to Norsha. Rubbish, he called her. Before he could protest the girl swiftly got down on all fours and backed away through the open door. It swung shut behind her. Now the old magician faced him again and Arnold to his joy, remembered:

"Stacca yaccas, O Necro."

The old man gave him a look of pure amazement.

"You speak Klaptonian?"

"Zitto. I invented it!"

Necro smiled, a charming, toothless, old man's smile then nodded. He waved his hand towards the massive round table that stood under the curtained window.

"Grovli, fold, O Replic," he bowed towards the chair. Arnold stepped forward and pulled on the high backed chair, then suddenly cringed as with a searing hiss and a flash of tongue and fangs, a snake uncoiled itself and reared up at him. Frantically he jerked at his sword, but he was clumsy and his elbow knocked against the chair back.

"Num, num, O Dirtwon," cried the old man. "Do not mob Clarence. He's quite harmless, unless he takes a dislike to you. Wicci wipper, naughty boy," he said gently to the snake. It's head dropped and it slid off the chair and over to the corner of the room. As it went it brushed against Arnold's foot. He felt the blood drain from his head, staggered to the chair and sat down.

"My boy, you have gone all rosi-dirt, all dirty-pink." Necro passed Arnold a beaker. Without thinking he drank. It was strong. It was the sort of thing you get to drink when you're eighteen, if you have a head made of concrete. But it made him feel better.

Necro sat down: "Amazing, a Dirtwon who yurbs Klaptonian."

Arnold felt offended.

"What do you mean, 'Dirtwon'? I'm a lot cleaner than you," he burst out.

Necro hooted.

"No, no. Dirt is our name for your world. What you call Earth. Dirtwon means earthling. You are not Dornal. You are Arnold."

Arnold's mouth fell open.

"How do you know?"

Necro moved his hand over the table. The surface glowed, became clear like a mirror, clouded over, then cleared. Images appeared and focused as on a TV screen. Arnold saw, to his amazement, the Arndale Centre. A pang of homesickness struck him. then the picture vanished.

"I knew that you looked like our Himsir Dornal. I am amazed that you speak some of our language. You even know my name."

"I made it all up," said Arnold.

Necro slowly shook his head. "I do not think so," he said. Then went on:

"Klaptonia's people came from Dirt – your part of Dirt, aeons ago. In their new home, they gradually made a new language. Did you know in Dirtyurb there are many sounds, word beginnings, word endings. Put together they make millions of words. But you use only a fraction of them.

"On Klaptonia we make use of sounds that you neglect. We make up words as we go along. If we like the sounds we keep them. If not, we throw them away. He began to recite, eyes half closed: "Dirt, girt, hirt, jirt, lirt mirt, nirt quirt, rirt, sirt, tirt, virt, wirt, yirt, blirt brirt, glirt, trirt, shirt, skirt, spirt, slirt ... and so on. On Dirt you make use of only one or two sounds."

"Yeah, 'cause the rest are nonsense," said Arnold.

"How do you know?"

"Well, you learn that when you start school ..." Arnold began.

"Do not always believe your teacher. Even teachers do not know everything. I know. I am a great teacher myself. And I know that the more you know, the more you know you don't know ..."

"OK, OK. So Klaptonian is a real language then ..." Necro raised his eyebrows as if in pain.

"Klaptonian is a very developed language. It is divided into Nurbul Yurbul, spoken by the best people, and Rabbul Gabbul spoken by the lower sort."

"Wow," said Arnold. "Two languages. But how do you tell the difference?"

"There is no difference," said Necro, airily. "Exactly the same words. But Nurbul Yurbul sounds much nicer."

"Oh like that. I've heard that one before," said Arnold. "But listen, if you make up words all the time, how can you be sure everyone understands you?"

Necro shook his head.

"You cannot be sure. That is Klaptonia's great problem. It is very easy to insult someone without meaning to, or to try and insult someone and make no impression. For example, the word for fist is gorner, the word for idiot is gormer. Tell someone to ding it means wait. Tell them to dang it means hang. Call someone a freeber, it means they are generous, call them a froober, it means they are a sweetheart, call them a fryber, it means they are worth only five yoggles, almost worthless."

Arnold laughed: "Dirtyurb's a lot more sensible than that."

"Oh yes? Is a boot something to wear, or part of a car? Is a ball a grand dance or a bladder to kick about? Is a plot a piece of ground or a secret plan? Is a blow a breath of wind or a knock on the head ..."

"All right, all right. But Klaptonian sounds a lot more complicated. I mean all this misunderstanding. It must lead to quarrels."

"Endless dispute, wrangling, fighting, injury, death," answered Necro. "A great deal of time is spent either trying to kill people or avoiding death. Hence to avoid total disaster, we have a complete system of greetings or yaccas, and a complete system of apologies or submissions, called grovels."

Necro fixed Arnold with a glittering eye and bored on:

"The most usual greeting is Stacca Yaccas. Then there is Brecca Yacca or good morning, Nacca Yacca, good evening, Sacca Yacca, good night. Snacca yacca means Bon Appetit, Pacca Yacca means Bon Voyage. Licca Yaccas is good health or cheers, Flagga Yacca is the soldier's salute, Fracca Yacca, the greeting before a big fight, Mocca Yacca, the coffee table greeting, Mecca Yacca means Salaam Aleikum, Wacca Yacca is for your closest friends ..."

"I'll never learn those. It's too complicated ..."

"Indeed it is," said Necro complacently, "and the system often breaks down. But then, there is the grovel. Grovels help equals to avoid too much conflict, and inferiors to avoid punishment (if they are lucky)."

He raised his eyebrows.

"There is the civil grovel or level grovel among equals, the travel grovel for journeys, the revel grovel for celebrations, the swivel grovel when you have offended two people at once, the navel grovel for your superiors. For the lower ranks there is the hovel grovel. In deep trouble, the gravel grovel is called for. And when all hope of forgiveness has gone there is the shrivel grovel."

He folded his arms.

Arnold gasped. "It's incredible. I never dreamed ..."

"I thought you did nothing else," said Necro ironically.

"Turn it up," said Arnold, "I mean how can I learn it all? I'll need a crash course."

"Ha, hm," Necro said evasively.

A sudden uneasy feeling attacked Arnold's stomach again.

"Hey, look. Just why have I been brought up here?"

Necro's eyes wandered. Arnold stood up.

"Look, mate. Come on. Tell us. What is it all about? Why *have* I been brought here? How long am I staying? How do I get back? You must know. You organised it all, didn't you?"

Before Necro could open his mouth, there was a

hammering at the door. He marched to it and swung it open a foot. Arnold heard a servant's voice.

"Occul Necro, the Zalti Yurbon is roobing."

Necro hesitated, then slammed the door in the face of the servant. He turned and looked guiltily at Arnold. He waved his hand. The image bloomed on the table surface. Arnold stared at the walls and scratched desks of his classroom. Old Dracula was up front. It must be history . . .

His eyes ranged round the tables . . . Cor, there were the Yobs, there was Sharon (he felt a sudden pang) and there was . . . But that was incredible . . . He was sitting there himself. But it couldn't be. He was up here.

He gasped: "That's Dornal sitting in my clothes."

"As you sit here in his."

"So, what is it all about . . . Come on!"

Again the knocking sounded at the door. For a second Necro looked at Arnold. Was that regret in his face? Then he strode to the door, opened it, slammed it behind him and had gone.

"Hey, what about me?"

Arnold rushed to the door and jerked at the handle. But it would not budge. He was locked in. Amid the silence of the darkened room, he heard the slither of Clarence the snake. He shivered. Now he was sure this was no dream. Or if it was a dream he was stuck in it and had to play it for real.

He was stuck up here on Klaptonia and — Dornal was stuck down there on Dirt. Who was worse off he wondered?

Chapter
12

DOWN ON DIRT, at Denfield Comprehenshive, Himsir Dornal, Hodbung Shredder of the Premi Moblot, was having a quiet freaker. It lasted all day and a good bit of the evening and it was due to carry on for several days more. For the first time in his life, he was being pushed around and he could do nothing about it. He, who until this morning had been undisputed hero and future leader of an entire planet, was being treated like a grafton, a clodder, a mere wallock basher. There were lots of humiliations that day, and the next and the next.

For a start the clothes were all wrong. The jacket was tight under the armpits and the trousers were flappy round the ankles, whereas anyone in their right bonce would have known that a tunic should be loose round the shoulders, so you could swing a sword and behead someone and tight round the ankles for when you were leaping on your shreddi nedder and galloping off into the Bashi Rangles.

Then this place, this school. When he got back to Klaptonia he would have Necro hung up by his thumbs, no his heels. ''School is sinters, Nurbul Replic,'' he had said. ''I know all about schools on Dirt. I've read lots of Dirti-Scrolls about it. It's one long run of excitement and fun, lots of wheezes, japes and jests. All good fellows together. You will not want to leave when the time comes to slyp back to Klaptonia.''

The fact was – it was a prison. The only difference was it was above ground, not down in the dungeons like home. You had to stay in one room. You couldn't move until you were told to. Then you had to get up, gather your gear and traipse down corridors, up stairs, pushing and shoving until you reached another cell. And in each cell the interrogation started again. If you ran away, they sent people to fetch you back. But if they really wanted to punish you, they threw you out and wouldn't let you come back. Wangi! It was so yonco, it was numpo.

He felt helpless. He Dornal, loved or feared by everyone this side of the Prussy Peakers – helpless. He would have been totally lost but for this tall dark girl who sat behind him, all the time. How she did it with all the moving round the buildings, he did not know, but she managed it. And at the right time she would whisper, he could feel her breath on the back of his neck, telling him what to do or what to say.

She seemed to think he was out of his head. She said everything twice and kept on asking, ''Are you OK, Arnie?'' That was even more humiliating. He hadn't taken help, advice or anything from a woman since he was two years old and he couldn't remember that very clearly. Even Topma daren't speak to him like that. And the thing that made him grind his teeth until sparks came was that there was nothing he could do about it. He felt wound up. But Necro had warned him that if he lost his temper he would blossom out in his original tanji Klaptonian colour and his cover would be blown.

So, he had to keep quiet, do what he was told, say the right thing and let this girl look after him. And he didn't know how long he had to keep it up.

Later that morning, they were all let out into an exercise yard. He was separated from Sharon. The custom seemed to be that males and females got together in groups and hurled challenges and insults at each other. He could see some of the bigger boys and girls getting together across the yard behind a shed where peculiar wheeled machines were kept. But he had no idea what they were up to. And for the moment he was not interested.

Here and there were signs of familiar activity – fighting, shouts and cries of pain. He watched and found it stranger. No swords, no daggers, just punching, eye gouging and kicking, very primitive, rather like the sports indulged in by clodders and hodders on national feast days. There was one difference, though. Now and then the fighters were evenly matched, but often two or three would be attacking one, usually smaller. That he did not understand, how anyone could be interested in fighting someone smaller, though the bigger ones clearly enjoyed it. There was much about the rules of this planet he must study. Uncertain of the language he hesitated to ask.

He did not know that while he strolled round the school yard he was being watched. Eenie, Meanie, Mynie and Mo had gathered by the low wall near the playing fields muttering together. To be honest, they were still a bit bruised, battered and bewildered after the early morning events in the telephone box at the Arndale. Even Eenie, who could do joined up thinking, still hadn't worked out what had happened. What started out as a bit of early morning fun, torturing Arnold, had suddenly turned into a duffing with them on the delivery end. What was worse was that some of the bumps and bruises showed. Mo had a duck egg sized swelling that peeped through his skin cut. Meanie had a large black eye. Only Eenie had managed to escape actual damage. He always set things up, but never got lumbered.

But who had thrashed them? It couldn't be Arnold, thought Eenie as he watched their intending victim wandering round the yard studying everyone.

"You know, there's something funny about little Arnie," he mused.

"So, what else is new?" demanded Meanie, gingerly stroking one part of his body which had suffered more than most in the morning's fracas. "You know the little sod's bent, so?"

"Yeah, but look at the way he's wandering round. He's acting like he's just arrived. There's something different about him."

"Too right," grunted Mo. "He worked us over today."

"Pull the other," said Mynie contemptuously. "He's got minders."

"Him never. Who'd look after him, and what for? How can he spend on minders?"

"Leave it," muttered Eenie soothingly. "Like I said. There's something funny about Arnold. What we have to do is find out what."

"So, let's go and pull his wings off," said Mo.

"Don't be stupid," said Eenie. "No I beg your pardon. That's an unfair thing to ask, isn't it? No, we do this by being friendly. Come on."

They surrounded Arnold as he sat on the low wall. Eenie smiled at him, like a boa constrictor measuring up a lamb.

"On your own, Arnie?"

Dornal looked up. Eenie noticed that the boy's eyes were steady, his gaze unafraid. That puzzled him.

"Oh, hello chaps," Dornal stood up and extended his hand. "We haven't met. Are you fellows prefects? Or," he hesitated, "are you the school bullies?"

The boys fell about, except Eenie, who grasped Dornal's hand.

"No, we've noticed you about the quad," he fitted his tone of voice to Dornal's.

"Yer," added Mo, "we've often though we'd like to play with you."

Mynie turned away, while Mo's shoulders began to shake. Eenie ignored them.

"How about our getting together after school? We've got a ripping wheeze. It'll be a great howl."

Dornal's face brightened. "After lessons you mean."

"We-ell, not exactly. You see us chaps have been detained this evening. Frightful bore. So a touch later, maybe."

"Ah, you mean, in the dormer?"

Mynie's mouth dropped open. Little Arnie had flipped his lid. But Eenie's eye did not even flicker.

"Ripping," he said. "We'll be in 3H."

"Oh, I'll wait outside then."

"No, no." Eenie shook his head rapidly. "Keep out of the way. The rest of them are day pupils. Frightful creeps. They'll be going home. School gets very quiet then and we don't want anyone else in on the jape, do we?"

Dornal grinned. This was sinters. He'd made friends already and boys too. The others grinned back and turned to walk away. The school yard was emptying. Dornal made his way back into school, a cheerful glow warming his inside. Meanie watched him walk away.

"Did you see that, eh? When he grinned he started to go this funny orange colour. Think he's on gas?"

Eenie shrugged: "Dunno. Have to sus it out. But whatever, I think we are going to have fun winding Arnie up. We just have to point him in the right direction and let him go off . . ."

Chapter 13

ARNOLD STARED AT the images in the table top. He watched as Dornal, arm in arm (well, almost) with the Yobs strolled back into school after the morning break. He saw the hurt look on Sharon's face, as Dornal, busy chatting to Eenie walked past as though he did not even see her. Could anyone be such a wally? he wondered. That berk wasn't fit to rule a planet, now or later.

He was brought back from his contemplation of the dear old school in the magic table mirror, with a start. There was a gentle but insistent pressure on his legs. He looked down. His heart stopped beating. Two unblinking eyes regarded him from a distance of six inches, below them a forked tongue gently moved in and out. That flaming snake Clarence had climbed(?) up on his lap. Suddenly he realised the ghastly creature wanted him to stroke his bonce, just like Moggy at home. Swallowing, he gingerly touched the flat head. To his amazement it felt dry. He stroked it. Clarence hissed gently. The beady eyes closed. Arnold felt comfortable. He began to doze off, himself.

"Himsir Dornal!"

The whispered words jerked Arnold out of his thoughts. He swung round in the chair, sending

Clarence cascading to the floor. A face suspended between floor and ceiling peered at him between the curtain folds. The handsome, dirt-streaked orange face and tangled hair, brought his heart beat back to normal.

"Norsha! What are you doing there?"

She seemed puzzled. He realised he was talking Dirtyurb. She pushed the curtain fold aside, stepped down to the floor and grovelled.

"Nurbul Replic. The Zalti Yurbon is roobing. They are yurbing you have shivanned. Been snaffed."

"It's shaccot," he said, pointing to the locked door.

"Ha!" She nodded, then beckoned him. Arnold moved towards her. She turned and vanished through the curtains. He followed, then drew back in horror. He found himself by an open window, staring down the side of the palace walls to a paved court yard fifty feet below. His head swam. There was no sign of Norsha. He looked round wildly. Then he saw her, six feet away, clinging like a fly to the rough masonry, just below the window. Freeing one hand, she beckoned him on. Oh no, thought Arnold, choking back a desire to be sick. What do I do now? What would Dornal do? He knew what Dornal, the dimmo hero would do. He'd be out there on that ledge, walking round the wall like a fly. Was that what made heroes? Being too thick to notice things like the possibility of falling and smashing yourself up?

He closed his eyes, swallowed once more and heaved himself over the sill. For a second or two, the sword trapped between his legs, held him back. Fat lot of use this flaming magic sword was. Nearly done himself a mischief.

His scrabbling feet found the ledge. It was narrower than he thought. Norsha must have size twos as well as a head for heights. His waving hands found the rim of stone almost a yard above his head. Forcing his eyes round he saw Norsha again. She was half way round the block. She pointed across the space to a window on the far side. Arnold looked across then couldn't stop himself. He looked down. His head started to turn. He was going to pass out. For a second or two he thought of climbing back through the window and then realised that he was now about ten feet away from it. Going forward was diabolical. Going back was unthinkable. He pressed on, keeping his eyes on the girl's lithe back through the cloth of her dress, which she had tied between her legs. Why was she doing this? Come to that, what was Necro up to?

Between each thought he mechanically slid his hand to the left, then his foot, then drew his other foot after, then his other hand. One – two – three, he counted. Don't look down, Arnie. The sun was warm on his back. His mind wandered. Why had they swapped him with Dornal? Who was putting it round that Dornal was kidnapped? Was it the same people who had kidnapped Hermiss Roshan?

His hand touched something warm. It was Norsha's arm. He was right up against her now and they were clinging to the wall just below a window ledge. From beyond he could hear voices. First a babble, then one voice, hard edged and louder than the others.

"The Gloami Kojers have snaffed Hermiss Roshan. And now they have snaffed Replic Dornal. An inslam is immo. We must mobilise the Dongon, all bladers, crushers, skullers and shredders. Zalti Shredd, Supreme Power must be freebed to the Dongwon, Commander-in-Chief."

"But the Dongwon – that's you, Slamboss," came another voice, pompous but uncertain.

"Zitto, it's me, O Topwon."

"And how long do you hank Zalti Shredd for?"

"As long as I think fit, O Topwon."

Norsha's hand rested on Arnold's arms. She pointed up and then moved away from him. The message was clear. He should climb up and through the window. He didn't know how he could do it, but when he thought about it, he didn't know how he could carry on doing the fly walk along this two inch ledge. He wished he had done press-ups and chin-ups more willingly at school, but he'd always found P.E. a bore.

You didn't need muscles for fantasies. But this was different. Maybe in the future, he should stick to having safer fantasies. But that would be dead boring.

He reached up, grasped the window ledge. His feet came free of the stonework and he was hanging by his elbows. His legs kicked out wildly. Please don't look down, Arnie. He pressed with all his might. His body weighed a ton. He heaved and felt it slowly move upwards. An agonising effort and his knee was over the edge. The window was open. He reached out and gripped the wooden frame. Cramp suddenly seized the hanging leg. He longed to reach down and rub it. But he daren't.

He heaved again and then he was on his knees, half in, half out of the window opening. Now he could see them all gathered in the huge hall. Row upon row of richly robed figures, their backs to him, looking upward to a raised platform with two thrones. He recognised Topma from earlier this morning. That fat oaf with the red face, sitting next to her, must be the Topwon. And the great, hairy bloke built like Big Daddy must be the Slamboss. He stood just a little behind the Topwon's throne, but he still seemed to be in charge.

Now or never, thought Arnold. If he was supposed to be Dornal, he'd better make like Dornal. Hand on sword, he sprang lightly to the floor. At least he meant to, but the cramp in his thigh, pulled him back and he fell like a sack of potatoes, rolling into the backs of the last row of the Great Council. He was barely on his feet again when there was a tremendous stir in the crowd. They turned round as one and gazed at him in astonishment.

"Himsir Dornal," shouted a hundred voices. Then he heard Topma say, complacently,

"I scrolled you the darli wipper was jotto somewhere in the Shotto. A stacca fratch over nothing."

From over on the right, a tall bloke in red suddenly put a trumpet to his lips and blew a blast that almost did in Arnold's eardrums. Then he shouted:

"A humbul mumbul and a navel grovel for the Nurbul Replic Dornal."

At once the crowd began to mumble. The sound grew louder and louder then all of them bent as if they were touching their toes. All Arnold could see between him and the throne was row after row of well clothed rumps.

He looked round hastily. There was no sign of Norsha. And the window was closed. There was only one way – forward. He braced himself and marched up to the dais. Behind him as he walked he heard the swish of robes as row after row stood up.

The three on the dais looked at him. Topma was smiling. Topwon looked baffled. Slamboss looked furious. Arnold cleared his throat. The way to play this, he knew, was to pretend he was dreaming it.

"Nurbul Topwon. Why is the Zalti Yurbon roobing without me?"

There was an awkward silence. Then from the first row came a gentle, persuasive voice. It was Necro.

"The Shotto flunkers could not find you."

Oh, you liar, thought Arnold. Should he reveal that the two of them had been together? But no. Necro knew he was not Dornal. But he wasn't telling anyone so he had better play along with him.

"And what has the Yurbon been roobing about?"

"Oh, er numdo," muttered the Topwon clearly embarrassed.

Necro spoke again. "Nurbul Replic we were roobing about a puzzler. When the Sizla, the sun, shivanns behind the Prussy Peakers to the East every looma, how do we recc it will rise again from the depths of Necoa in the brecc, the morning. Talwons scroll us that beneath the Prussy Peakers is a cavern, the Groobi Choob, the Cavern of Doom, and the Sizla returns after setting, through the Choob. That is why the inpo of our mondo is more sindi, hotter than the expo. But numko, no one has ever ibed this. So how do we recc?"

What a lot of yoyos, thought Arnold. Flipping sun going down behind the mountains, travelling through a tunnel and coming up in the East through a big lake. He cleared his throat and played for time.

"What does the Yurbon wig about this?"

Slamboss put on a cunning look.

"Numko could wig. We all bonzed: if Replic Dornal were here, he would freeb us a scroller."

All nodded and began to mumble. I bet, thought Arnold. He could see Necro looking nervous. He began to speak slowly making up words as he went along and hoping they sounded Klaptonian.

"This is a seeni Talwon. But it only scrolls us what we wing. We imagine, we wing what we cannot iball.

I wing that our mondo is round, rol, like a ball, a lobber."

"A lobber," glowered Slamboss. There was a burst of muttering. Topma looked baffled. Topwon, for some reason looked uncomfortable. Slamboss, though, had an evil smile on his face and Necro looked really worried. Arnold pressed on.

"When we do not ibe the Sizla, it is on the far side, the yondo poz of the lobber, of our world."

A venerable old man arose. "You yurb, Nurbul Himsir, that the Sizla shanxes round, rol our mondo doolo daj, every day?"

"Num, num," replied Arnold. "It is our mondo which revs like a lobber and shanxes rol the Sizla. We only imagine – we only wing that the Sizla goes round, shanxes rol our mondo."

In the hushed silence a very young councillor said:

"If our mondo revs, why don't we flomp off it, Nurbul Replic?"

Amid the laughter, Arnold thought: Gordon Bennett, if our earth revolves round the sun why don't we fall off? Then he realised, it was a fair question.

"Gravity holds us to the ground," he answered. All stared at him.

"Er – a wonzo shredd seccs us to the grav," he translated rapidly.

All of them, except Topwon, began to shake their heads.

"Nibbic," called Arnold. "If you don't believe me, jump in the air. See how long you can stay up. Er, skimp in the bree. How long can you ding in the bree?"

To his amazement, all the rows of councillors began to jump up and down. It was clear that in Klaptonia, orders were orders. Doosos were doosos and he was the one who was freebing them. How long his feeling of power might have lasted he could not say, but the brutal voice of Slamboss sounded.

"Frij it." All froze and came down to earth, looking foolish and frightened. Slamboss turned to Arnold, his face full of malevolent guile:

"If what you yurb is crozmi, Nurbul Himsir, then the Sizla also spangs on the Gloami Kojers, our yarbon hostos."

For a moment Arnold quailed. This bloke was a real frightener. Then he gathered his courage and spoke up.

"Yumda. The sun shines on everyone — the Sizla spangs on dooliwon — Tanji, Gloami, any tinjer."

A burst of whispering swept through the hall, then Slamboss spoke again.

"But we recc that the Gloami Kojers are gloami and not tanji because they nocca ibe the Sizla. They are gloami with frij. That is why they gruj us. How can the Nurbul Replic yurb that the Sizla spangs on our hostos?"

There was a silence you could cut with a knife. All eyes were on Arnold but his brain had seized up. Then he heard the voice of Necro.

"Aha, I bonz it. Nurbul Himsir Dornal is testing us with zotti yurbs and bonzers, to chex how well we recc our mondo. Shiners."

There was a nervous, relieved laugh from the crowd. "No," called a councillor at the back. "Not shiners. Dazzlers."

Topma rose. "Not dazzlers. Sinters, abso sinters. Now I have had enough of this slaff. I shall tring my wizzi wipper for a nice chumb of flork."

She stepped down from her throne, swept up to Arnold, tucked his hand into the crook of her arm and walked him away to the great double doors at the farther end of the hall while the whole council grovelled in admiration. As they left the hall Topwon rose swiftly.

"The Zalti Yurbon is dismissed," he said rapidly before Slamboss could speak.

The hall emptied. Slamboss, his face set and grim, leaned towards Topwon.

"So?" he demanded. "What do you bonz of that?"

Topwon grinned: "Well, if that's the shuff for Dornal, I wig he's slecca. That wipper's got it up here," he tapped his head. "I've not luxed a Yurbon so much in yexes."

Slamboss bent closer.

"How do you recc," he whispered, "that it isn't really Dornal, and not the Dirtwon?"

Topwon blinked.

"But you scrolled me Dornal had been slyped down to Dirt and this wipper frang up."

"How do you recc it is not Dornal, who hanks us to creed he is down on Dirt, when crozmi he is here? How do you recc Dornal is not in the shredd of the Gloami Kojers?"

"Oh," replied Topwon. "I hadn't bonzed at-won. The Gloamis are grooso diddli."

"Nibbic," said Slamboss quietly. "There is a way to find out . . ."

"That is?"

"Put him to the barbic."

"The torture?" Topwon's voice rose.

"You eeroled," said Slamboss, looking round. "The Lurci Flunkaj can barbic him. If he isn't Dornal, we'll recc it, immo."

"Finkle he is?"

Slamboss grinned evilly: "If he is Dornal, *they'll* recc it, immo."

He turned round, violently. Necro had quietly come up behind them.

"What do you hank?" he demanded.

Necro bowed. "A stacca grovels," he murmured then turning he slunk from the hall. Slamboss watched him go, eyes full of suspicion.

Chapter 14

DORNAL WENT BACK into school after break feeling more cheerful. With his new friends around him like a bodyguard, he found he was the object of much attention. Boys and girls stared at him, nudged one another and whispered. He could not guess what they were saying, but supposed they were remarking on his having found a place in the fast set. Certainly his friends seemed to command respect. Everyone got out of their way. Their manners left a lot to be desired. But they were no worse than he expected among the bladers, crushers and skullers of the Klaptonian Dongon. In fact, he thought, as he watched Eenie, Meanie, Mynie and Mo, from the corner of his eye, they would make excellent military material – the close cropped bullet heads, the flat noses, the massive shoulders and swaggering hips. Yes, he thought, a fine body of lads. With the right kind of weapons and training, he could make a splendid troop out of them.

Then he remembered he was no longer Himsir Dornal, but a Third Year pupil in a Dirt school. What was it Necro had told him? Not to step out of character, not to get excited, or he would lose his colour-cover and become the object of ridicule. He looked at the strange dirty-pink of his hands and arms and the faces of the boys and girls who swarmed around in the school corridor, and he wondered for the tenth time that morning how he could endure being this slaff, this ridiculous colour, when at home, his skin would glow a magnificent orange. He shrugged. He had to put up with it until they sent to bring him back.

The dark girl Sharon brushed up against him near the classroom door.

"Are you out of your bonce, Arnie?" she whispered.

He stared.

"Why are you running with those nut-cases?"

"My friends? What has that to do with you?"

Her lips tightened: "Because you do not know what day of the week it is. They are poison. The Yobs. No one goes near them. They are playing you up for their own reasons."

"I know what I am doing," he answered, exasperated, "woman!"

"Oh, stop messing about will you, Arnie," she snapped. "Got to go now – sports – got your proper gear?" She smiled suddenly.

Dornal felt himself begin to glow. He frowned and controlled it.

"Of course."

"OK. See you after school. I've got drama this afternoon."

He shrugged: "My friends have plans for a splendid wheeze."

She tossed her head and turned away. Then turned back. "Listen – I'll wait for you outside. See you get home, OK."

Dornal said no more, but turned his back and hurried after the Yobs, who were heading through the cloakrooms. He went to search for his locker and more by luck than management, he found it. And his sports gear was there. He examined it curiously. Two garments, a kind of tunic without sleeves, and a slaff pair of short hose. Then a pair of low shoes such as the poorest clodders used in the wallock-meds, battered and scuffed.

On the far side of the school, a mob of lads, laughing, shouting and pushing one another round turned and looked at him.

"Arnie's got the wrong gear, as usual. What a dimmo."

They gathered round, shaking their heads.

"He's a sad case. Look at it." One snatched at Dornal's bundle. He plucked it back. Another pulled at him from behind. He swung round, fist raised.

"Oooh, he's getting his mad up," they cooed.

Dornal felt a hot flush sweep up his body.

"Hey, look, Arnie's going a funny colour."

For one passionate moment, Dornal was about to lay into his tormentors. But with a super-Klaptonian effort, he controlled it. The colour drained from his neck and cheeks.

"Hey, he's going white again. Do you do anything else, Arnie?" they taunted.

There was a surge of energy through the crowd. There came the sound of head banging and ankle tapping. The circle around Arnie melted away and there were his new friends grinning at him. Eenie, hands on hips looked around him.

"Who is winding our Arnie up? Come on, own up. No, tell you what. Arnie, you tell us which one it was. Put the finger on one of 'em."

Dornal looked round. Now he saw fear in their faces. He saw the smile on Eenie's face and the crowd grew quiet. Something held him back from pointing. There were rules, doolis, he should know, about how to behave. What was the right thing to do? Necro had not prepared him for this.

"Come on Arnie. Pick one out, any one'll do."

"What's this, what's this? Why aren't we on the coach?"

The crowd shifted. Eenie melted away leaving Dornal on his own. He turned. Behind him was a tall man in a blue tunic, his chest and biceps bulging through the cloth. His face below the shining baldness of the head was square and red, his eyes small, blue and dangerous. It reminded Dornal of Slamboss. And he was nearly right. This was Maxwell Boardman, the Games Master, known throughout the school and if not loved, if not respected, then feared by all. His favourite phrase was "I'm trying to help you, lad," and the sound of the words sent a chill down the spine.

"Ah, yes, little Arnold, making trouble as usual, eh?"

Unused to his new name, Dornal looked round, baffled. The rest of the crowd shifted nervously. One giggled.

"I'm talking to you, laddie."

The Games Master's face was close to Dornal's. A cloud of aftershave and manly sweat swam around him. But Dornal, despite Necro's training, had not mastered the art of submission. He stared back and for a second the other's eyes wavered. Dornal knew that look. He had seen it in the eyes of many a hosto. When they did not know what to do after the first move had failed. A brief temptation struck him – to dismiss this clodder with a haughty word. Then it left him. The Games Master changed tack. His eyes darted to one side. His hand reached out, plucking Dornal's sports gear from his hand.

"What's this?" he asked. The gigglers had got the message and were laughing openly now.

The Games Master raised his hand and allowed the bundle to unfold, shorts, singlet, sports shoes. They dropped one by one to the ground.

"And what are we going to do in the swimming baths with these, eh? Walk on water?"

Boardman's index finger struck home on Dornal's chest.

"You have done this once too often. You are not stupid. You can only make mistakes like this because you are trying to wind me up. Well, two can play at that game."

He looked round, raising his voice.

"The rest of you, on the coach. Mr Hargreaves is taking you, God help him. So I have time for our little joker here. A personal course of treatment." The crowd vanished. The Games Master pointed to the gym.

"Get in there. Get your gear on. Then get out on the field and do press-ups until I tell you to stop."

Dornal entered the gym. To the right he saw a long room with wall hooks and lockers. The familiar smell of sweat and leather he knew from barracks swept up to his nostrils. Slowly he began to peel off his clothes then stopped in horror as his briefs dropped to his ankles. Necro was right. Across at hip level, was an unmistakeable band of bright orange. Frantically he plucked up the shorts and tried to drag them on. He slipped and fell against the bench as a shadow loomed over him.

"What's up with you lad? Need help? How old are you?"

Under the Games Master's gaze, Dornal fumbled with the pants and the low shoes. How did the thongs fasten? He hastily tucked them into the side of his foot and sprang to his feet.

"Out on the field, then."

Dornal ran. That voice was getting to him. As he came from the stuffy shade of the changing room, the sun's warmth hit his face. But it was not the clear, dry heat of Klaptonia's Sizda, but more like the humid warmth of the Bashi Rangles. He felt drops of sweat roll down his forehead into his eyes.

"What's up with you , lad? Sweating before you've even started? Right. Down on the grass. Go on," he urged as Dornal hesitated, bewildered.

The Games Master's chest swelled in frustration: "Don't push your luck ..." Then in a sudden rage he advanced on Dornal. Dornal braced himself. Their eyes met. And again the Games Master looked away. Suddenly in exasperation he threw himself down and began vigorously to raise and lower his body on his outstretched arms.

"Like that, like that. Now you carry on until I tell you to stop, right?"

Dornal fell to the ground and began to lever his body up and down. As he did the breath filled his lungs, his muscles responded and for the first time since he landed on Dirt, a sense of well being filled him. He fell into the rhythm of the exercise. And he thought to himself: this I must try on the bladers when I get back. Too much time drinking wallock root juice and lounging about with dimas. All soft. This'll get them back into condition. Maybe he could get the Games Master to slyp up the Beam with him when he returned. He never noticed that the Games Master had left him and walked away towards the school.

From her second floor office Ms Heathcote, the Head, raised her eyes from the desk work (returns for County Hall) which quite frankly bored the pants off her, an expression she only used to herself. Her gaze ranged the school yard, the playing fields, the windows of the science lab. She could see, from her desk what most of the school was doing. She liked to watch that.

From time to time she took up from her desk the field glasses she used when out bird watching and swept the horizon with them. With their help she could detect and identify not only the deed, but the doer thereof. What these lenses had seen behind the bike sheds, in the lab prep room or even round cupboard doors in the staff room, would fill a small book. What she saw she kept mostly to herself. Just as she kept most of herself to herself. To some of the staff and most of the pupils, she was a quiche-eating wimp, and she hid herself behind that disguise. Head-teachers often need a disguise.

Her eyes picked up a lone figure on the edge of the soccer pitch. She fiddled with the binocular screw. The image came nearer. She saw the boy in sports gear, arms pumping up and down. Press-ups. Now what was he training for? Sports Day was months away. And why on his own? She finally got the focus right. Why it was little Arnold Radleigh. No! She could imagine him training for creative writing, but this?

The 'phone rang. She put the binoculars down and picked it up. "Yes – ye – es." Her voice changed as she recognised Oliver Edwards, chairman of the Education Committee. She knew what he was on about, pompous fool. Plans for cutting the local schools down from eight to five and which were candidates for the chop. Funny how slow they were when you wanted help, and how quick they were when they were closing something down. She mentally switched off while his voice droned on. Minutes passed. "Yeerrs, yeerrs," she muttered.

The 'phone went down. A knock on the door and the Deputy Head entered with more problems. The Head listened again, gripped the side of the desk and waited for peace and quiet to descend on her once more. She looked at the pile of work on her desk with distaste, then idly picked up the binoculars again. He was still at it! Little Arnold was still doing press-ups. She raised her wrist. It couldn't be. Forty-five minutes press-ups. She stood in agitation. Nearly a thousand press-ups. It wasn't humanly possible.

A sudden thought struck her. Snatching up her binoculars she trained them on the staff room. Yes, there he was, track suit hanging on the chair, legs raised on a table, coffee cup in hand, talking to two student teachers. He'd set that poor little Arnold to do press-ups and skived off to sit on his bum in the staff room. People like Maxwell Boardman, she thought, kept Human Rights campaigners going all over the world.

Skirts flying, long legs striding, she was out of the door, along the passage, down four flights of stairs and out on to the playing fields, leaping the small wall like a gazelle. As she came closer to the mechanically working body, she noticed that Arnold's body, face, arms, legs, had gone bright orange. The boy was going to have a stroke. There'd be an inquiry. The school would be sued. Insurance claims.

"Arnold, stop it. Get up," she commanded.

The boy shook his head. "I must go on until the Games Master commands," he grunted.

The Head bent down and hauled Dornal up by his singlet. As he stood and faced her, his face slowly adjusted to a more normal colour. She breathed her relief. "Do you mean to say the Games Master told you to do press-ups for nearly an hour?"

Dornal nodded. He was baffled by the appearance of this slim lady with the grey eyes and short blonde hair. But he knew authority when he saw it.

He bowed low. She stared.

"That is true," he said.

"Oh, is it. Well, go back to the gym and lie down. Are you feeling all right?"

"I never felt better," he stammered.

"Now," she said, "I shall go and speak to Mr Boardman myself."

She turned and strode away, leaving Dornal puzzling over his latest experience. Of all the strange aspects of life on Dirt, the women were the most amazing. He would never understand it. He shook his head and wandered away to the gym.

By afternoon it was all over the school. Little Arnold had landed the Games Master in it up to his nostrils, just by doing what he was told. What a cunning little sod he was, they all marvelled.

Eenie rubbed his hands as he marched his little band away from their daily detention.

"We are going to have jolly japes tonight, chaps," he said.

Chapter 15

TOPMA LED THE way, down the passage from the Council Chamber, talking over her shoulder as she went.

"Sinters, darlo Dornal, abso sinters. The scan on the blushers of those gormers, when you yurbed our mondo revs round the Sizla. They credd it was crozmi. What a stacca soggers."

Arnold wasn't sure whether to be pleased with himself or whether he was simply getting himself deeper into trouble. And there was a lot of trouble about. Not only had Hermiss Roshan been kidnapped, but there was a plot to kidnap Dornal. And since Dornal was suffering down in Denfield Comprehensive, that meant a plot to kidnap Arnold.

And who were these Gloami Kojers, these Purple People? They were purple because they lived on the wrong side of the mondo and the Sizla never shone on them. A right load of wallocks if ever you heard. But what were wallocks? They sounded a bit like something you had every Friday for school dinner. There was a lot about this place he didn't understand, which was frustrating because he'd invented it. Or maybe they had invented him. That was an alarming thought.

They passed through another hall, with two

thrones, Topma with her arm through his. He felt
foolishly comfortable. If Mum had walked with him
like this, at home, he'd have blushed down to his
socks. But up here he could get away with it. Down
there — on Dirt — what was Dornal doing? He
thought rapidly. What day was it? Tuesday. Oh no, it
was swimming, and he'd brought his sports gear. So
he knew what Dornal was doing — press-ups with
the Incredible Hulk leering at him. A smile came on
to his face. Topma smiled back at him.

The door ahead swung open. Beyond Arnold saw
the mysterious servant girl Norsha. Now she'd
washed and put on a green tunic. Her eyes were
lowered. She did not look at him and to be honest, his
eyes were elsewhere. In the middle of this sump-
tuous apartment with its ornamental couches and
curtained alcoves, was a massive table laid with
dishes of all kinds, grouped around a huge metal
plate bearing a cooked and steaming animal as big
as a baby elephant.

"Twanged on the flap this brecc," trilled Topma.
"You'll lux this, Dornie."

Shot on the wing? Arnold giggled. It beat the
school cafeteria. Topma pushed him playfully.

"In you todd and have your dosh. You look quite
sindi and fratched with all the graf."

Hot and bothered. I should coco. But a bath?
Where?

He marched to the nearest door. She stopped him.

"You are in a chimpi tem. That's the dimas poz."

Ladies side? Arnold swerved desperately and
lunged through the other door. The room beyond
swirled with steam which condensed and ran down
his face and filled his eyes. He reached blindly and
struck not stone, but flesh. Someone chuckled.

"Grovli . . ." he began. But already hands were busy

round his middle. The sword belt was twitched away. Next the hands smartly slipped the tunic off his shoulders. He panicked. She'd be after his strides next. He gathered his wits.

"Staccot," he commanded, his voice going up the scale. "Bego!" The girl vanished. He looked around him. The steam thinned out. He could see tiled walls and floor. There were two baths at ground level, one looked cold, still and green. The other looked boiling hot and it was red.

The bathroom seemed empty now, but he took no chances. In the corner was a tall screen, painted with pictures of creatures as fat as pigs, flying over a weird forest landscape. Must be prehistoric he thought. Nothing as big as that flew these days unless it was on charter. Behind the screen he slipped out of his hose and stared in amazement. It was the first chance he'd had to look at his own body since he arrived in Klaptonia. To be honest it looked far out. His skin was stained a deep orange down to his navel. After that came a strip of more or less normal colour. Like you get when you sunbathe in trunks. The orange colour started again at his thighs. Would he revert when he got home? he wondered.

He peered round the screen. Now the room was empty. He tiptoed across and tried the first green bath, with his toe nail. It was freezing. He took another couple of paces and tried the second bath. It was boiling. He thought the skin would peel off his foot. He went back to the first. Now it felt a bit better. He stuck his leg into the hot bath – aaargh, then into the cold one. The relief was incredible. He sat down on the tiles. Swung his legs into the hot (neeargh!), then back into the cold (aaaah!). Each time it was more bearable. Elbows bent, he rested his hand on the edge, slid in his legs up to the hips, counted one, two then neeargh, swung up, back and over into the cold. Rolled back into the boiler, then out again. No wonder they were mad as hatters on Klaptonia if this was their idea of bath night. He was kicking cheerfully, seventeenth time round, in the cold bath, when he looked up and saw Norsha waiting at the edge with a large fleecy cloth held in front of her.

Panicking he sank below the surface, She mustn't see his white bit, but how long could he keep this up? He let his head break the surface. She was looking at him in pure amazement.

"Zoff!" he shouted in desperation.

He pointed down, then to the door. She shrugged, dropped the towel and stalked to the door. As it closed behind her, he clambered out of the bath, wrapped the towel round him and raced behind the screen He dried himself furiously, then struggled into his tights. Funny business this – in a world where men were men and women were walked over, the men all wore women's clothes.

He slid on the tunic and hose. That was easier. Bit funny without the briefs, still, it saved time. He looked for the belt and sword. It was gone. Norsha must have removed it. What was that girl up to?

"Norsha," he called. There was no answer. How thick were these walls? If the rest of the palace were anything to go by, they were two feet wide. Now, which door did she go out of? And which was the dining room? There were three doors, all fitting close to the wall and each with gold door knobs.

Ah well, Eenie ... on second thoughts, no. He took the nearest one. It swung open and revealed a pitch dark passage beyond. Wrong, he thought and made to step back into the bathroom. But he found he couldn't move. His tunic was caught on something.

No, someone. Somebody had hold of him. He struggled and hit out. Someone in the darkness grunted, then pulled closer to him. He smelt foul breath. Whoever it was had been drinking, sump oil or similar. Someone else was behind him, gripping his arms. He lashed out with his heel and heard his attacker groan.

But the grip from the front was stronger. He was lifted up. A hand was clapped over his mouth and he was thrown over a shoulder. They were so big it must be Kitten Kong. Just as he began to realise dimly who was hi-jacking him, he was in mid air, being carried forward into the darkness as though riding on the back of a mad elephant.

Chapter 16

THE MAD RIDE through passages, down flights of steps, more tunnels, each one gloomier, danker and smellier than the one before, ended when a door in front was kicked open. Arnold's nostrils filled with a choking mixture of grease, burning coal and foul air. Torches, smokily flaming, stood out from the wall, not lighting but throwing into shadow the objects on the rush-covered stone floor. As Arnold was dumped down, hands grappled at him, rushed him forward, swung him round and bent him back. His spine crunched on a hard surface, above the floor. He was on some sort of table. He tried to jerk up, but a huge hand slammed him down. Busy fingers strapped ankles and wrists. He was spread out like a letter 'X', unable to move, save for his head.

As he turned his head, he wished he hadn't. For now he saw where the burning smell came from. In the centre of the floor was a brazier, full of red glowing lumps of coal or charcoal. Sticking out were metal rods. It didn't need much imagination to know these weren't toasting forks. His innards underneath the white patch started to freeze.

"If he'd had his Misti Sticcer with him, we nocca champed it," said a voice near Arnold's foot. A young voice. He could see the fat little squit. It was the couple of charlies who had brought him up here. So it *was* a magic sword. Right, if he could lay hands on it, he knew what he'd do to this dynamic duo. Convert them to a quartet. A soprano quartet. It was amazing how this place got to you. He'd not been there a day and he was getting quite brutal. Still they were going to be brutal to him. They hadn't come down here for toasted teacakes that was certain.

"I wonder where that sticcer is? You didn't slep it on the todd, did you?" asked the boy, Nobbin. He had a funny way of talking to his Dad, but Arnold guessed it was Nobbin who did the thinking while Hitman took care of the action. It was a deadly combination.

A shadow passed over him. Man Mountain was moving round to the brazier. A bare muscular arm poked out of the jerkin sleeve and a hand like a bear's paw touched the iron.

"Ooooh, that's sindi," he mumbled.

"Yum, Dadwon, wing what it's like the other end," slavered little Nobbin. Hitman scratched his head. "I'm fratched about that sticcer. You don't wing he's lurced it sumloc, do you?"

"What, up his jumper? Don't be gormi, Dadwon, he couldn't put a sticcer up there."

"You yurb to your Fawon a bit more grovli, Nobbi, wonzo when there are yonco kojers about."

"Grovels, Dadwon," Nobbin whined. What a cosmic creep he was. For a moment, Arnold almost sympathised with Hitman. Was there a Mrs Hitman, he wondered?

Then his sympathy vanished as the great oaf licked his fingers and started touching the torture rods again.

"I bonz I'll dib a diji nan iron," he muttered.

Hitman pulled up the iron and waved it in the air. Arnold's eyes crossed. A number nine iron? Sparks flew and the cherry red end suddenly glowed white.

"Hey, just a nimmot, Dadwon," said Nobbin. "You haven't wigged what to doople him."

"Doople him?" Hitman looked baffled.

"Zitto, you've got ask him puzzlers. That's why we're putting the barbic on him."

"Like what?" Hitman looked disappointed.

"We have to wig if he's Dornal or not."

Hitman thought carefully, then put the iron back to heat up. His eyes brightened.

"Yum, but he'll porc just to stop us sizzling him, won't he?"

"Yum, Dadwon. But if he doesn't know what sort of answer we hank, he won't recc what to yurb will he?"

Hitman looked at Nobbin, then slowly counted two fingers.

"Too kojers, too brands. Replic Dornal, that's won. Then, there's the yondo kojer, the Dirtwon. What's his brand?"

"We don't recc. That's why we're freebing him the barbic, Dadwon."

"Yer."

"But," Nobbin went on, "if this *is* Dornal, he won't know what the Dirtwon's name is, will he?"

"Well, if he doesn't recc, that chex he atta be Dornal."

"Yum, but how do we recc he crozmi doesn't know it? He could be the Dirtwon wanging not to know his own brand, jotto to stop us sizzling him."

Suddenly Hitman smiled an evil inspired smile.

"We'll barbic him, premi, then doople him puzzlers afto."

"Suppose he naccs on us, or ..." Nobbin paused, "morbs on us."

Hitman nodded slowly.

"Well, you ding with the bucket and tosh sogger on him if he naccs. Don't waste it. Just a glob now and then."

"Ah, Dadwon, I lux to use the irons. Can't we take turns?"

"Num. I've scrolled you. These are not trinkers. You have to be seeni — like wonti-too yexes, before you get to use barbic irons."

Arnold had a sudden thought. In fantasies it was all action. But nothing was happening here, though he was getting wound up. Just the dialogue was upsetting him. Still talking was better than burning. If he could keep the conversation going, that would put it off a while. Better still, if he could separate them. But how?

If he could get the big wump out of the torture chamber, the little one wasn't allowed to use the irons. If he could get the little one out, then the big one wouldn't know his number nine from his niblick would he? Then he remembered — the Misti Sticcer, the magic sword. Where was it? He hadn't a clue, but he felt pretty sure Norsha had taken it. She seemed friendly, but how did he know she wasn't a twister, a spy, an agent from the Gloami Kojers? But if she were an agent of the GKs, then she might lead him to where the Hermiss Roshan was. She was bound to be on a different side to these two animals. But she wasn't here, was she? Always around when not wanted, never there when she was. She must be an agent, perhaps a double agent.

All this ran through his mind in a mini-second. He could think fast under pressure. He noticed Big Daddy had the number nine iron in his hand and was waving it about again. Now it was coming closer. He could feel the warm breath of it making his little hairs curl. It stopped.

"Maybe we atta cop his chooner off. Pity to pog that, it's classi cloot," said Hitman slowly.

"Num Dadwon. To cop his cloot off, we have to slep him. If we slep him he'll morb us. No, barb him a bit. Wyp the cloot."

The heat moved closer. Arnold felt the sweat run in rivers down his body.

"The Misti Sticcer," he gasped. "I'll freeb the Misti Sticcer if you slep me."

The heat vanished again. Hitman's face lit up. He put the iron back in the fire and held out his hand.

"Nibbic. Freeb!"

"Don't credd him Dadwon. He's hoking you."

"If he does, Sonwon, I shall be siccers."

"But that'll be too dilli, Dadwon."

"Eerol," said Arnold urgently. "I lurced the Misti Sticcer somewhere."

"Where did you lurc it?"

"I'm not scrolling."

Hitman grinned: "Sinters. Now I've got a puzzler for you. I can barbic you."

"Num." said Arnold. "I'll todd with Nobbin and he

can fring the sticcer to you, while you keep the charcer sindi."

Hitman shook his head.

"How do I recc you'll come back?"

"Do you doubt the Yurb of a Himsir?" Arnold said haughtily.

"Num. But suppose you're not a Himsir. Suppose you're a diddli Dirtwon."

Arnold thought desperately. This was worse than choose your own adventure talking to this pair.

"Eerol. You slep me. I'll todd with Nobbin and cop the sticcer. I'll freeb him the sticcer and yurb him who I am — crozmi."

Hitman thought carefully, then finally shook his head.

"Num. You scroll me where the sticcer is. I'll todd off and cop it, then I'll meho and barbic you, and you'll scroll me who you are, crozmi."

"Hey, Dadwon, that was sinters, real pozzi bonzers," gasped Nobbin. He turned to Arnold. "Zitto. You scroll us where the sticcer is, jacco, or Dadwon starts the barbic."

Arnold took a deep breath.

"Nibbic. The sticcer is lurced in the doshi-cham."

Hitman grinned. Placed the iron across the top of the brazier, then turned and marched to the door. There he turned again and shook his finger.

"Nimmo, Sonwon. Don't dib with those irons. You can get charco that way."

Arnold knew it. No sooner had the ape gone when an evil little smile came over Nobbin's face.

"Dazzlers. Now's my occ to dib the irons. Dadwon's so miggi, I nocca cop the occ. I mean how can you improve, if you don't dib? All I ever do is swib the grav and make yoot beer."

What a dredji little turdwon he was, thought

Arnold. Out of the corner of his eye he saw the door had swung open. Hitman had forgotten to close it. But Nobbin was too busy by the brazier. The podgy little hands reached out. But clumsy Dadwon had put the iron down across the top of the coals. It had heated all the way up to the handle.

"Yaaargh," howled the little creep as his fingers closed round it. He jerked in agony and the iron flew across the floor. In an instant the rushes burst into flame and vile smelling smoke billowed up. The little git was running round in circles. Arnold spotted the bucket, full of water.

"Dosh it with sogger from the cubber," he yelled.

But Nobbin wasn't listening to friendly advice. He was stamping madly on the rushes. Next moment to Arnold's surprise, he was backing away through the cloud of smoke, hands held out in front of him and whimpering.

"Num, num, grovli."

Beyond Nobbin, Arnold now saw the familiar figure of Norsha, no longer in her green bathrobe, but once again in her dirty kitchen smock. In her hand was the smoking torture iron which she waved in front of Nobbin's quivering cheeks.

"Slep Himsir Dornal."

"Numdo. Dadwon'll flake me."

"If you don't slep Himsir Dornal, you won't have any flake."

She touched Nobbin's jerkin gently. A sizzle and a cloud of smoke and he was gibbering at Arnold's side, frantically picking at the leather straps.

"Oooh my poor piccers," he moaned.

Norsha flicked his rump with the hot iron and drew a howl of agony from him.

"Blinki twinki," she jeered. "It's barely glom. I'll sind it up," she added helpfully.

Nobbin dragged open the last strap and Arnold rolled, in agonised stiffness off the table on to the floor. As he dragged himself up, Norsha was busy bent over the prone figure of Nobbin, stretched out on the block, fastening the straps. She stood back and plunged the iron into the fire. Then she bowed low to Arnold, and pointed to the handle.

"Nurbul Himsir. Would you lux to charc the bitti pog?"

Arnold looked at the outstretched limbs, the quivering orange features. Would he like to give him a taste of his own medicine? A savage Dornal thought came into his mind, then he pushed it away and Arnold took over again.

"Num tocc for that," he cried. She looked at him curiously, then nodded.

"Zitto, O Replic. Nimmo — heel me, but jacco. Your bree is in rix."

"So, what else is new?" said Arnold in Dirtyurb as they fled through the open door and down the foul winding passage beyond.

Chapter
17

SHARON RAN INTO Dornal at the end of the school day. At least she caught up with him after following his erratic progress round the school. He was behaving very strangely, but not in his usual strange manner. She was determined to find out what was going on. She found him in the small passage that led from the cloaks to the battery of small rooms where the caretaker kept cleaning materials and did all those other mysterious things which caretakers do. He was looking down the corridor first in this direction, then in that, and then sneaking back into one of the broom cupboards.

She caught his arm. "Arnold, are you all right?"

He glared at her as if he did not recognise her.

Then he grinned sheepishly and put his finger to his lips. "Can't talk. Can't tell you. Must wait for my friends."

"Friends? You're off the wall. Those aren't friends. They're reptiles. They're using you. They'll land you right in it."

He glared at her indignantly.

"Garbers. What do you know about my chúms? How can a girl understand the japes that chaps can get up to. Girls are so wet, always worrying about what's going to happen. That's why they spoil everything."

"Thank *you*, Arnie." He really was strange. Was he high on something? She moved in closer to look at his lips. He jerked his head back. Funny, he didn't look as though he was high, but he was acting like it. And if he had started hanging around with the Yobs they might have given him anything.

Dornal looked round then whispered: "I'll tell you, if you don't split on us. We're having a midnight feast."

"You're WHAT?"

Her voice rose and he reached out to place a hand over her mouth. The hand was rough and strong. She didn't know Arnold had it in him. She knocked the hand aside and the two of them struggled together briefly.

"Listen, Arnold, are you coming, or not?"

"Coming where?"

"Home."

He gawped at her. She was not getting through to him.

She took a breath. What should she do? Get hold of him and drag him out of school? In his present mood she doubted if she could manage it. But if she left him here . . .

Footsteps sounded along the corridor. It was Big Bertha, head of the cleaning ladies, who had more clout about the school than anyone, including the Head. She strode along, swinging her bundle of plastic bags.

"What are you doing here, then?" she called. Bertha always started talking to you when she was miles away. By the time she reached you, you were too dazed to say anything.

"Er," muttered Sharon, her eyes swivelling wildly. Arnold had vanished. Bertha advanced.

"What are you doing here? You know you shouldn't. Oh, it's you, Sharon . . ."

"Yeah, Mrs Bennett, I lost an earring on the floor."

"Serve you right; shouldn't be wearing them in school, should we? Shall I help you look? Don't want it in the Hoover do we?"

"Er, no thanks, Oh, it's down here." Sharon bent and pretended to be scratching around on the floor.

To her relief Big Bertha was satisfied.

"All right love, off you go. There are too many kids hanging about here after school these days. Nowhere else to go, that's the trouble. If I had my way . . ."

Her voice died away down the passage.

"Arnold," Sharon whispered.

His voice came back from beyond the open cupboard door.

"Thanks old girl, for not letting on to the beak."

"The beak?"

She shrugged. "Listen Arnold. If you're not coming out, that's your lookout. But you can't stay here for any midnight feast or whatever caper the Yobs have dreamt up. But if you won't come now, I'll stick around for a bit outside."

Dornal heard Sharon's footsteps moving away. Then he crouched down behind a pile of boxes. He was beginning to feel hungry and a little sleepy. It had been a wearing day. How long was it till midnight, when they would start the feast he wondered? Feasts to him usually meant smoking platters of sliced flork, washed down with yoot wine. But Necro had told him that mightnight feasts meant toasted crumpet, cream cakes and bottles of pop. What these were he did not know, but he was looking forward to them. He wished his friends would hurry up. He began to doze off.

The door opened. A man's voice boomed.

"Bertha. Where's that new carton of Harpic? You lot must be eating the stuff."

Dornal heard someone rummage among the containers and brushes. He crouched down and after a moment or two with a muttered oath, the man left the room. Time passed slowly. Dornal's mind wandered. Life on Dirt was turning out to be interesting in its own strange way. What, he wondered, was happening to his double, his shuff, back in Klaptonia? He couldn't imagine that he could last long before he was found out. But that was a problem for Necro and Slamboss not for him.

"Arnie boy. Wakey, wakey!"

The door was open again and his new friend Eenie poked his head round it.

"Come on."

The others were outside in the passage. They studied him with interest. He could not understand why they looked at him in this way. But he supposed it was a look that indicated friendship on Dirt.

Eenie led the way back through the cloaks. They moved swiftly and silently, ducking back behind corners when they heard the clatter of buckets or the whine of Hoovers.

"Up here."

They climbed two short flights of stairs and turned into a

narrow passage to stop outside a green door. Eenie twisted the handle.

"Our lucky day," he grunted. The door opened and Dornal's nostrils were met by a strange smell, sharp and strong which made him sneeze.

"Hey, pack it in," Eenie nudged him.

Dornal looked round. Along the sides of the walls were two beds. Or so he guessed. White metal frames, a mattress, sheets. One of the sheets was brown and smooth. More strange smells.

"Dormer, old boy," whispered Eenie. "Only two beds per room for prefects like us."

"Good egg," replied Dornal. "Shall we have our feast in here?" His stomach rumbled. "Is midnight soon?"

Meanie looked at him sharply.

Then he turned to Eenie: "Hey is he putting us on?"

"Nah," Eenie shook his head. "He just thinks it's Christmas."

"I don't like it. Suppose he's up on something. We could be lumbered."

"Listen mate. If he's got that kind of gear, we need to know what it is."

"Come on chaps," Dornal interrupted, puzzled by their conversation. "Let's unpack the food hamper."

Eenie shook his head.

"No, old boy. We've a much snappier wheeze. We're going to feast in the Head's study."

"You what?" Mynie's mouth fell open. Eenie jabbed an elbow into him.

"Follow us, old fruit," he said to Dornal. "The jape is you sneak into the Head's study, and open the window. We pootle off down to the tuck shop and get lashings of grub."

"Cor yes," added Mo, "and a pack of lager, and ..."

"Stuff it, boardhead," interrupted Eenie. "Then we hand it in to you through the window ..."

"Why can't we use the door?" asked Mo. "It's two

floors up and I don't like heights."

"Stupid, we have to keep the door locked, so old Baxter doesn't know what we're up to . . ."

He jerked his head. "Come on."

Swiftly they made their way down steps, along corridors, with the stealth and precision of break-in artists. For the second time that day, Dornal admired the dedicated energy and craft of his companions. What a splendid bunch of bladers they'd make, as his personal bodyguard. If only he could slyp them back to Klaptonia.

They slid to a halt outside the Head's study. From his pocket, Eenie took out a bunch of keys, selected one, tried it, swore, tried another, swore again, and then, at the third attempt, the metal grated and squealed. With a jump the door swung open. As it did, they heard footsteps on the floor below.

"Get in there."

They tumbled into the room.

"Get the door shut, quick. Get down."

"Can't make the key work, that's what. 'Ere, Mo, stand against the door."

Heavy footsteps pounded outside. Baxter was humming and cursing under his breath as he walked. At the door he paused, rattled the handle, then pushed.

"Funny, that," he mused as the door yielded then stuck as it met Mo's weight on the farther side. "Have to see to that tomorrow."

He moved off. The five looked at each other. Dornal's excitement mounted. Eenie clapped him on the shoulder.

"Right, we're off. Now we're going to lock the door behind us, so the beak won't suspect. You keep cave and when we come back, let us in by the window."

Dornal nodded: "Don't be long, chaps, I'm ravenous."

The door closed behind them and he heard the grating sound as Eenie's key finally made the circle in the lock. Now he looked round the study. A pleasant room, he

92

thought, with a faint smell of woman's perfume and a small vase of flowers on the desk. He thought back to the early afternoon and his encounter with the Head. A strange person, so agitated over his exercises on the playing field. A pleasant face though. He sat down in her chair and looked out over the playing fields. Well, his first day on Dirt had turned out better than it had begun. Perhaps now he had friends and had the hang of the strange customs, he could overcome his disadvantages, like not understanding all that was said to him, or not being able to read.

His thoughts were suddenly interrupted by a great crash and a bellow from the far end of the building.

"Hey, what are you up to?"

Dornal recognised the voice of the caretaker. The building now resounded to the clatter of boots and scrabble of feet on the stairs and in the passages. Then the voice came again.

"Kevin, get on the blower and get the police. We'll get one of 'em at least."

His friends had been rumbled. Dornal's instincts told him. And he was locked in. Trapped. He heard the shouting come nearer, a rush of footsteps outside that rose and died again. Then silence for a few moments. In the distance, through the evening air, he now heard a strange wailing sound that came closer and closer.

Again there were voices outside.

"Anything missing, Kev?"

"Not that I can see. They've been in the sick bay."

"Oho. After drugs, I'll bet."

"None of the cupboards touched, though."

"What about this? The door was a bit dodgey when I tried it earlier on."

Keys scratched in the lock. Dornal leapt from the chair, looked round swiftly and then dived under the table crouching behind the swivel mounting of the Head's chair.

From the floor, he saw the door open, two pairs of legs, boots.

"Nah, nothing in here. Must have been mistaken."

"Better go down. The Old Bill's here."

"Late as per usual. Run down and let 'em in, Kev."

The door slammed shut. Dornal heard the key turn again. He was locked in for good, now, hungry, trapped until the Head returned in the morning. His first adventure with his new friends on Dirt, had gone chossy.

Chapter 18

"STACCA TACCAS," MUTTERED Arnold as he followed Norsha down the winding passage that led away from the Torture Chamber. She stopped and sent him a puzzled look with a ghost of a smile, then abruptly masked it with her usual glowering expression and pointed forward.

"Jacco, before the gormer mehos."

Arnold needed no urging. He stretched his stiff and bruised limbs to keep abreast of her.

"Where to?"

"Jacco, Jacco. Your bree is in rix."

She kept saying his life was in danger. She was right. If it wasn't sudden death from unseen Gloami Kojers, or falling three million feet from the castle walls, it was a slow roast in Hitman and Nobbin's microwave. How long had he been here? Half a day

and already he'd enough material for three full scale
fantasy adventures. The only snag was he couldn't
switch them off. He puffed with the effort of keeping
up. She ran like a deer, twisting and turning in the
gloomy warren of tunnels beneath the castle.

"My Misti Sticcer," he gasped.

She nodded and abruptly turned into a side tunnel.
He staggered, regained balance and followed her up a
spiral stairway. A door opened and they were in a
room lit by a narrow slit in the wall. It was like a
prison cell. You could reach both walls at once with
your hands. On the floor was a pile of straw and an
old blanket. He didn't need telling — this was the
servant's quarters.

Norsha cast aside the blanket and there, it's
ruby and emerald crusted hilt gleaming in the faint
light, was the sword, with the belt neatly coiled
round it. She raised it up with care and stepped
towards him, slipped it round his hips and swiftly
buckled it in front. She bowed down low and
stepped back.

"I must cop a nedder and plog to div Hermiss
Roshan," said Arnold, who now remembered he was
Dornal again. A shadow of irritation appeared to
cross her face. The green eyes glittered.

She shook her head. "You atta rig. They will dib to
morb you."

"Who, and why?" demanded Arnold. She shrugged
as though his questions were pointless, as if she had
no idea of the answer.

"Where?" he demanded.

She spoke, half to herself:

"If we todd by the wallock-meds and yoot orchards,
we can shanx more jacco. But we shall be scanned.
Num, there is singo won todd. Dro the Bashi Rangles.
There it is murgo and we can shanx in lurc. But it is

rixi. I don't recc the todd. We could be chumbed in the slurd."

Her face brightened.

"There atta be a scimmer in Necro's cham. He is the jenko about Klaptonia. We can shim up the bricca and inco dro the spanger."

Arnold swallowed. Climbing round walls and in through windows — that was not a brilliant idea. He had to have a more brilliant one.

"Numdo," he said with more firmness than he felt. "We shall inco the Occi Cham and cop the scimmer," he hesitated, and grasped the sword hilt "at the nicc of the sticcer."

She nodded and led the way from her room, Arnold close behind her. In a matter of seconds, through narrow ways and up winding steps, they came into the half-lit passage outside Necro's great studded door.

Arnold drew a quick breath, slid out his sword. He'd got the hang of it now and the blade came free smoothly. Pushing past Norsha, remembering in time not to say "Excuse me," or anything unprincely like that, he lunged at the door. It gave way, he shot forward, down the steps and into the gloom and smell of the magician's den. It was empty. But as the rush of his entry carried Arnold forward to the table, something uncoiled and shot through the air at him. Before he knew it had wrapped itself like a scaly bandage round his arm and the sword dropped from his shocked grasp. In an instant Norsha was at his side, grappling with his attacker. Then she stopped, eyes wide as the snake (for it was he) nuzzled the side of Arnold's face.

"Oh, zoff, Clarence. You put the frij up me."

The snake unzipped and slid away under the table.

"Jacco, Norsha." He nodded towards the chest.

"Lets mol in the dumper there. Num, you doo that. I'll mol dro the doofers on this yonco eezer. Cor what a mess," Arnold muttered as he began hastily to pluck up parchment after parchment, from the pile on the chair.

"Num doob to pog my doofers," said a quiet voice behind them. Norsha and Arnold jumped. Necro stood there.

"How did . . .?" Arnold began.

"Aha," began Necro, then he added: "I scanned you in the Misti Crist and lurced in the danglers. I recced you would todd here."

He walked to the door, opened it. He gestured angrily at Norsha who silently crept out. Arnold was about to protest, but remembered in time who he was supposed to be. Necro closed and bolted the door then pointed to a chair. Then he waved his hand over the table top. One by one the interiors of various rooms in the Shotto came into view. Arnold saw Topma with her waiting women, at work on a new tapestry with monsters on it. The Topwon was sleeping off his lunch. The Slamboss had company and Necro speedily switched channels. In the torture chamber, for a brief chuckling moment, Arnold saw Hitman with little Nobbin across his knee, spanking away. The image roved the walls and towers outside. Guards dozed in the now setting sun.

"Tranco," murmured Necro. He spoke now in Dirtyurb.

"You must leave. Your life is in danger."

"I know. But no one tells me why."

Necro looked crafty. "It is not easy. There are agents of the Gloami Kojers about."

"Huh, Purple People," said Arnold. "The only ones who are trying to kill me are that dynamic duo, Hitman and Nobbin."

Necro put his finger to his nose.

"Aha, but who are they working for?"

"Well, they must be Slamboss's minders," snorted Arnold.

Necro's eyebrows rose. "Can you be sure? The one thing is, you must leave the Shotto and escape into the meds."

"So," said Arnold. "But can I trust you?"

Necro suddenly smiled a wicked smile.

"Perhaps not. But I am the only one who can show you the way through the Bashi Rangles."

"OK, so give me the map."

"There is no map," Necro chuckled, "the map is here," he tapped his white head. "If you wish to escape, I must go with you. But the question is whither."

"Whither? Why to rescue the Hermiss Roshan."

"Brave boy. You realise that this means not only a journey through the terrors of the Bashi Rangles, but a voyage down the Great River, through three unknown Topwondoms, over the hostile rugged reaches of the Prussy Peakers and on into the land of the Gloami Kojers."

"Er," said Arnold. This was the kind of project he'd never undertaken, a kind of serial fantasy. And he might never get back, or wake up. On the other hand if he didn't go, someone might morb him messily here in the Shotto. It wasn't exactly multiple choice.

"Well, so be it," he said, more boldly than he felt. "I'll go to the Gloami Kojers and offer to make peace, if they release Hermiss Roshan."

Necro crowed with laughter.

"Do you believe they will agree? Our sworn enemies, yarbon hostos for a thousand years?"

Arnold leant forward.

"Necro, between ourselves. You know I'm not

Himsir Dornal so you don't need to give me any bullshit. Have you ever met any of the Gloami Kojers?"

Necro murmured "Hm."

"For all you know, they may be just as afraid of you, as you seem to be of them. They may be ready for peace talks."

Necro looked at Arnold in amazement.

"If you go around saying any more things like that, even the dimmest clodder will realise you are not Dornal."

"True, but what's wrong with the idea?"

"It is – er – very interesting. And that is the point. Replic Dornal is brave, honourable. But he never had an interesting idea in his life." He smiled whimsically: "Interesting ideas are not useful to heroes like him. They tend to slow one up."

"You mean, I've got to be brave and stupid?"

Necro made a face.

"Sometimes it is easier to be brave if you are a little thick."

He rose. "You and I must make ready to leave. It will soon be looma, night. We shall leave by a secret passage. I have nedders waiting beyond the Shotto walls."

"Just you and me?" said Arnold jerking his thumb towards the door. "What about Norsha?"

"Pff. A graftona, a woman servant. She is of no account," he said carelessly.

Arnold said angrily: "We are not leaving her. She ..."

"You are right," Necro interrupted. "It would be fatal to leave her. She might betray us." He studied Arnold's face. "How do you know she is not a double agent, saving your life now, to betray you at a moment of her own choosing?"

"Well, OK, if we take her with us, we can keep an eye on her."

Necro nodded: "Very well, as you wish."

"Call her in then and tell her what we've decided."

An expression of disgust spread over Necro's features.

"One does not discuss plans with graftons. One gives them orders. You must swiftly get used to our social structure on Klaptonia. You are mastering the language. Your performance in the Yurbi Cham today was sinters. But there is still much for you to learn."

He paused as if making a decision.

"As we travel and make camp, I will try and instruct you in all you need to know as Replic Dornal. Otherwise your disguise may not save you. If the Gloami Kojers think you are Dornal, they may try to kill you. If the Klaptonian Bladers think you are an alien who has been shuffed for their beloved Himsir, they will slice you into small pieces."

From a recess in the wall, Necro took out garments which he handed to Arnold. "Put these on over your chooner. They will disguise you as my groom. People will think we are going to collect magic herbs."

"What about the sword? Will it notice?"

Necro held out his hand: "I will hide it under my cloak until we have passed the city walls, then I will return it." He chuckled. "I hope you know how to use it."

Arnold flushed. For a second he felt like whipping Necro's smiling head off his shoulders. But he had to admit he didn't even know how you started chopping off someone's head. He didn't even know if he had the strength, even if he — yeeuch — wanted to.

Gritting his teeth, he drew the sword and handed it over.

"I'm ready. Call Norsha," he said grumpily, as he drew on the clothing.

"One moment," said Necro. "Before we start our journey, I must see how it goes with Replic Dornal on Dirt. I hope that by now he has settled into his new life." He grinned. "A safer, but more humdrum existence than you are destined for on Klaptonia, I fear, my friend."

The table mirror clouded, the clouds swirled and cleared. Arnold leaned forward eagerly. His suddenly homesick brain took in the details. There was the school. It was evening.

"Look," he gasped. He pointed downwards. By the school gates were police cars, lights flashing. Along the school wall were figures climbing and running. He recognised the Yobs. But where was Dornal?

Necro waved his hand again. The image changed. There was a room, a table, bookshelves. A figure hunched by the door seemed, vainly, to be trying to open it. It was Dornal.

Necro stared. He was baffled.

"Cor," blurted Arnold. "Dornie's been locked in the Head's study and the Law's come. He's in dead trouble, on his first day."

Chapter
19

TRAPPED IN THE Head's office, with the school building alive with pounding boots, yells and curses, Dornal began slowly to realise that there was more to this jape than he had thought. And he had a suspicion that his new friends were not going to do the decent thing and rescue him. Even now they were racing for the wall round the school yard and heading for the hills. The blood-curdling sound of the siren wailing, drew nearer in the evening air, pulsing higher and higher like the shriek of a charging monster.

For the tenth time that day, Dornal pulled himself together and came out from under the table to crawl on hands and knees to the window. Beyond the school wall, in the street under the greying evening sky, a light blue vehicle had arrived. From its roof a circling light sent out brilliant flashes. Four men all dressed in uniform climbed out. How could they all fit inside? He guessed there was menace about them. Were they armed? he wondered. What did they do to the people they attacked? Did they kill, maim or simply capture?

He dropped back from the window. It seemed they were looking right at him. Though he realised that with the room unlit they were unable to see him. What to do? He could not get out of the room without being caught. He was trapped, unarmed and uncertain of his enemy's intentions.

Voices in the passage outside. He slid round the wall and listened at the door.

"Do you reckon they got away, Eddy?"

The familiar gruff voice of the caretaker answered.

"Dunno, Kevin. I just have this feeling they weren't all together."

"How d'you mean? Two lots?"

"Well, I thought they'd split up. One lot's got away over the wall."

"Who were they then?"

"I've got my suspicions. Look Kev. You talk to the Law while I check each room, just in case there is one lying low."

"Right-ho, Eddy."

Dornal heard them move away. Then came a new sound, the grating of metal. He guessed the caretaker was opening the doors one by one. The sound began to come nearer. This time, he knew there would be no way he could hide. He flattened himself against the wall. When the door opened he would make a dash for it. But dash where? Could he go back to the dormer and pretend to be asleep? Some instinct told him this might be part of the trick. If they searched this room and found him, they would question him. What would he say? Only a cad would give his pals away, even if he weren't very sure about his pals. Suppose they tortured him? Well, he braced himself. He would have to face that. The key turning sound came nearer. He crouched and made ready to spring.

What was that scratching noise? It wasn't the key. It was quieter and nearer. There it was again. He turned. His mouth fell open. At the corner of the window, beyond the glass was a face, suspended in air. Even in the fading light he could recognise the girl Sharon. The head jerked beckoning him. He tip-toed to the window and craned his neck. His eyes popped. Sharon was leaning sideways dangerously from a foothold on a long metal column that ran up the side of the building. She raised a free hand and signalled to him. He shrugged, spread out his hands. She made an angry face and pointed again. He looked down, bewildered. She made angry gestures, her hand moving to and fro. He looked down again and now he saw. At the base of the window was a metal bar. He pointed to it. She nodded.

He fumbled with the window catch. It would not move. He pulled this way and that. Outside in the passage he heard the footsteps trample into the next room. A few more seconds and the caretaker would be here. He shook his head. The girl, leaning out more dangerously from her perch made twiddling gestures with her fingers. Now he saw a small knob in the middle of the bar. He turned it. He heard the door slam in the next room. Sweat broke out on his forehead. He turned the knob the other way. It loosened. He pushed at the bar and suddenly the window swung sharply outwards.

"Come on Arnold," he heard her whisper. "Climb out on to the drainpipe."

Behind him he heard the key in the lock. Now he understood and, warrior like, wasted no more time. On the window ledge he stretched out hand and foot and made contact with the pipe. Sharon had slid further down. He transferred his weight to the pipe and pushed the window shut behind him. As he began his sliding descent, he saw a light go on in the room above. As he reached the ground at the foot of the wall, he could see the figure of the caretaker silhouetted against the light. Sharon grasped his arm, pulling him along in the shelter of the wall. He did not hesitate. For the third or fourth time that day, this girl had got him out of a tight corner. He followed in her wake, hand touching the wall for guidance. Behind them came more shouts. More rooms lit up.

"Keep in to the wall, we're nearly there," she whispered.

His head cracked on a hard structure in front. They were in the angle of two walls. Already Sharon was scrambling up the brickwork. He followed so closely that her foot struck him across the shoulder as she swung over. He gripped the top of the wall and swung tightly over it to land cat-like on the ground on the farther side. As they climbed to their feet she took his arm and walked him along the wall. The street was quiet now and darkening. There was no sign of the blue carriage and its crew.

"The Law's round the corner," she muttered. "What were you doing in there, you great nana?"

He gulped.

"My friends and I had planned a midnight feast in the Head's study, as a big lark before going to bed in the dormer," he said.

She stopped and took his shoulders. She looked closely at him.

"Arnold, you are OK, aren't you?"

He was suddenly angry. "Of course."

"Well, you're doing some very funny things, just lately. And, listen, mate, they are not your friends. They are putting you on for their own purposes. They are fitting you up for something. Why have you started in with them now? You always hated the Yobs. So, what's changed with you, Arnie?"

He did not answer. He could not. He had an impulse to explain to her. She deserved an explanation, he knew. But he could not share his secret.

A quiet humming noise in the street behind them, made Sharon stop and take a quick look round. To Dornal's astonishment, she took him by the arm, swung him round and pushed him against the wall. She draped her arms over his neck pressed her body against his and began – she actually began to push her face against his and make little movements around his mouth, with her lips. What was she doing Dornal wondered? Then he felt a sensation the like of which he had never known before. It began at the base of his spine and worked its way up to the top of his head.

His hair bristled. What was happening?

"What's this?" Someone else was curious. Behind them, Dornal saw the blue car. A large man in dark tunic had climbed out and stood close by.

Sharon turned. "Do you mind?" she said. "This is supposed to be private."

The man in blue sniggered. "All right, Snowball. Pardon our intrusion. We're looking for some herberts who've been seen climbing over the school wall. One might be your boyfriend."

"Pull the other," retorted Sharon. "He's got better things to do than climb school walls. We've been in there, all day."

"Come on, leave it," said a voice in the car. The man turned and the vehicle slowly moved away. Dornal's breath returned. Sharon took his arm and they walked along. Dornal made a decision.

"Sharon," he said.

"Yes, Arnie?"

"I must tell you a secret."

"Go on." Something in his voice made her eyes open wider.

"I am not Arnold, as you think. I am Himsir Dornal, Replic of Klaptonia. I am here only for a while, taking refuge on Dirt, to defeat an attempt by my enemies, the Gloami Kojers, to kidnap me."

For a second she eyed him seriously, then she smiled.

"All right, Arnold. Have it your own way. Just between you and I, we know you're really Dornal from Klaptonia. We'll keep it our secret. But let's pretend you're funny old Arnold, and you live just across the other side of the main road, and your Mum and Dad are probably wondering what you've been up to, and if I know your Dad, he is going to be very stroppy."

"But," Dornal protested. She was not taking him seriously at all.

"Come on," she said firmly. "We'll make up some story about needing to stay behind to help in drama class. They might just believe that."

"But – I – I stay at the school." He searched for the word. "I'm a – boarder. I sleep in the dorm."

She shook him. "Arnie, will you pack it in? You are Arnold Radleigh. You live in 16, Hornby Gardens, with your Mum and Dad. You are 14, you have lived here all your life. You are really very intelligent, but now and then you behave as though you were a nine year old and right now you are off the wall. And I am taking you home. So shut up."

Dornal shut up. There was something mesmeric about this girl. But since she had saved him from unknown fates several times today, he owed it to her, at least to follow. Not least because he had no clear notion of what he should do next. Necro had told him nothing about his Dirt family. Was that because there had not been time, or was Necro concealing something from him? The thoughts circled slowly round his brain. When he got back to Tipacal he would have certain questions.

"Here, we are, Arnie. I'm off. See you tomorrow. And do stop messing about."

Again her lips nuzzled his face. Dornal felt again the vague, unusual sensation. Then she had gone leaving him alone on the pavement. The door to the house was open. A large man, belly looming over his belted trousers, shirt unfastened to show an expanse of hairy chest, stood on the step.

"Where have you been?" he demanded.

Dornal was thinking of his reply, when the man moved to one side, and as Dornal passed him, gave him a short, sharp swipe on the head which projected him into the narrow hallway.

"Oh, leave him, our Dad." The calm, woman's voice sounded from the lighted room. Dornal entered. She was plump and dark. The round face with its brown eyes was smiling. "We wondered what on earth you were up to, Arnold. Oh, and you've left your bag and sports gear at school, and what have you done to your clothes. They're all dirty."

"You know what that lad wants." The man was standing behind him now and Dornal braced himself for the insult of a second blow to the head. Should he turn and punish this insolent clodder? But he had a feeling that on Dirt fathers had authority to beat their offspring. He had to be careful.

He looked at them both, then bowed. "A thousand grovels, Dadwon, Mawon," he muttered.

The man stared at him suspiciously. But the woman smiled warmly.

"It's all those books he's reading, our Dad. He gets confused. Now Arnold, you go upstairs and get washed. I've kept your supper warm. We were just going to watch Dallas."

Arnold followed the direction in which she pointed and climbed the stairs. Where should he wash. He opened one door. Inside was a bed, a table, a broken armchair. The floor was littered with clothes and books. And on the walls were lurid posters of fantastic landscapes, brutal figures in sword and armour, half clothed women, dragons spitting fire. This must be Arnold's room. He walked out again, found a small room with a deep bowl. Close by was a metal lever. He pulled at it experimentally and with a tremendous gurgle, water rained down into the depths beneath. Taken by surprise he had just time to hold his hands under the flow, raise them to his face and then the water was done.

He went slowly downstairs, rubbing his face dry. In the room below the man and woman were eating. Were these really to be his parents? They turned towards him, then the father turned away to look at the small box on legs in the corner of the room. It was like a magic table mirror with images that came and went. They seemed to be mostly of women, and men, who clung together, lay down on beds, bounced about, then rose, took drinks and shouted at each other. Perhaps people were amused to look in on what their neighbours were doing, he thought. Did that mean, though, that neighbours could watch them? He would have to be careful what he did. He did not relish the idea of being watched.

He sat down at the table. His mother smiled.

"It's your favourite, chicken and chips," she said.

Dornal took up the knife, raised a piece of meat in his fingers and began neatly to cut off slices. At once he felt again the slap of the man's hand across his head.

"Use your fork, you little pig."

Dornal was bewildered. Then he saw the metal pronged object and picked it up. After one or two false starts he got the hang of it.

"He's doing it on purpose," grumbled the man. The mother shushed: "No, he's not. He's just tired. He's had a long day, and he did apologise for being late."

"Load of rubbish if you ask me." The man turned to watch the picture in the corner and Dornal managed to finish his meal. But he could see that the woman was watching him curiously. He did not know what to do or say now, so he watched the picture too. Now the action made more sense. Two men were fighting, throwing one another about the room, smashing the furniture, striking blows which Dornal knew ought to have killed them outright. But each time they rose, shook their heads and resumed the battle.

"You can pack that in," said the father, brusquely.

Dornal was puzzled.

"If you think you are going to sit and watch the box all evening, you've got another think coming. I'm not going to sit and look at you all evening. Get upstairs and do your homework."

"Perhaps he hasn't got any dear," said the woman.

"So, let him get up there and read one of those stupid books."

"You've got his latest one. You took it off him at breakfast time."

The man gestured with his thumb to a cupboard near the door. The mother smiled at Dornal.

"Take your book and go on up, Arnold. I'll come and see you in a bit."

Upstairs Dornal suddenly began to feel tired again. He pulled off his clothes and dropped them on the floor. That seemed to be where the boy Arnold kept them. He climbed into bed and pulled the sheets round him. He was dozing when the woman entered the room. She tutted and picked up the clothes and placed them over the back of the chair.

"You daft haporth, why aren't you wearing your pyjamas?"

He looked blank. She picked up a striped tunic jacket from the side of the bed and a pair of trousers of the same colour and held them out. He pulled on the jacket and buttoned it, but did not dare to get out of bed to put on the trousers. She smiled at him.

"You're getting shy." She moved towards him and ruffled his hair.

"Don't you want your book?" She held it out. He looked sheepish and she began to laugh.

"I know what you want. You want me to read for you. I haven't done that for ages."

She came closer and sat on the bed. Her comforting warmth was near. She opened the book.

"I think you were here." She raised the book and began to read.

"Keen-bladed sword in one hand, wicked, needle sharp dagger in the other he leapt lightly on to the stone steps that spiralled into the depths of the castle."

Her voice murmured on, the adventure unfolded. But Himsir Dornal, Replic of Klaptonia, Hodbung Shredder of the Premi Moblot heard nothing. He lay back on his pillow, sound asleep, with one finger in his mouth.

Chapter 20

SLAMBOSS LOOKED UP from the steaming flork joint he was carving, as Hitman and Nobbin shuffled into his fur-lined chamber. He grinned wolfishly.

"Have you tremmed the barbic? Have you scanned his brand? Is it Dornal or not?"

His eyes became dreamy.

"Did he argle, or was he tranc like a gormer? I hanked to ibe it but slecca not for me to ming in cloddi doofers like that. Well?" he demanded as they stayed silent.

Hitman looked dimly at him: "But, it's yarbi to yurb when you are yurbling Shrefful Slamboss."

Slamboss suddenly rose from behind the table, carving knife in hand and walked round to stand in front of Hitman. Little Nobbin had already dodged behind his father.

"You are lurcing sumdo from me, aren't you?"

"Er," said Hitman, moving backwards. "Er, we ..."

Slamboss moved forward violently, carving knife held out like a bayonet. Hitman jerked back with equal violence, fell over his crouching son and both sprawled among the rushes while Slamboss, his rage controlled stood over them.

"You slepped him. You slepped him, didn't you? You nocca put the barbic on him."

Hitman lay on his back, unable to move. Little Nobbin, quick as light scrambled up and scuttled to the door. From a safe distance he said,

"It was that Norsha. She liffed him rig, while we were moling for the Misti Sticcer."

"You nocca even put a sindi iron on him?"

"Well, num. We had him all zupped up and triggo for barbic. He was timpi."

"Yumda, Shrefful," said Hitman from the floor. "Abso numdo it was the Dirtwon. If it had been Replic Dornal, he'd have chimpled while we charced him."

Slamboss kicked Hitman in impotent fury.

"Gormer! Wing he was hoking to be timpi?"

"Oh num," said Hitman. "Replic Dornal's too dimmo for that."

Slamboss looked about to explode, then he said:

"On your pats."

They stood up and waited by the table, as he took a cup of yoot wine and drank deeply. He stared at them hatefully, then:

"So, this Norsha liffed him rig, did she?"

"Yumda, Slamboss. Like you yurbed. She atta be a nebber for the Gloami Kojers."

Slamboss glared at Nobbin: "You slep the bonzing to me, you bitti slurder."

His massive forehead creased in an enormous ugly frown. He drained the wine cup.

"Todd and fring Necro," he ordered

"But, Shrefful Slamboss," said Hitman eagerly, "we are your Lurci Flunkaj and we natta be ibed. We're lurco."

Slamboss's cheeks swelled, then he gritted his teeth.

"Zitto. I'll todd and yurb him myself. You heel afto, but ding out of ibe."

Two minutes later, Slamboss crashed through the heavy door of Necro's Spell Chamber. The room, still lit by two great candles, was empty. Slamboss with a roar of uncontrollable anger rushed across the floor. Cringing outside in the passage, Hitman and Nobbin heard the crashes, squeals, hisses and squelches as Slamboss hurled chests and caskets, spiders, toads and snakes this way and that as he rampaged across the room. But it was clear that Necro had gone. Hitman and Nobbin tiptoed into the room just as Slamboss brutally kicked Clarence into the window ledge.

"Shrefful Slamboss. The Misti Crist," urged Nobbin.

All three leapt for the great chair and stood before the magic mirror table. In time Hitman and Nobbin remembered to stand back and let Slamboss sit down. Necro had left the table operational. The two who stood behind their master heard him swear a terrible oath. The image showed the sky outside turning from pale orange to grey as dusk fell. The guards at the city gate were slowly closing the great iron gates.

"Iball that," said Nobbin who had dodged round his father. He pointed. On the darkening trail outside the city were three figures, two on nedder-back, one loping behind. Slamboss ground his teeth.

"Necro's bego with them."

"Oh, that's slecc, then. He'll scan them," said Hitman comfortingly.

"Num," snarled Slamboss. He turned: "Todd afto and heel them."

"But Shrefful Slamboss. They're shanxing into the Bashi Rangles."

"Zitto. They're fonzing to shivann there, bonzing we won't heel them."

"But we will, Slamboss."

"Num. *You* will. Heel them. Choose your nimmot, and then cop him."

"Who? Necro?"

Slamboss cuffed Nobbin and hurled him across the room to land by the curled up Clarence. He leapt up even more quickly.

"No, Dornal — or the Dirtwon. Cop him."

"Oh, and fring him back to Tipacal?"

Slamboss gave Hitman a look of such hatred that the two of them stumbled in panic out of the room, tripped up the steps and fell into the passage. Left to himself, Slamboss sat elbows on the table, glaring at the fading image as night fell on the gloomy wastes of the Bashi Rangles.

Chapter
21

"I SPEAK MORE in sorrow than in anger," said the Head, her grey eyes sweeping over the massed ranks at morning assembly. The troops shifted in their places and prepared for a longer stay than usual. But this time, they did not switch off. There was an air of excitement about the school as there always is when SOMETHING has happened which the troops know all about, the staff knows something about and the Head knows almost nothing about. In this case it was the carry-on last night. The break-in at school, the Law called, chase-me-charlie through the school buildings, sliding down drainpipes, clambering over walls. Sick bay broken into, morphine tablets stolen (that wasn't true, but no story's complete without a little adornment is it?) Head's study broken into. And of course everyone knew who had done it. At least the troops did. The staff thought they did, but how to prove it? Would they finger print the entire school? Not on your nelly. The Head on her human rights kick would never agree to that.

"What is so unacceptable about this episode is that the image of the school has been damaged. You can imagine the stories which will appear in the local press this week: 'Drug raid on school sick bay – squad cars chase intruders.'"

"It is particularly bad because the authorities are now considering whether schools in this area should be closed down or amalgamated with others and of course schools which acquire a bad name will be under great pressure."

The Head allowed her eyes to wander along the middle ranks. She was not half as innocent as some people thought her and she knew she was looking in the right quarter. Her eyes met Eenie's. He looked back levelly, his handsome, brutal face calm. Meanie stared back insolently. He had no style. Mynie's eyes were narrowed to the point of being closed. Mo looked blank. The Head had left him behind at the first two syllable word she used.

Her eyes paused a fraction of a second. Arnold Radleigh, sitting a little way along from the Yobs looked strange. He was changing colour slightly. Funny, she thought. When she had found him on the sports field he had turned rather a strange colour. But then he was a strange boy and very shy. He was the type who looked guilty when they weren't. She was strong on psychology was the Head. She breathed deeply. This was always the hardest bit for her. The awful warning.

"It grieves me to have to say this. But if those involved in last night's episode are detected, they will have to leave the school . . ."

There was a silence. This was strong stuff, for her.

". . . at least until the end of term."

Several hundred minds made rapid calculations. No big deal. Still strong for her.

After assembly, Dornal avoided the Yobs. He avoided them because he was not certain how a good chap dealt with a situation like this. On the one hand the honour of school was at stake. He had heard enough stories to know how important that was.

On the other hand, a chap did not sneak, or snitch, on his fellows. That was another code of honour. And Dornal did not have the mind that could cope with two different codes of honour at once. He also avoided Sharon because he knew that she knew. And he knew that she had rescued him. The more he brooded on that the more uneasy he felt. Why was it that at home he could manage totally without the help of women (except to pick up clothes or serve a dish of flork) while here he seemed to be totally at their mercy?

As he struggled back into the classroom with the dismissed troops, he heard Eenie whisper from the side of his mouth: "Hey, Arnie, see you at break. Right?"

Dornal ignored him and walked back to his desk. He was in for some heavy thinking. He did not want to depend on Sharon. He was uncertain whether to trust his new friends. So for the moment he was on his own. He had to be prepared. And so this morning, on leaving the house, he had made sure he had his swimming gear with him. He could not understand why anyone should want to wear clothes when swimming. They only got wet. On the other hand he knew that the trunks would protect his Klaptonian colours from view. The problem would be how to get in and out of them without being spotted.

Lessons came and went, each one more baffling. History in particular. Why did they spend time discussing battles from the past, when none of them were being trained to fight today? He was amused by the teachers attempts to explain the course of battle to the class, but with his soldier's instincts, he gave no sign of this. He kept his head down. He discovered that by bending over his desk pretending to read or write, or by hiding himself behind the large head and shoulders of Mo, who sat in front of him, he could pass whole lessons in peace and quiet without a single question.

At break time, the Yobs, eyed carefully by the rest of the troops, stationed themselves in a corner of the yard. They resisted all attempts to find out what had really happened the previous night. No one dared ask them directly. And the more cunning hinters gave up when they saw the expression in Eenie's eyes.

"How about him?" Mynie jerked his square head in the direction of Dornal's lone figure as he sat on the low wall next to the sports field. "Is he going to grass? What do we do if he does?"

"What're you fretting about?" asked Mynie. "Just tell him we'll break his legs off, if he does. No sweat."

"Shut up," said Eenie, deep in thought. "He's not going to split. For one he's as deep in it as we are. For another — how did he get out last night?"

The others were silent. Then Mo said: "Hey, right. I'm going to ask him."

Eenie reached out and took Mo's tie. Carefully he slid the knot upward, waited until the large face had turned puce, then said: "No you are not. There's no need. There's only one way that wally could have got out."

He slid the knot down and Mo's colour and breathing returned to normal.

"She got him out."

"What, Heathy?"

"Nah — Thompson."

"Her, never. How?"

"How do I know? She's his minder. That's the only way."

"Anyway," muttered Meanie. "That's blown him for now."

"Knock it off, son. There's miles of stretch in that little wonder, yet."

"How do you mean?"

"Just belt up and let me think. Something'll turn up."

The Yobs fell silent, as they always did when Eenie was thinking.

Bursting out of his purple track suit, brick red face shining, small blue eyes flitting here and there, large hand fiddling with the whistle that hung round his neck, Maxwell Boardman, the Games Master was making a speech in the staff room. Most of the staff ignored him or rather they tried to, though his voice was so loud he made sure they heard him. And he did have a small audience of PE teachers, plus one small member of the English department who had got himself trapped between the Games Master and a filing cabinet. He winced every time the Games Master's index finger stabbed towards his chest. At times like this, he wished he had gone in for professional hang gliding or something else quiet and safe.

"Reputation of the school? This dump has no reputation. Shall I tell you what will decide whether we're closed down or not, next year?"

The little teacher nodded like a mesmerised rabbit. Boardman went on.

"It'll be who wins the district sports event. I know the people on the Education Committee. As far as they're concerned, it is sport that counts. Stands to reason. Character building. Results. You can see the ability in the results. 'O' level Art," he went on, his voice rising up the scale,

" 'O' level sociology. And half of them can't count or spell properly."

"How does winning the soccer cup help you spell properly, Mac?" called the bearded Head of Science through his cloud of pipe smoke. His colleagues chuckled quietly. Boardman was undeterred.

"Character, mate. That's what counts when it comes to getting jobs. Can you rely on people. Team work," boomed the Games Master. Suddenly he remembered something. "How can you train people when you get taken to the Court of Human Rights every time you try to straighten out some little squit who's forgotten his swimming gear?"

"Oh, who was that, Mac?"

"Arnold Radleigh."

The Head of English raised her head from her bundle of papers: "If you imagine third degree will make Arnold remember anything, you're mistaken."

Boardman ignored her and thundered on. "This school will be down the pan next year. Merged, jobs up for grabs. Unless we pull something out of the bag, and sports is what is going to count, God help us."

Out on the field, the Games Master looked at the mob in football gear. He was feeling disheartened already. Five minutes ago, he had discovered Arnold in swimming trunks, while the rest of the changing room were rolling around with laughter. To their amazement, the Games Master controlled himself and simply found the lad a spare strip, while the others ran out on the pitch. He had an uneasy feeling that Arnold was setting him up, daring him to punish him and then getting him in dirt with the Head. He felt manipulated but could not work out what to do. He decided to wait for his opportunity. Best keep little insects like that out of his hair and concentrate on the District Cup.

He ran his eye over the players as they ranged aimlessly about the field then blew his whistle to assemble them. He knew right away his luck was out. The team was one short.

"Right," he shouted. " 'A' team over here. Now I want one from the 'B' team to make up, and one from the scratch mob to make up the 'B' team."

"Sir," a voice at his elbow made him swing round. Eenie, captain of the 'A' team, stood there.

"Yes, Crawford?"

"Sir, I didn't reckon much to the reserves last time. I'd like to try Radleigh."

"You'd WHAT?"

Three or four of the team clustered round: "Yeah, sir. Arnie's a great little mover, really. If he's fed properly."

The Games Master stared. Could this be the start of an elaborate piss-take? But Eenie looked at him, eyes free of guile.

"Sir, just give him a trial, please."

Boardman shrugged.

"OK, but no messing about. There is no time and I am not in the mood."

"You won't regret it sir."

The Games Master breathed deeply, then blew his whistle.

"All right," he bellowed. "Let's be having you."

Chapter 22

ON THE OUTSKIRTS of the city of Tipacal, as dusk merged with the thicker darkness of the forests ahead, Necro turned to Arnold and spoke quietly.

"Change out of those old clothes and mount your nedder. Then I will return your sword."

Arnold hesitated. He was staring at the mounts. He had expected horses. But these were like a small dinosaur, with six legs and a long neck. Necro swung his long shanks nimbly over the beast's broad back.

"Hurry," he said.

Arnold stripped off the evil smelling jerkin. Then as he moved to put his left foot into the leather stirrup loop, he remembered.

"Hey, we've only got two mounts. There are three of us." He nodded towards Norsha who stood, head down, a little way from them.

Necro shook his head and handed Arnold the sword.

"No, no no. Graftons do not ride. Let her run behind. Come, do not argue, we must get into the cover of the trees."

Reluctantly Arnold clambered up. He saw that the old magician was sitting half way up the beast's long neck. It seemed incredibly uncomfortable.

It was. He gripped the tapering neck with his knees and immediately felt a violent pain in his most sensitive parts as the motion of the nedder shot him up a foot then brought him heavily down. Then up again, then down. He was in agony. He slid back into the centre, his feet splayed out across the nedder's spine. But at least it felt normal, not like riding a giraffe. A moment or two later as they pushed under the trees, he felt a violent blow on the back of his head as though he had been struck with a yard brush. Clutching the reins he looked back wildly as he received another flap, this time blindingly across his face. The nedder had an incredible fan-like tail which came up at regular intervals and swept across its back. Arnold gritted his teeth and shinned up the animal's neck just as the tail came sweeping down for the third time.

He soon found out why. Under the trees, amid the tangled undergrowth the day's heat had gathered and sweltered in the damp air. Around them in the dank twilight of the Bashi Rangles great clouds of insects now swarmed with high pitched buzzing. They flashed past his head and eye at high speed. They seemed in the dimming light to be as big as bees. He crouched down. The massive tail swept up from behind and the tormentors were gone. Another few steps, the manic buzzing began again, and slap went the nedder's tail. Arnold clutched the reins, the nedder's neck and hung on, while the six legs made long strides into the mouldering gloom. The city was lost to sight behind them as they were swallowed up in humid reeking haze of the wilderness. They forged ahead and to left and right came the night sounds of a ferocious jungle, slitherings, hissings, snarlings sudden roars and agonised screams as teeth met in the flesh of trapped prey.

Arnold's stomach chilled. He clung on, barely seeing ahead where Necro rode, unable to look back where Norsha the servant girl ran ragged and barefoot behind him.

Abruptly Necro halted, backing his beast up along Arnold's.

"We are being followed."

"Course we are," muttered Arnold, waiting in tension for the next cloud of attacking insects and the slap of the nedder's tail. "Norsha's coming up behind. I can hear her."

"No, no. Further back. We are being stalked, whether by man or animal, I cannot tell."

"Animal, what sort?"

"In the Bashi Rangles, there are every sort. But all

meat-eaters, all swift and utterly voracious. That is why one never travels here except in search of adventure."

"What do we do, then?"

"I will lead the way off the track, a little ahead. We shall move on to higher ground."

He called to his nedder, which surged ahead and in the same movement Arnold's mount reared up so suddenly that he found himself flat out on the beast's back swinging madly from side to side like a sailor on a storm-tossed raft. Without warning the nedder swung to the right. Now Arnold was hanging off the side, only keeping his grip on the reins. Now left and like a trampoline artist he was across to the other side. As they climbed the nedder slowed down and with a huge effort Arnold managed to regain his place on the neck. He locked his feet together in front of the animal's throat. Now he was secure. He could ride. As for his sensitive parts, he found they weren't sensitive any more. And this was no time to worry. Snorting, heaving, its great body bunching and lunging the nedder was struggling up away from the track, but its speed was slowing step by step. Then suddenly, it stopped, sat back on its haunches and allowed Arnold to slide off backwards onto the rough ground beneath the stunted trees.

"Hurry," commanded Necro from in front. "We must climb higher."

"What for?" demanded Arnold, puffing and panting as he struggled almost on hands and knees, while the great creature, its breath hanging like a cloud around him slipped and scrambled by his side.

"No time to explain. We must get higher."

Rocks stood up in front of them like a wall, dark and menacing. And within them was a darker darkness. Arnold heard Necro pushing about amid the bushes. "This way," he called. Arnold followed. Now they were inside the rock, a narrow cleft, with barely room for himself and his mount. More shoving and then they were through into a larger space, a cave. Ahead was a red glowing light that danced up and down.

Arnold stared. Necro had somehow lit a fire which threw glare and shadows on the curving walls. A larger shape beyond the blaze showed that Necro's nedder had slumped to the ground. Necro was seated comfortably against its back, rummaging in his saddle bags. Arnold felt a great push behind him as his mount collapsed on the cave floor. He sat too. It was like being on a great plush divan. Necro passed him food. Flork again. Still he hadn't eaten at the Shotto had he? He was hungry, and it was very tasty. Then he remembered again.

"Where's Norsha?"

Necro's eyebrows rose.

"Outside, of course. Making her bed."

"Can't she come in here?"

"Indeed not. She is a graftona. You are a luxon. I am — never mind. Mixing is not allowed."

"Besides," added Necro quietly. "She may be a nebber, a spy. I do not want her to listen to us. Fear not. She will be perfectly all right. Graftons do not have feelings as we have. Here put this round you."

Necro handed him a large, deep-red cloak. Arnold took it. He was too sleepy to argue any more. The excitement, the ride and now the softness of the nedder's back, the food, the yoot wine Necro passed him in a leather cup, all combined to send him to sleep. Before he drifted away, he asked:

"What's all this business about getting up high. Why?"

"Because it is going to rain tomorrow."

"Rain?"

"Yes. All day. Very hard."

"How do you know?"

"It always soggs on Soggerda," answered Necro. "Zizz well."

Chapter
23

NECRO WAS RIGHT. As soon as Arnold woke from his deep sleep and slid from the nedder's warm side to the ground, he heard it. Not like a rain shower or storm or even a cloud burst. It was like a waterfall.

Necro was seated by the fire busy with some brightly coloured stones he had arranged upon a dazzling white cloth spread out on the ground.

"Brecca yacca, O Nurbul Replic," he said, smiling.

"Brecca yacca O Necro."

"If we are to be toppo, you must brand me Occul Necro."

"Did you say it would rain like this all day?"

"It does, every Soggerda."

"You're making it up," said Arnold.

"But it does. Tomorrow, on Murda, Murg or Mist Day, we shall have heavy fog as the Sizla takes up the water. The next day, Blizda will be cold, with heavy snow. Then gales will blow on Wafda. Next comes Verda, and the grass grows again, then Gloda, when it gets warmer. Finally on Sizda, great heat returns and so on."

"You mean, the same weather for each day of the week?"

"Every daj of the weeg, every weeg of the monz, every monz of the yex. It is a very fine system."

"But it must be boring," protested Arnold.

"Who," asked Necro, "wants to get excitement out of the weather? There is abso numdoo to discuss. Rain is wet. Sun is hot. End of conversation."

"You haven't lived," said Arnold. "But is everything more or less fixed in Klaptonia?"

Necro shook his head.

"On the contrary life is full of excitement. You never know when you may be killed or injured."

"Well, that's a bit like home. You can get knocked down crossing the road."

"No, no, Nurbul. You must not say 'like home'. You are at home. Try and remember. But you misunderstand me. We do not have accidents on Klaptonia. Accidents are a sign of a badly planned universe. Everyone should live as long as they ought, then die."

"So, what's this garbage about getting killed then?"

"That is on purpose."

"You mean, someone trying to kill me?"

"That is it."

"But why?"

"Because you have offended them. Because they have a grudge. A hundred reasons."

Arnold tried to take this in: "You mean, I might get murdered at any time, just because someone has taken a dislike to me."

"What better reason? Imagine someone killing you, as happens on Dirt, when they do not know you, have never met you and have no reason for killing you. Our system is just, and much more exciting."

126

"But no one's got any reason to kill me."

"How do you know? Klaptonian is such a flexible language, you could have given offence without knowing it." Necro bent forward: "That magnificent speech of yours – don't blush – in the Yurbi Cham. How do you know, as you chose your words, you did not offend someone, who may even now be seeking revenge?"

"But how do you stay alive?"

"Mainly on reputation. You are probably safe because you are – or rather Dornal is the greatest warrior for your age in Klaptonia. I have such magic powers that I am immune to envy or hatred."

"But, they can still try."

"They can indeed, and hence," said Necro, waving his hand over the white cloth and stones, "each day, I carry out the Morb Wilber or Death Forecast, for a select number of people, of course."

Arnold went white.

"Including me?"

"Including Dornal, which must mean you," said Necro slyly.

"W-w-what does it say?"

Necro swept the stones into the centre of the cloth, bundled it up and stowed it in a saddlebag.

"It says you may expect a murderous attack before nightfall."

"Can't we clear out then?"

"No, no. The whole area is flooded. Besides it is in bad taste to try and fix results like that. It is like knowing the result of a race beforehand and placing bets accordingly."

"I'm not having anybody placing bets on me." Arnold's voice rose. Then he looked at Necro. "You haven't ... have you?"

Necro looked coy. "Sometimes I do. The truth is the

murder forecast isn't all that accurate. Sometimes people don't get killed after all."

Suddenly Arnold leapt to his feet. He could have kicked himself.

"You said it was flooded, didn't you?"

Necro nodded.

"Well, what about Norsha?"

Necro shrugged. "Quite safe. Probably roosting in a tree somewhere, waiting for us to summon her to make breakfast."

"But, she can't stay out there. She'll catch her death." Arnold set out for the mouth of the cave.

"Wait," commanded Necro. "Sit down, for a moment and let me explain. If you are to pretend to be Replic Dornal, you should know more about the world you rule."

Arnold sat down reluctantly.

"Did you imagine that a world like this, of mighty warriors engaged in continuous warfare, non-stop adventure, sudden death, great feats of arms and so forth, could exist just on its own? Who would provide their weapons, their food, their clothes, who would rear their nedders, groom them, prepare them for battle? For everyone who performs noble deeds, twenty must perform humble tasks."

Arnold waited. This looked like being a long lecture. But he needed to know. Necro placed his fingers together and closed his eyes.

"Klaptonian society is divided into two groups. There are luxons whose job it is to consume food, clothes, etc, to be gracious, important, brave and beautiful, to be perfect. If they had to bother with where the next meal came from, what chance would they have of being perfect?"

Arnold yawned, but listened.

"Luxons include the top moblots of the army,

skullers and shredders, as well as court ladies, councillors, Topwon and Topma. The common soldiers, slammers and bladers, etc, come of course from the graftons, who do all the work.

"Graftons are divided into ..." Necro's eyes half closed as he began to chant, "prodders who herd cattle, codders and rodders who catch saltwater and freshwater fish, hodders who build houses, todders who make the yoot wine, nodders who arrest wrong-doers, quodders who look after the prisons, godders who see to religious matters and swodders who are recruited to the Dongon and become bladers.

"There are also seven grades of flunker or servant. Norsha belongs to the seventh, the flunker-dimas, who on Dirt are called maids-of-all-work."

Necro cleared his throat and pressed on remorselessly.

"Relations between luxons and between graftons and luxons are regulated by the grovel and the yacca, as I told you. And beyond that everything is regulated by physical combat. Since physical combat is messy, the whole business of killing, maiming, etc, and all other chivalrous matters are controlled by the Slamboss or Games Master. He masterminds all encounters in the Bashi Rangles. Here the various monsters prowl on whom warlike luxons can test their virility. This also means the wallock-meds can be kept free for cultivation."

Necro paused and raised a small bone whistle to his lips.

"Enough for the moment. I shall now summon Norsha and she can prepare our breakfast."

He blew and in a moment footsteps sounded inside the cave entrance. Norsha entered. Her long hair hung down wetly around her orange, heart-shaped face. Her clothes were dark-sodden with rain. She lowered her eyes as Arnold greeted her, and began to busy herself at the fire. Soon the smell of frying flork rose. Necro turned again to Arnold.

"Now, O Nurbul Replic, what are your scims for ma-da, when the sogger tremms and the Murg wonzes?"

Arnold had a feeling he was just being asked out of politeness, since Necro knew that he was in charge. But he spoke out.

"I bonz we atta shanx to Hermiss Roshan's shotto and scan if there are chexes as to where she has been tringed."

To his astonishment he saw, out of the corner of his eye, Norsha frown and shake her head. If Necro saw, he ignored the gesture.

"Numda, O Replic. If I may freeb my doolus. Hermiss Roshan is in the shredd of the Gloami Kojers. We have two pinners. The Gloami Kojers secc her and clim a yoggler. Or we inslam and shredd them to slep her."

"Huh," snorted Arnold. "You yurb like Slamboss. There is another pinn," he added.

"Oh."

"Yumda. To shanx to the topwondom of the Gloami Kojers and neb out the grav, then wig what to do."

Necro looked grave: "You recc that this means a rixi shanx, dro the Bashi Rangles, to the Drago Soggon, dro a stacca yonco topwondoms, dro the Prussy Peakers, before we ibe the Gloami Kojers."

Arnold was silent. He should keep his big mouth shut. Always trying to be clever. Trouble was up here if you said something you had to act on it. He had the feeling Norsha was watching him.

"I doos we bego, ma-da in the yorni brecc."

He picked up a piece of flork from the platter by

the fire, winced as the hot meat sizzled on his fingers, then went on: "A-da, though, Norsha shall ding in the chib, here. I doos it."

Necro shrugged. "Yum, Nurbul. She may ding and zizz at the tremm of the chib."

Breakfast done, Norsha stole away into the shadows and lay down inside the cave near the entrance. Necro got out his white cloth and stones and began to mutter. "Ah, Replic Dornal . . . very interesting . . ."

Arnold his stomach full, his back warm against the nedder's side; it smelt like a dishcloth, but it was comfortable; drifted off to sleep again.

He woke in darkness. The fire was out. He was lying on the dirt floor. Someone was on top of him, grappling at his neck. Foul breath gusted into his mouth. Around him were the sounds of struggle in the darkness. He heard Necro cry out, then a dull thud and silence. He tried to throw off his attacker and draw his sword. He made a superhuman effort to break free, rolled sideways, half winded and plucked at the sword hilt.

It came free just as a tremendous blow on the back of his neck sent him sprawling to the ground and a darker darkness filled his eyes.

Chapter
24

DORNAL WAS SETTLING in on Dirt. The weeks began to slip by. He was relieved to find that he could survive, if he remembered certain rules. Every night he repeated them to himself as he went to sleep, like magic charms to keep him from harm in the day ahead.

He was learning. He learnt the difference between the two little rooms in the house, the one where you washed and the other across the landing. The second was rather entertaining when you got used to the way the water shot up your rear. Later on he learnt to stand up before he pressed the lever. He learnt how to eat his food with knife and fork. He was amazed at the wallock mixture he was given for breakfast and the noise it made when milk was poured over it. Flork he only saw at weekends and they called it pork. He supposed it didn't fly.

He learned to call the man and woman Dad and Mum. He guessed they were graftons, though Dad, he observed, had luxon habits. He sat around while Mum bustled here and there serving, clearing away, sorting out and soothing.

He learnt how to cross the road without getting killed. It was easy to get killed on Dirt even if no one had a grudge against you. He suspected the innocent were in more danger than the guilty. And those who murdered on the roads were only punished if they were caught. Imagine killing someone, then trying to hide it. No Klaptonian would kill unless proud of it and expect to get killed in return.

He learnt to eat his sweet and main course in the right order at school. He remembered his correct gear. He put it on under his clothes so he couldn't forget it. And when sports finished, he put his clothes back on top. No one spotted his little orange secret that way. It was uncomfortable after swimming sitting with wet trunks under his trousers, but he had learned to endure hardship from an early age.

In school he grew more confident in his reading, helped out now and then by Sharon. But best of all, at night, when he went to bed, Mum would sit by the bed and hold out the book, while he moved his lips silently — "Keen-bladed sword in one hand . . ." He enjoyed these stories of killing and sudden death, swamps and monsters. They were the nearest he could get to normal life. Though the heroes could not have a fight, it seemed, or leap off a cliff, without turning to another page to find out if they were going to kill someone or drown themselves. What a bunch of gormers, he thought. But he never told Mum. He would do nothing to stop her reading to him at night.

In other lessons he learned to keep his head down and let other people answer questions. His training as a soldier stood him in good stead. He became skilled in avoiding trouble. However, if he thought he had escaped notice he was quite mistaken. In fact, one day, he was the subject of two conversations at opposite ends of the staff room — at one end the Head of English and the other end the Games Master, both discussed with their colleagues the problem of Arnold.

"It's strange the way Arnold is performing," the Head of English said with a frown.

"Or not performing, Karen," said her deputy.

"Or not performing as you say, Keith," she replied. "He seems to have lost all interest in English. His marks are atrocious, almost as though he were trying to convince us he knew nothing about his favourite subject. Sometimes he behaves as though he can barely read.''

"Something psychological," murmured the new English teacher, not wanting to be left out.

Karen shrugged: "Something could be upsetting him, but I can't think what. This has always been the subject he did well in even if things were going to pieces elsewhere. I think I'll have a word with his parents. There could be something wrong there.''

"Personality problem, perhaps," added the new English teacher. "You know how people sometimes get involved in their own fantasies and lose touch with the real world.''

"Hm," said the Head of English, "that's usually been a help with this subject.''

At his end of the staff room, the Games Master boomed: "What happens when the biggest wally in the school starts lining up for the 'A' team? When Crawford said let's have Radleigh on the team, I thought pull the other.''

"It could be a take on," said one of the PE teachers quickly.

Boardman shook his head: "No, mate. That is one thing Crawford does not mess about over. Football is his religion. So what is little Arnold up to, I ask myself. It's weird to watch them, the way they bunch up round this little no no, on the field. They feed him, they carry him right up in front of goal, then . . .''

He paused for effect.

"Do you know what happened the other night?" He wasn't asking really, but went on: "He puts one through so hard that it broke the net, went on over someone's garden wall, through their back window and nearly out the front again. Bill for damages and one goalkeeper still recovering from shock.

"Yet, at the same time, he doesn't seem to know whether he's playing soccer or rugby or what side he's on, or whether it's Monday or Tuesday."

"That's Arnold all right," said the other PE teacher.

"I know. That is what's so bloody funny. Something's going on with that boy. But so long as he scores at the right end, he can be Frankenstein for all I care."

Chapter 25

SLAMBOSS STOOD AT the side of the mirror table in Necro's chamber and surveyed Hitman and Nobbin. Hitman's domelike head had been made a more interesting shape with a large swelling which shone purple in the half light of the room. Little Nobbin had a black eye. Their clothing was in ribbons and Hitman still held two or three inches of shattered sword blade in his hand.

Slamboss's eyes bulged:

"Yurb it. Yurb it! You flumped. I recc you flumped. I ibed you in the Misti Crist. You made a pogser of it. I atta have you danged by your piccers."

"Ooh that's numpo, Shrefful Slamboss," said Nobbin, "You can't dang your Lurci Flunkaj up by the piccers."

"Why not?" asked Slamboss incautiously.

"Who would doo it?"

Slamboss gave an incoherent roar of rage and aimed a savage kick at Clarence who had poked his head round the table leg. Then he sat down heavily.

"That chib was too loomi for me to ibe dooli. But I recc you were pogsing it up. But what did occo — nibbic?"

They looked at one another.

"Shrefful Slamboss. We don't recc, crozmi. Won nimmot we slurged into the chib. Necro and the Dirtwon were zizzot. We were copping Dornal when, fliccot, it all went blunt. We were slammed from afto."

"Yumda. Poggi slam. Sumko donged me on the bonce. Then the nedders shanxed about. Won of them patted Dadwon. The other folded on me. We were bingi to exo breeli."

"You'll be bingi to exo breeli from here," roared Slamboss. "Now bego and slep me bonz."

"We could slamber them when they shanx to the Drago Soggon," said Hitman hopefully.

Slamboss waved his hand.

"No. I'll piccle it this tocca. I'll freeb Replic Dornal a doocum he can't numyur. That will crozmi chex if he is Replic Dornal or num."

Chapter 26

MIST SHROUDED THE great sweltering mass of the Bashi Rangles, cloaking every hill, ravine, bog bush and stunted tree in a pale, green haze. The nedders plodded on steadily, their feet squelching in the soil now drying out as the floods went down. Above, the sky had vanished and they travelled under a hanging green curtain. It was oppressive and conversation died.

Before they set out at dawn, there had been a dispute between Arnold and Necro, as he had demanded that Norsha be allowed to ride behind him on the nedder's back. Necro shook his head vigorously.

"Impossible. A grafton riding behind a Replic Luxon."

"Well, I'm not a Replic anyway, so what yonc does it make?"

Necro looked alarmed and put his finger to his lips.

"Sh," he muttered. "Once word gets out there is no telling what may happen."

"OK, then I'll walk and she can ride."

Necro passed his hand over his eyes.

"That would be ten times worse. Imagine what would happen if you were seen."

"Who's going to see us in this rubbish dump, except Dracula?"

Necro looked shrewdly at Arnold, as they wrapped their cloaks around them and mounted their nedders.

"We are being watched all the time and will be until we get clear of the Bashi Rangles. How do you think the attempt was made on us last night?"

Arnold looked down. He felt very embarrassed: "I'd rather not talk about that. I'd have been done for, if it hadn't been for ..." he jerked with his head towards Norsha who was stowing away the food.

Necro smiled.

"Nonsense. It is the duty of a grafton and particularly a servant grafton to do anything for their masters, even lay down their lives. After all if a luxon should sacrifice their life for a grafton, that would be a total waste. If a grafton sacrifices their life for a luxon, everyone benefits. It even improves the value of their life."

"How can it improve the value of their life if they lose it?"

"They will know they enabled a noble, gracious person to go on living and seeking perfection."

"How will they know it if they're dead?" asked Arnold disgustedly.

"Ah, if the grafton does not know it, the luxon will."

"Won't they feel ashamed like I do?" muttered Arnold.

"On the contrary, it is your duty to remain alive."

Arnold pulled at the harness on the nedder's sloping back.

"I know, Necro."

He suddenly felt as though he were talking to an old uncle.

"Listen, at home, I mean down there on Dirt, I've always felt it made sense to avoid trouble, to keep out of the way, to use your loaf to get clear when things start to drop on you ..."

"Well, you are a Dirtwon."

"Yeah, I know, Necro," Arnold slapped the reins down so that the great beast started and jerked up its long tapering neck.

"But, just since I've been here, I've started to think ..."

"Think what, O Nurbul Replic," said Necro, his eyes twinkling.

"Sometimes you have to stop thinking and start thumping."

"Ah, now you are beginning to think like a real Himsir. Do you still want the graftona to ride?"

Arnold blushed furiously. He had been caught out.

He glared at Necro, then turned and called to Norsha, who was bent down amid the bushes, raising a bundle on her back. He called and pointed to the nedder. For a second he thought there was a faint glint in the deep green eyes. Then she frowned, looked stupidly at him, and bent to her task again.

Arnold heard Necro chuckle softly. He turned round and urged the beast forward.

"Ding, O Nurbul," called Necro. "Let me show the way."

He pushed his beast to the front. Arnold followed and some ten yards behind came Norsha head down, long legs striding.

At first, they rode in what seemed to be a great circling slope, as though they were trying to get down into an enormous valley buried into the green gloom. Arnold heard from either side in the tangled, dripping undergrowth the sliding, rustling movements of unknown animals. But he was beginning to get used to this hideous place. He could judge the distance of the sounds, could recognise when they were near or far, what seemed to be coming his way, with menace, and what meant distress or death for some other creature. He realised that he was hardening himself, because there was no other way of carrying this through than to try and be the Dornal he was supposed to be inside this richly bordered, but now mud spattered tunic. To be a hero in fantasy was one thing. To be a hero in real life was a much more humdrum thing. It was more a matter of keeping your stomach in place, your teeth clenched and doing a hundred every day things without an outward care, when inside you really wanted to crawl away and hide under the bed.

But, where was his bed now? It was down there on Dirt with the real Dornal fast asleep in it perhaps.

Arnold shivered, despite the warmth of the thick red cloak. The air grew colder as they rode. Above there was no sign of the sun, no rays or beams struggling through the mist.

As they moved down into the valley, coolness and gloom increased. Arnold dropped the reins and thrashed his arms around his chest. He looked to the side. Necro's jaffa face and white stringy hair had disappeared inside his cloak. Behind him the green miasma closed in and there was no sign of Norsha's bare-legged loping figure. Still they moved on and down and as they moved the droplets on the bending branches turned to slivers of glass-clear ice.

The green mist swirled closer, grew darker and the heavy beasts moved more warily. They hesitated front hooves raised and sniffed the air.

"What's wrong with them?" he asked Necro, his voice crackling in the emptiness.

"They are afraid. They do not know what they fear but they are afraid."

"Why?"

"Because this valley passes through the range of the Murgru, the Mist Monster.

Arnold jerked on his reins: "What are we going this way for?"

"That is not what Replic Dornal would have said."

"I know that. But," added Arnold cunningly, "I have a duty to protect my life. It's valuable. I want to perfect it."

Necro laughed slowly: "You have a mind that is far too quick to play this part, O Dirtwon. But, if we are to reach the Drago Soggon, the Long River, then through this valley we must go."

"And if we meet the Monster?"

Necro shrugged: "What can I say? The Monster's

gaze paralyses all it falls on, so that he may devour them at his leisure."

"Can't we dodge round him?"

"He has eyes at the back of his head."

"Then if we meet him, we're done for?"

"Replic Dornal would, nevertheless give battle and take his chance."

"Idiot!"

"An hour ago, you said — 'Sometimes you have to stop thinking and start thumping.'"

"Yes well ..."

Necro raised his head. The trees were parting, arching to form a clearing.

"Let us stop and eat here. If we then ride on, we may get through the woods to a safe place before the snows come."

"Are you sure it's going to snow, Necro?"

"Zitto. It always snows on Blizda. Always has, always will."

"OK, then, what about your death forecast. Have you made it today?"

Necro swung down off his nedder. Norsha ran past them lightly and set to work in the clearing, snapping twigs that broke from the frozen trees with a musical twang. Necro and Arnold stood and watched while flames leapt up in the clearing.

"Grovli fold, O Replic," Necro bowed.

They sat down near the fire. The flames glinted and flashed from the iced trees. They sat in a green cavern as though in the centre of an iceberg. But Arnold now felt the warmth seep back into his bones as he huddled into the thick cloak. He watched Norsha's quick bare limbs at work around the fire and felt guilty again that he should sit warm while she worked in her rags. But he was trapped in his role as Prince, trapped inside his own dream, unable to change it.

Norsha was singing as she worked, a little smile on her lips;

"When the yoot froot is in blosser.

We will frooble, you and I."

Arnold nudged Necro.

"What does that mean?" he whispered.

Necro made a face.

"Oh, some grafton song that young people sing. I expect she has a froober or two beneath the city walls."

Arnold felt a strange feeling inside. Somehow the idea of Norsha and her lovers at play beneath the city walls made him feel uncomfortable. He looked at her. Her eyelids dropped and she came forward, bending low with platters of food.

"Snacca yacca, Nurbul Replic," she murmured.

They ate and she slipped away to the other side of the fire. The little song began again. Arnold looked up quickly and saw the old magician studying him. Something was baffling Necro.

But before he could speak, the nedders on the edge of the clearing let out a shriek of alarm and reared up. Their huge eyes rolled at the peak of their long necks and they pushed at each other. Necro raised his hand and called. The nedders sank down again, but remained alert. A small breeze began to blow down the green tunnel of the trees. The fire died down, the flame flickered, the ashes scattered. Inside his red cloak, Arnold felt a chill that turned the marrow to ice.

There from the direction of the wind, a white shape was emerging from the green, paler than pale, formless, high, advancing, growing, spreading.

Necro was suddenly on his feet.

"Gid, gid, Nurbul Replic. It is the Murgru."

Arnold turned wildly. He grasped Necro's arm.

"Norsha, where is she? We can't leave her."

Necro's hand tightened round Arnold's like a vice.

"Will you stay and fight?"

Still looking round bewildered Arnold was dragged across the clearing, bundled on to the nedder's back, which pitched like a ship in storm as the animal lashed out with its legs. Then Arnold saw Norsha, crouched beyond the dead embers of the fire, eyes fixed on the advancing white light. And from the centre of the light rose an eerie, knife thin howling.

"Away," yelled Necro and while Arnold watched helplessly, he smote the nedder on its flank and the two beasts burst from the clearing, branches and twigs snapping and tinkling before them. Thrashing hooves carried Necro and Arnold away into the green depths, while the clearing behind them filled with blinding whiteness and the eerie howling of the Murgru.

Chapter
27

MUM CAME OUT of Dornal's bedroom and looked at Dad quaffing his Guinness by the flickering light of the old TV set.

"Switch that thing off will you, our Dad?" she said wearily.

He grunted, rose and lumbered to the set. Bright lights, dancing girls all dwindled to a point and vanished.

He waved his glass. "Want one?"

She shook her head: "I'll make myself a cup of tea. I'm a bit worried about Arnold."

He made a face: "So, what's new? Nothing but problems with him."

"No, I know he's a bit absent minded, but he's always done well at his English and History and his reading's always been, well, you know ..."

"I do know. He'd read Yellow Pages or his Snibbles packet all day if he had nowt else."

"Well, you heard what the English teachers said. He's doing very badly. In fact he's not performing well at all in any subject. And," she lowered her voice, "he seems to want me to read to him every night, now, just like he did when he was small."

"Well, if you're daft enough to do it."

She smiled gently: "Oh, I don't know. I never minded that." She looked at Dad. "You never did it, did you? You missed that anyway, having a read with him when he went to bed."

Dad looked embarrassed: "Well, I never did think much of reading anyway."

"The other thing," Mum's voice was lower: "It's very funny. Sometimes he reminds me of you, you know when we first got married before he was born ..."

"Eh, what do you mean?" Dad put his glass down and stared.

Mum looked away: "I don't know. It's when he gets excited. He seems to change somehow."

Dad changed the subject. "The daftest thing the teachers told us, though, wasn't his English. It was his sports. They reckon he's suddenly turned out to be a long distance swimmer. Gets into the pool when they go there and doesn't come out till the end. And at one time, you couldn't even get him in the bath. Then his football. They've chosen him striker for the 'A' team. I don't believe it. I don't believe he even knows one end of the pitch from another. But they reckon he has star potential."

"I don't like it," said Mum, pulling a face. "What good is that going to do our Arnold, when he leaves school?"

Dad took a long drink of his Guinness. Conversations like this always bothered him.

"Well, he could always turn professional."

"Oh, be serious, our Dad. I mean a real career, something secure."

"I don't know. Don't look at me like that. We'll just have to keep pegging away at him." Dad put down his glass and looked round vainly for another bottle.

"You mean, I'll just have to keep pegging away at him," said Mum.

Dad gave up his search for the bottle and turned to her.

"Look. I'll take him down to the Rovers' match this Saturday. I'll soon find out whether he knows what he's doing or not. If he really has got soccer potential, I'll take him in hand."

Mum shrugged and went into the kitchen.

On Saturday, Dad took Dornal to the match. It was a baffling experience. The lad's attention seemed barely to be on the match. It wasn't much of a game. The Rovers, as per usual, were performing like ruptured crabs, but luckily the visitors were no better and after some pretty humdrum play the match ended up one all. Dad tried to sound out his son as the match progressed, passing comments, waiting for his reaction, inviting his views on tactics and foot work. But as the match went on, his impression grew that his son knew as much about football as he knew about quantum physics. The only time the game really seemed to grab Dornal's attention was half way through the second half when he suddenly spoke, half to himself.

"What a stacca wallock chumbling gormers. Any blader could morb them in too nimmots."

Dad stared at him. The lad blinked, then said:

"No sense about how to attack or retreat. They could wipe the floor with the other mob if they really went in at the centre."

Baffled, Dad looked at the field. The two sides were wandering aimlessly up the left wing putting the ball in and out of play.

"How do you mean?" he asked. Then he saw that Dornal's head was turned the other way. The mouth was slightly open. His colour was changing as he grew more excited. Down below, behind the goal, two rival groups of supporters, fists and boots whirling, were trying to get a more conclusive result than the game on the pitch offered.

"They should outflank and fall on the rear," muttered Dornal.

Dad saw with amazement how his son rose in his seat, bright flush mounting to his cheeks. Reaching out, he yanked his son back into his place. The lad's cheeks slowly went back to normal.

"Ah, the umpires are coming, they're stopping the game," he said.

Dad blinked. The game on the pitch was still going on. But on the terrace the Law had moved in, grabbing collars and tapping kidneys. Slowly the two struggling groups of fans were separated.

Dornal and Dad went home in silence. Dornal was still baffled by the game. Without the Yobs around him to point him in the direction of goal, the movement of the two sides still puzzled him. Dad's remarks and questions made matters worse. He had the feeling Dad was suspicious about him and was probing. Dornal was determined not to give anything away. He was vaguely aware that in his excitement at the match, he had revealed both Klaptonian language and colour. He must be more careful.

146

He wished he felt more warmly towards Dad. Deep down he had a strong vein of contempt for him. It couldn't be just because he was a grafton. So was Mum and Dornal didn't feel contempt for her. Instead he felt a kind of foolish warmth. If he stayed on Dirt much longer, he was afraid that Mum and Sharon together would totally change his character. How long before he went back he wondered? He guessed that might be when the Gloami Kojers (or someone else), had disposed of the gormer who had taken his place, time would be ripe for him to go back and be Replic Dornal again. Then, he thought, there would be changes. He would do some straight talking to Topwon and Slamboss about the way they were running the Topwondom.

Meanwhile, he had to play his part down here, keep his head down in the classroom and his boot in on the field. If only he understood all this changing ends, in and out of play, off side and so on. He wished there was someone he could ask about the meaning of soccer, without revealing his total ignorance.

It was after tea that night, in his own room, rummaging through Arnold's books, that Dornal suddenly found a battered set of paperbacks, their corners turned back and furred over, their spines broken and pages falling out. On each jacket, in garish colours were soccer players hurling themselves about. And in bold letters was the title "Hard-boots Hogan".

He sank down on his bed and slowly began to pick out the words of the story inside. He was still at it, two pages on when Mum peeped into the bedroom.

"You've not got enough light, lad."

She switched on the light and Dornal jumped. He held out the book and Mum smiled.

"You want me to read this one. You haven't touched that since you were nine. I thought you'd grown out of that. I can't understand your craze for football these days."

She sank down on the bed. Dornal moved closer. Their heads touched and Mum began to read.

"Hogan's team are up against it. Two minutes to play and two goals down. And some joker has fixed Hogan's leg. Can he pull the team through at the last moment? Read on . . ."

Chapter 28

NIGHT WAS FALLING as Necro and Arnold made camp just clear of the tree line on the sloping ground above the Great River. Already the ground was white with snow and the air shimmered with cold. They discovered an old shelter such as shepherds use, branches placed like a tent against a tree trunk. Necro made a fire and pulled from the saddle bags more blankets which they wrapped around them. Last of all he commanded the great beasts to come close and lie down on either side of the fire so that Arnold and he were enclosed in two huge walls of warm, smelly flesh. At first the rough roof above them dripped with moisture, but this soon rose up as steam, and in the end, the dark reeking cave of branches, leaves, cloth and flesh, with the fire at its mouth winkling like a red eye, grew warm and dry. Necro took out cold meat and offered it to Arnold.

Arnold refused. He lay stunned by his thoughts and looked out at the blinding cold night. Behind them the dark forest was silent as the grave as though all beasts had crept to cover in the snow. But Arnold's head still rang with the unearthly scream of the Murgru as it closed in on the little clearing and Norsha the servant girl, while Necro and he clutched the necks of the panic stricken nedders as they blundered their way through the undergrowth to safety.

"Eat, Arnold," said Necro quietly. "The night will get colder, the fire will die down. Those who do not eat, grow weak."

Arnold shook his head. He felt sick — in his body and mind.

"Why will you not eat?"

Arnold turned to the old man in exasperation, though he knew he was really angry with himself.

"You know why. We shouldn't have left Norsha." He glared at Necro. "Dornal would have fought the monster."

"Yes, but you are not Dornal."

"What difference does that make?"

"A great deal. He is a Prince and Hero. You are a schoolboy with a vivid imagination. This is real, not fantasy."

Arnold picked up a piece of meat and chewed morosely.

"I know. In real life, I usually get out of things, if I can. But in my dreams, I'm brave. Why can't I just for once ..."

"Stop thinking and start thumping?" finished Necro.

The old man's eyes met Arnold's. They seemed to glow red inside the orange of his face in the cowl of his long, black cloak.

"I will tell you why. I believe that what you are enduring now is a test to find out if you are Dornal or not. Until you stand and fight, it is impossible to tell.

149

Once you attempt to fight, the difference will be clear. Once it is known that you are not the Replic, that the Replic is not in Klaptonia, then our enemies will rejoice and our people will lose heart."

"So, I've got to go on being a coward so that Klaptonia can survive?"

Necro smiled.

"You are doing something very difficult. Dornal would find it impossible. Running away — he does not know how to."

The old man stared into the dying embers of the fire.

"On Dirt, Dornal will now be suffering because he has to do what he does not know how to do — let other people decide what will happen. Here, one sweep of a sword and problems are solved for him. Down there, no swords, no desperate action, just thinking things out and muddling through. It is a test for him, though he does not know it."

"Are you saying that all this business, all this escaping, struggling and fighting in the Bashi Rangles is all fixed? Well, who's doing it?"

The old man was silent a moment, then abruptly changed the subject.

"I promised that each camp night I would tell you more of Klaptonia, which as its Replic, you should know. Tonight, I will tell you about animal life. Outside the Bashi Rangles, where beasts and monsters are of infinite variety, life is really quite simple. There is one main domestic animal, the pog, some of which are kept by luxons as pets, but most are herded by prodder graftons until they reach a certain size. Then they are transformed into two kinds, a flying animal known as flork and a swimming animal known as shork. Both are hunted for their delicious meat.

"If they escape being twanged or rodded, they grow and grow. There is no limit on their size. There are legends of Giant Flork, bigger than a house, that flies over the desert regions to the West and a Giant Shork which haunts the depths of the Long River which runs beneath the Prussy Peakers. But few have seen such and none have lived to tell the tale.

"Flork or shork meat is not unlimited and thus can only be eaten by luxons just as the strong wine made from the yoot froot, can only be drunk by luxons. Graftons live on wallocks. But it is believed that they have secret orgies in which they chew the wood of the yoot tree and become intoxicated. This is punished severely since it reduces their capacity to work. A yooty grafton is useless."

"Yeah, useless graftons. That's why we ran off and left Norsha."

Necro ignored Arnold and continued:

"Insects are divided into various groups, eetles, geetles, feetles, meetles, treetles and so on. The eetles are risky because in sufficient numbers they can devour you. That is why the nedder is equipped with a fan like tail so that the eetles of the swamps do not devour all heroes before they are free to die in combat.

"But," added Necro, "the real danger comes from the feetle. That, my friend is something to fear. The feetles – when they come, there is only one thing to do, even for a hero – to flee."

"Why, what's so drastic about them?"

Necro turned away and pulled the cowl over his head. The fire had died out. The nedders slumbered, their bodies rising and falling like sea waves on either side.

"They come in the night in thousands and they . . ."

The old man's voice died away. He was snoring.

Arnold stared into the white night. His body was weary but his head would not let him sleep. In front of him in the dark he saw the face of Norsha and heard the plaintive little song she sang:

"When the yoot froot is in blosser,
　We will frooble, you and I."

He eased his body along the ground away from Necro and down the narrow channel left by the nedders' massive bulk. As his feet pushed into the still warm embers of the fire, he silently rose to his feet and leaving the snoring heaps behind him, he clutched the cloak round his body, gripped the sword hilt in one hand and moved out across the snow, following the sound of the voice.

Chapter 29

THE TRAIL HAD been covered. The forest floor was white below and the trees bent stiffly, each branch under its frozen epaulette of snow. Arnold walked first, then ran, but could not catch up with the singing. It went before him like an echo, but came no nearer. Instead it seemed to retreat into the forest and the darkness. But he could not stop even though he knew he was going further and further from the track and could not find his way again.

He ran on and his feet struck into the snow which clung and mounted up until he rose on thick soles which he stamped away in a flurry of spurting white. His feet leapt higher with the effort, his cloak pulled from his clutching hand and streamed behind him and he ran in great strides and called as he ran:

"Norsha! Norsha!"

He ran into the thicker reaches of the forest, away from the thinly wooded slopes above the river, back into the depths of the Bashi Rangles, their tangled ravines and frozen swamplands. He forced his way through thickets that broke and snapped and jangled as twigs and branches splintered. He ran as though he knew the way, but he had no inkling where he was. He simply ran and called as he ran:

"Norsha! Norsha!"

And suddenly he burst through briar and bushes into a circle of space under the trees and found her lying in her rags on the snow covered soil. Her body was still, but soft. He threw himself down and thought or felt he heard the whisper of a heart beat in his ear. He pulled at her shoulders and the body bent and slipped away from him. He slid his hands beneath her back and pulled her up to him. Her face against his was deathly cold, the eyelashes pinpointed with ice. He pulled back upright, her body leaning on his, then bracing his legs until the strain behind his thighs was like a pain, he thrust his shoulder beneath her and lifted her on to his back. Then he turned and struggled back into the forest.

Each step was heavy now and his feet sank deeper into the snow. Each branch and twig pulled at him, at hair, clothes, feet. His face was lashed time and again by twigs, but he did not bother to protect it. He used both arms to hold Norsha's body over his shoulders and pushed on, heading back to the river. But he was not heading for the river. His feet were wandering in a huge circle. He had no sense of direction any more, but only strove to keep away from the deathly clearing where he had found her. His shoulder muscles creaked with the strain. Inside his head, his mind groaned with the effort, his teeth ground against one another as he forced himself to struggle on all the time, wherever his feet and strength could carry him.

Ahead was light, a dancing red like a camp fire. It grew from a point to a star, from a star to a stain on the snow, from a stain to a curtain of crimson light, throwing the tree trunks and the tangled thorns into sharp relief, and glistening on the snow beneath.

The trees fell away to right and left and in front was clear space, alight with a glow that was not day, but was as bright. And the space was ringed with shapes and shadows, some human-like, some animal-like and some monstrous, weird, unnatural, slender, snake-like, gross giant-like, looming grotesque and breathing menace, slobbering hate. Now they were all around him and the weight of the girl's body was almost unbearable. The creatures ringing him in stretched out arms, tentacles, demanding her back. He would not let her go. But he could not hold her and he could not carry her further. Norsha sank from his grasp to lie on the snow at his feet. The circle around him drew in grew huger, more distinct, the features of horror, the foul breath more real. And he must move, now or never.

With a supreme effort, breaking the paralysis in his limbs and mind, he put his feet astride the prone girl, raised his left hand and with the right, dragged at his sword.

"Pat hander and I'll morb you!"

The last word flew away repeating like an echo in the fire light and in answer came crazy sneering laughter that rippled round the clearing. The sword refused to clear the scabbard. His heart seemed to burst and fly up into his head in the effort. And now from out of the monstrous circle swelled a great, grey mucous mass, its glistening folds topped with a small obscene horned head and winking black eyes. It enlarged, yeast-like as it came closer, blooming out in ghastly bulk above him to left and right, its quaking pleats swaying like a tent in the wind.

And still the sword would not clear the sheath. He took the scabbard in his left hand and jerked until the tension drove into his stomach. Then from the air behind him, out of nothing came a voice enlarged and powerful like a giant calling between cupped hands from a distant battlement.

"Replic Dornal. Replic Dornal . . ." the sound wailed away into the forest. And from the clearing came a shrieking chorus: "Dooooornaaaal. Dornaaaal."

"This is Slamboss," came the giant voice. "O Replic, nimmo is your zaltest chex. Slurd Slug Replic shall have oba for his fawon's morb. You atta morb him with won dong or he shall chumble you. You can," the voice ran on cunningly, "make a jacc for the timmer. All you atta doo is freeb the grafton dima, to Slurd Slug. His ganner will be sluffed, staccot for you to rig."

There was a silence. The scarlet flames danced. The grim circle breathed its evil and waited. All he had to do was abandon Norsha to Slime Slug Son, and he could escape with his life. A choice?

The voice sounded again.

"Pinn, O Replic. Let us ibe the crozmi bree of our Replic!"

A mad dizzy rush of fear and anger spiralled up into Arnold's head. All his desperation flew into his hands and with a heart-stopping jerk, the sword

155

came free, its white steel flashing with a hundred points of light from the fire – red, green, blue, yellow, a cascade of sparks.

He charged forward blindly, blade swinging in a great circle of pouring light, slashing madly at the grey glabrous mass before him. The sword met no resistance, it swung on and back in crazy pendulum and as it swung, dark blood spurted at each point, boiling and foaming, showering him with indescribable filth. Above and beyond came the howling, writhing, shrieks of hatred from his foes.

The Slamboss voice blasted out behind him.

"You have morbed Slugma, the mawon of Slurd Slug. That was a dredgi doo."

Arnold's eyes swivelled wildly towards the grey hulk that lay collapsed like a fallen tent. Slime Slug's mother?

"I didn't recc that," he cried in despair.

"Slurd slugs," came the answer, "are shreddi goron kojers, strong family folk. For them no freebon is too zalti."

"Where is Slurd Slug?" yelled Arnold. "I'll morb him."

"He is yondo. You have champed his mawon. A reppi champ." The great bellowing laugh from Slamboss reeled away into the darkness, while around the grotesque audience echoed its foul laughter.

"Now, there is won graf you atta doo. If Slurd Slug had champed, he would chumble you. Now you have champed, you must chumble Slugma."

Eat her? Nausea rushed into Arnold's throat. He choked back. And in the midst of his nightmare came a gleam of cunning. Salt, he thought.

"Crisper," he shouted, "I can't chumb Slugma seppo crisper."

From the ground in front came a gigantic oozing,

156

slithering, dragging on the ground. Evil eyes winking the monstrous heap was heaving, moving away
and with it was going the whole rout of enemies.
They vanished with bubbling shrieks of rage and
fear into the darkness of the forest night and Arnold
was alone.

The fire had died out and Norsha, too, had gone.

Chapter
30

"WHAT I WANT to know," said Meanie, idly kicking the
wall on the edge of the soccer pitch, "is how long this
stupid caper's going on for?"

"Yer," said Mo. "I thought it was going to be a right
giggle. But . . ."

He paused because he couldn't remember how he'd
intended to finish the sentence. Eenie slowly raised his eyes
as if to ask heaven why he should be saddled with such a
bunch of intellectual failures.

"That's right," put in Mynie, looking sideways at the
leader. "For weeks now, we've been carrying this little
wimp around, letting on he's a great striker, when he's the
biggest disaster area to hit the game since . . ."

He tried to think of a player bad enough, but none came
to mind.

"Listen," said Eenie, contemptuously. "This is why you
woodentops spend half your time playing pontoon for
matchsticks. You've no flair."

They looked at him, hurt. Beyond them, on the field, the

opposing side were already in possession, belting balls in and out of the goalmouth. Near the changing rooms, the Games Master was assembling the 'A' team, Junior League for a final pep talk. In a moment, he would be bawling for them to come over. Eenie spoke quickly:

"'Course he's the biggest wally to hit the game since the year dot. But, who has passed him off on Godzilla as a potential star? Who's got him into the 'A' team? Who's kept him at it through all these fixtures, right up to today, when we've got to the semi-final?"

Like any good leader, he did not wait for followers to answer. He stabbed a brutal finger into each chest.

"We have. We put him up and we will let him down, when it suits us. Right? But you have to play clever. We're going for maximum effect. Get that? Maximum effect. We get through into the final. And when's the final? It is the same time as they are making their minds up – do they close the school down and flog it off or do they keep it going. And what is going to decide?"

His finger ranged round the circle again.

"Performance is going to decide and that is when we let little Arnold go. We not only lose the final, we make Pokeface look stupid. We get the school closed down. And it's our doing. Everybody will know it is our doing and nobody will be able to do anything about it."

"Hey," said Mynie, "suppose we overdo it and go out at the semi-final?"

"Don't be a noggin. Of course we don't overdo it. We just keep Bozo under control, slip him one or two now and then. I'll score the goals we need at the right moment. OK? Just you lot concentrate on carrying him around for this match. In the final you can let him go and fall about laughing. And afterwards, we collect, as well. Remember."

The others smiled, relieved. That they understood. At the third yell from the Games Master they trotted obediently back to the rest of the team.

Eenie moved in closer to Dornal as they ran out on to the pitch. As they passed a crowd of girls from 3H cheered them on with appropriate comments. Eenie muttered to Dornal.

"Listen, take it easy. I'll let you know when to go for goal, right?"

Dornal turned and smiled broadly.

"Don't worry. I've worked everything out."

Eenie stared at him. A faint suspicion formed in his mind, then vanished as the whistle went for kick off.

The first half was slow, with both teams nervous, but after half an hour it was clear that the visitors were on the offensive. By half time they were one up. Half way through the second half they had made it two nil and though Eenie, acting to his plan, got one in for the home side, the visitors then made it three-one. Eenie began to feel slightly apprehensive. This was going further than he intended. And he noticed, too, that little Arnold was overdoing it. He was messing about, but really messing about. Not his usual half-cocked way of doing things. It was as though he were playing around on purpose. Two or three times he had the ball and kicked wide or over. But not wild – as though he had aimed to miss.

Eenie found himself galvanised into action, quietly whipping the Yobs up to make raids on the opposing goal. They were baffled by their leader's sudden burst of enthusiasm. Twenty-five minutes from time, though the score was still three-two for the visitors.

"Listen Arnie," whispered Eenie, as they trotted back to the centre. "Stop pissing about. We've got to equalise. Then we get extra time, so when I tell you to put it in, put it in will you?"

Dornal grinned at him. "Not to worry," he said cheerfully.

Ten minutes before time, the score was four-two and still Dornal was trotting to and fro with that amiable smile on

159

his face. It began to dawn on Eenie that something had gone wrong. For once one of his schemes was not working. Was little Arnold taking him and the boys on the roundabout?

There were seven minutes to go. The school supporters, convinced the match was lost were drifting away from the field and the Games Master was grinding his teeth till the sparks came. The Head, watching the game from the touchline wondered for the umpteenth time why men thought this game was so exciting. But she feared all the same that not only the game, but the school might be slipping away into a hole in the ground. Just at that moment, something happened that took them all by surprise.

Dornal, who had been loitering in the centre of the field, suddenly walked into the opposing centre half and hooked the ball neatly over his flattened body. Like a local Lineker without the finesse, he tore down the centre of the field. He did not run rings round the opposing defence. He ran over them. They bounced off him like pin balls. Fifteen seconds later they were recovering the ball from a back garden and the net had a gaping hole in it.

Barely had the teams got back to the centre, when the little devil did it again. The school supporters suddenly turned back and crowded the touchline again. There was a brief lull in the action while the opposing team gathered round Dornal and tried to tie him down. The ball was kicked into touch again and again. Time was draining away. Three minutes, two minutes. But Dornal seemed quite unperturbed. One minute to go.

In the very dying seconds of the game, he came to life again and bore down on the opposing goal leaving a trail of battered bodies behind him. Just before the final whistle the goalkeeper lay in a state of shock and another hole appeared in the damaged net. It was five-four. School were into the final. Hardboots Hogan, or Replic Dornal, had done it again.

While a shocked and silent Eenie tried to work out how much of an idiot this idiot had made of him, Dornal surrounded by the rest of the team was heading in triumph for the changing room with the 3H girls trying to get near him. Once inside, Himsir Dornal, high on victory, made for the showers joining in a rousing chorus of "If I were the marrying kind."

And this time, all caution thrown aside, he stripped off and plunged boldly in with the others. From the changing rooms the cheers and singing suddenly changed to shrieks of amazement.

"Hey," the two teams howled in unison. "Look at Arnold. Just look at him."

Chapter 31

ARNOLD OPENED HIS eyes. It was dawn. Grey light flooded the sky in front of him. He viewed it through a v-shape formed by the towering bodies of the nedders who gently heaved and snorkled in their sleep. He was back in camp. How did that happen? He heaved himself up on his elbow struggling in the folds of the heavy red cloak. He struck the body of the old magician who had rolled close to him. Necro still snored. Above them the rough network of branches which had sheltered them last night, showed black against the sky.

That was funny, where was the snow? He pulled the red cloak from him and rose on to his knees. Through the space between the nedders he could see the dark network of bare trees stretching down the slope. Winter had come and gone in a single night while he slept.

Slept! He leapt to his feet. Had he been sleeping? Was that mad journey through the wilderness, that desperate, farcical attempt to rescue Norsha just a dream? He had struggled he had carried her through thicket and briar. He had defied foul and horrible creatures, the Slamboss's evil challenge, to save her. He had fought, wildly, violently. But she had vanished. It had never happened. He clenched his fists in rage with himself. The only time he could do things right was in fantasy. Norsha was gone, left behind in the glade where the blinding white menace of the Murgru swept down and he and Necro fled like cowards, all because he must not be put to the test for fear he should betray himself.

He sank down again. Then pulled at his cloak. It caught. He tugged again. Necro stirred. The old man opened his eyes.

"Do not venture out. Stay where you are. Today is Wafda, day of winds. As soon as the sun rises, the wind will blow. You will not be able to stand. Stay here."

Arnold launched himself upright.

"Norsha. I have to find Norsha."

Necro waved his hand.

"All this fuss about a graftona. Lie back. We shall have breakfast soon."

Breakfast. He stared. The old man grinned and wrinkled his nose and all at once, Arnold smelt frying meat. The delicate scent curled like invisible smoke along the narrow space between the sleeping animals. Behind it came like a whisper the crackle of flames and hiss of fat. And behind that, quietly came the song:

"When the yoot froot is in blosser ..."

He turned, bewildered, to Necro. The old man laughed.

"But, Necro. We left her. She di..."

Necro shook his head.

"No, you went back for her."

"I didn't move. I slept."

Necro raised his hand and placed it on his own forehead.

"You went back in here, Arnold. That is a journey Dornal could not make. Had I let you go in reality you would have died. But I could not stop you doing in your mind what you wanted to do, though why you should risk your life for a graftona is a mystery to me. There are things about Dirtwons which I do not understand, wise as I am."

Arnold forced his way to the outside of the shelter and stood jammed between the heavy flanks of the sleeping nedders. On the ground — it was swept clean, Norsha had built a fire and was bent over the iron grid on which meat was bubbling. She looked up, one eyebrow raised.

"Brecca yaccas, O Nurbul Replic," she said. She laid aside the long spit and bowed her shoulders. Arnold stepped close and without thinking reached out to touch her. She shrank away quickly.

"Norsha?"

She did not answer.

"Norsha. You atta yurb." He tried to command though he felt ridiculous.

"I grovel, O Replic," she said quietly, though she

163

did not take her eyes from the fire.

"You were in the shredd of the Murgru. It's scan is morb. You were singo. How?"

She turned. Her smudged face smiled, white teeth showing against the orange cheeks. With her left hand, she took out of her rags a piece of polished metal. It shone and she saw her features reflected in its round surface. Before she slipped it away again, he saw that its rim was studded with tiny stones that glittered like jewels in the light.

"A crist? You revved the scan? But how did you todd here? You were yondo in the rangles?"

She turned again, her face blank. She shook her head.

"I do not recc. But I am here. Let the Replic grovli fold and I will freeb the chumber."

He sat down near her. She frowned and pointed to the shelter.

"Inco. Jacco."

From within the shelter Necro called: "Jacco, O Replic. Inco."

Arnold had barely pushed in between the nedders when with a shriek like a soul in torment, the wind swept down, the ashes of the fire were flung into the air and the small trees around were battered flat. He flung himself down beside Necro and sat while the gale ripped overhead. Strangely the boughs which formed the shelter did not move, but sang like violin strings as the wind surged over them. The noise rose and fell with each gust. The noise continued; it did not diminish while the day lasted. It was as Necro said, a day of winds. There was no venturing out. He and Necro finished their meal in silence. Necro took out his white cloth and coloured stones and began to cast the wilber.

Norsha withdrew into the far end of the shelter by

164

the narrow gap and began to repair the torn sleeve of her shift. As she stitched she sang.

Arnold walked over to her.

"Why do you yurm that yurmer, Norsha?"

She lowered her eyes and would not answer. Arnold walked back to his place and she did not sing again that day. Necro put the stones away at last.

"Tonight," he said with quiet cheerfulness, "there will be a murder attempt."

"What?" gasped Arnold. "Then we've got to get away."

"No, no, no, that will not be possible. Besides, no one would dream of killing in a high wind. It must wait for nightfall."

"But can't we do anything about it?"

Necro looked embarrassed. "Unfortunately the forecast is not entirely accurate and it is not possible to say who will make the attempt or how they will do it. Almost anything can happen."

He shrugged: "However, rest assured, it will only happen if whoever it is, is really determined and has a really good reason for killing us. Although," he went on more quietly with one eye on the servant girl sewing in her corner, "since you are not entirely Klaptonian, the rule may not completely apply to you. That is very interesting."

"What do you mean," whispered Arnold, "not entirely Klaptonian?"

As always at such moments, Necro changed the subject.

"You are perhaps curious why Norsha would not answer your question about the song. If you had been entirely Klaptonian, you would not have asked it. It is bad form for a luxon to interest himself in the intimate affairs of a grafton since these are beneath notice. In any case these things are of no consequence, either for luxons or graftons."

"What do you mean? No importance. I mean, love, sex, and all that are very important. I mean on Earth — on Dirt, people talk about nothing else, well almost nothing else."

Necro's eyebrows rose. "Talk about froobling? Why should anyone want to talk about froobling? What does it matter?"

"Er well," said Arnold, "it does make the world go round."

"The world go round? A strange expression," Necro mused. "I remember your strange speech in council, about the world going round. But tell me, Arnold, how does froobling make the world go round?"

Arnold looked round, embarrassed. There was no sign that Norsha could hear.

"I mean, without froobling, the human race would die out. It's about having babies, in the long run, isn't it?"

Necro beckoned Arnold closer, then said in Arnold's ear:

"Let me make it clear. Froobling has nothing to do with having children. This is a Dirt custom of which I have heard vaguely from time to time. But it is frankly so ridiculous that I have never believed it. Sometime when we have the opportunity, you must explain more to me."

"No, mate," hissed Arnold, "you explain to me. What is this garbage about froobling on Klaptonia?"

Now Necro looked so amazed his old red eyes seemed to cross.

"On Klaptonia," he said, so quietly that Arnold could hardly hear him "froobling is only for pleasure. Children arrive as they are needed. The idea that children are born by chance just because some

166

luxon or grafton wants to enjoy themselves is barbarous. Children are far too important to be accidents. Think how many unwanted ones there would be.

"On Klaptonia both graftons and luxons live as children until frooble time. Then they begin to frooble. At the age of twenty-five years they are ready for their replics. They journey to the shores of the great sea, Necoa, in the East, graftons to one side, luxons to the other. And there, under the Twinki Tree, they find their twinkies, one wipper, one dima, to replace them. The grown-ups live for another twenty-five years until the children are fully grown. Then at the age of fifty, they auto-snuff, or self-destruct. Thus," said Necro, complacently, "the population is always stable, children are always wanted and parents are always fully mature."

Arnold rolled over and laughed until tears ran down his face, so that Norsha turned from her sewing and looked at him with a puzzled smile. He pulled himself together and hissed at Necro:

"You are putting me on. It's a lot of old cobblers."

"Cobblers, shoemakers?" asked Necro.

"Lobbers! Pogdosh! Talwons!"

Necro looked offended. "I will make a bargain with you. If you will accept my logical explanation of how our population works on Klaptonia, I will accept what quite frankly is a most bizarre story about Dirt, that people frooble and babies happen by accident. I do not believe that any people of your intelligence could possibly think of a more ridiculous system."

Now Arnold changed the subject.

"Hey, you are more than fifty, Necro. Why don't you auto-snuff? You're certainly more than twenty-five. Where is your wife, your replics? I think you can pull the other, it has janglers on."

"Night is coming," said Necro abruptly. The gloom in the shelter had increased, and Arnold had not noticed for his head had been full of the musical whine of the wind in the boughs and the strange things he had heard. The bent figure of Norsha had quite vanished in the dusk. Arnold had an impulse to go and talk with her. He wished Sharon were here now. Her cheerfulness and calm good sense were suddenly so real that he could see her there, dark face, white teeth gleaming in a grin. Then the image was gone and he was left feeling empty. How much longer must he stay in this crazy world? Would he ever leave it?

Then he remembered Necro's forecast. Tonight someone would try to kill them. He realised that he did not have the energy of mind to worry or even think properly about it. He just had to take things as they came and do the best he could or whatever it was Replic Dornal was supposed to do. He wished he were as bold and brave as Dornal, but he was thankful he was not so dim. He could use his head — if he tried. He looked round. The other two had gone to sleep, just like that, Necro stretched out, black robe around him, Norsha somewhere in the shadows by the shelter entrance.

How much later Arnold could not say, but there began in the darkness a strange noise, a rustling on the ground, a faint drumming as if from a million small spidery feet. It came from the dark outside and crowded into their shelter. The nedders heaved in sudden panic, raised their snake like heads in the air and brayed a high pitched, screaming laughing bray. Arnold heard Norsha gasp and chuckle in her sleep, then laugh a rippling giggling laugh that ended in a choke.

Beside him Necro reared up and shoved Arnold.

"Aj, O Replic. On your pats."

"What — what?" said Arnold bewildered.

Then he felt it. Something was at work on his feet, his ankles, a hundred small hairy touches, creeping further up the legs, setting his nerves a twitch, making his stomach curl. Despite himself he began to laugh. He bent and brushed vainly at his legs, but the unseen presence was too many, hundreds, thousands that ran over his hands and arms. He struggled to rid himself of them and keep his body under control as he jerked and heaved in remorseless weakening hiccupping laughter. He couldn't stop.

Around him the great fleshy bulk of the nedders reared up and shook, the massive bodies quaking and jerking. And he remembered between the agony of laughter what Necro had told him, about the insect life — Feetles. These were Feetles. And all of them, Dirtwon, Klaptonians, nedders were being tickled to death.

Chapter 32

IN A MOMENT of wild abandon, Dornai dropped his shorts and leapt into the shouting, splashing singing mob in the showers and almost at the same time he leapt out again, realising what he had done. But the singing and shouting had stopped for a micro-second while his team mates beheld his naked body with its incredible orange blush. Then the silence was shattered by a mingled cheer and shriek of affected astonishment.

"Look at Arnie. You never told us. He's been using blusher on the quiet the little raver. It's a birthmark. It never. He's been at the sun lamp. Oooh can I touch it, Arnie? Will it come off?"

Someone with a stock of old 78's at home began to improvise:

"Itsy bitsy teeny weeny
Little tangerine bikini."

Then Dornal was in motion. If he had gone up the field like a tank he went through the mocking mob like a bulldozer. They fell to left and right, their shrill cries changing to yells of alarm and agony as they fell and bumped various delicate parts, while the Replic of Klaptonia, covering what he could of his orange bit with his hands sprang to the bench where he had dropped his clothes and dragged on briefs, shirt, pants in a mad rush over his still damp and steaming limbs.

Before the team could recover from his violent reaction — they were only kidding, weren't they? — the swing doors had slammed behind him and the bruised players were shaking their heads and chattering like demented chimpanzees. Had he always been like that? Nobody knew for sure. After all, he'd never been on the team before. Yeah, because he was a right wimp, wasn't he? Wally of the year. But how come he suddenly played like a little Maradona? Was he on gas? Was it that, turning him funny colours? Where does he get it? Dodgey game. But fancy little Arnie going like that!

Dornal escaped from the changing rooms and walked blindly across the field. He may have thought he was heading for the gate and the road outside, but in his upset state he was heading in the opposite direction — towards the bike sheds. And he did not go unobserved.

Eenie stepped out of the showers and picked up someone else's towel. They started to protest then changed their minds. Eenie was clearly in no mood for messing about. He signalled to the rest of the Yobs and they silently gathered round their chief in a corner of the changing rooms.

"He's been making monkeys out of us, all along," he said.

Meanie made a face: "I told you mate. I said all along. But you wouldn't listen would yoouuuu . . .!"

His voice went up the scale as Eenie's right knee rose with deadly precision.

"I'm talking. Like I said. He's been pulling it and we didn't spot it."

"Meanie did." put in Mo helpfully, then smartly backed away as Eenie's knee trembled into action again.

"You know what that means?" Eenie asked.

No one answered. It wasn't that sort of question.

"It means," he went on, "that he is going to make bigger monkeys of us come the final. And what happens with the book we made, eh? We've got a couple of ton on the school team losing."

They knew that. They'd gone round collecting the money. They had the money stuffed up their collective jumpers. They'd offered five to one as well as reasonable threats to get it.

"No way is he going to mess about winning that final. No way is he going to stripe me up."

The others stared at their chief. He seemed unusually emotional.

There was a silence. Eenie was waiting for someone to ask. Mo did.

"So, what do we do?"

"Do?" Eenie stared. "We go out there after him and break bits off. That's what we do. He can't win the cup on crutches, can he?"

Chapter 33

ALL WAS PANIC and confusion. The nedders snorting and hee-hawing like drunken donkeys were heaving up and down, smashing the bough shelter to matchwood. Necro and Arnold rolled about in hysterical convulsions as millions of feetles pressing in out of the dark forest swarmed about them and all over them, little feelers and feet working madly.

"For your waaaaaha life, ho ho aaaah," yelled Necro as he blundered past Arnold. Arnold looked about him. The nedders were floundering, spinning ponderously round and round, their long necks waving crazily. No way were they going to ride them. He pushed his way forward in the half darkness. It was no use trying to brush the little tormentors off. They were like a live body stocking all over him.

"Nooo—oor—shaaha —ha —ha," he howled.

"Fooor ... aaaahaaa ... yooor breeee ..." came an answering cry as they all stumbled out on to the grassy slope. Then they ran, arms flailing, teeth clenched to keep out the feetles who now ran madly, delicately round necks ears, eyelids, touching, tickling, winding up their exquisite agony to a pitch that was becoming unbearable, paralysing.

"Soooooo — oggoooo—oon," screamed Necro.

The river! Now the ground sloped more steeply.

They ran, stumbled and fell, rolled and heard the blanket of feetles crackle under them as their bodies spun through bushes and grass. Now the trees had thinned and the slope was broad and clear. They struggled up, fell again, rolled, rose once more but never dared to stop, to look round to see where the others were, never dared to open mouths, or even breathe in.

And at last it was over, over in a couple of minutes that seemed like years. Arnold felt the ground open under his blindly stretching feet. He was falling through space and with a splash that sent cold shocks through his whole body he was in the water. Down into green depths, up into the clear air, the arch of a starlit sky above him, down again into the depths and up once more. How many times did you go up and down before you drowned? He lashed out with arms and legs. A darker shape loomed over him. His thrashing arms struck something hard, a timber baulk. He grabbed. His finger nails dug into it, snapped and dug in again as he was dragged along, feet trailing underneath, current tearing at his legs.

He heaved up, both hands scrabbling for a hold on the wood. Now his face came clear and he breathed the clean fresh air. At that moment he realised that the torturing insects had gone. He was free of them. A jerk of his arm muscles and he had his elbows over the edge of the timber. Now he saw that he was on the edge of a large rough raft of tree logs, which drifted with the river current. The banks of either side were low and clear of trees, the forests and thickets of the Bashi Rangles were being left behind. They were in unknown country.

He swung a leg up on to the raft and lay for a moment while the water streamed off him. He opened his eyes and to his surprise — no he wasn't really surprised — there sat Necro in the middle of the raft, arranging his saddlebags around him, while at the stern sat Norsha, long bough-oar in hand, her green eyes gleaming as if they picked up the faint light of the moon which had just risen.

"Pacca Yaccas, O Nurbul Replic," said Necro.

Arnold woke. It was daylight. The others were asleep, Necro in mid-raft and Norsha at the stern. The bough-oar was tied by a leather thong and the craft floated steadily on in mid stream. The sky was clear blue, with fleecy white clouds, but the air was cool. It was like spring and the banks on either side were covered with short moss and grass like a lawn. At a distance were trees like willows, bending over, crowned with tufts of pale green leaves. As he watched, the sun went behind a cloud, the cloud thickened and grew darker and down came the rain. Large drops lazily fell and trickled down his hair, and then the shower had passed as soon as it began and the sun came out. The air warmed a little. As he watched it seemed the grass and leaves were growing and unfolding like a time lapse picture. It must be a trick of the light. But it wasn't. He could see things growing as they passed.

Necro was looking at him. "A-da is Verda, grass day. Ma-da it will be Gloda, warm day ..."

"I know, I know," answered Arnold. "And the next day it will be hot then it will pour down and the day after there'll be thick fog, then we'll have snow, after that winds. And so on."

"You learn fast."

Arnold grinned, then looked to see if Norsha were awake. The girl dreamed quietly, one arm over the oar, a faint smile on her curved lips.

"Where are we going now?" he asked.

"Where? There is only one way to go on the Drago Soggon, the Long River — towards the Prussy Peakers. And beyond them lies the land of the Gloami Kojers."

Arnold thought a moment then said briskly: "Pull the other ..."

"Why are you so doubtful?"

"Doubtful," scoffed Arnold. "I just don't believe you. Listen, a river can't flow towards mountains. It's got to be flowing away. Water doesn't run uphill, does it?"

Necro turned and extended his long arm. Arnold followed the line of his finger down the river. At a great distance there were what seemed to be grey clouds on the horizon. But they were solid, they were mountains. And the river was flowing deeply, steadily towards them.

"But it doesn't make sense," he protested.

"The Drago Soggon, the Long River," murmured Necro, "flows to the Sizdo, the West, and runs through the Prussy Peakers.

"Then, when it reaches the edge of our mondo, it turns back through the Groobi Choob, the Tunnel of Doom beneath the earth and flows the other way towards the Sizzup, the East. In the end it feeds into Necoa, our Great Sea, and from Necoa flows into the Drago Soggon again."

Arnold listened open-mouthed as Necro went on: "The sun, when it sets in the West, travels by night through the great Choob and returns to its rising point where it lifts up out of the waters of Necoa. Every twinkie knows this."

"But it can't rise out of a lake," jeered Arnold, "and anyway, who's seen it going through the tunnel, eh?"

"No one," said Necro calmly, "but it is clear that it

does, which is why the inside of the mondo is hotter than the outside."

He paused, for effect, then: "Have you ever seen the Planet Dirt go round the sun?" he asked.

Arnold said nothing. There ought to be an answer to that, he reckoned, but just now he couldn't think of one and he couldn't think why it mattered. Almost without thinking, he answered:

"OK, if we stick with the river, then we'll come back through the Tunnel and we'll know for sure, won't we?"

Necro's wrinkled orange features turned pale. Arnold had never seen anything like it before.

"No one has ever made that journey and returned alive," said Necro.

Days passed, the river rolled and the day seasons came and went. The raft ploughed on through dark brown flood waters, burned under the cruel sun, drifted ghost-like through the mists, sparkled with snow and frost and surged on waves whipped up by the gales. Arnold lost count of time. They ate. The supply of meat in Necro's saddlebags was never ending, and so was Norsha's ingenuity in cooking it. Arnold tried now and then to speak to her, but she would only mumble and turn her head away. And in the quiet evenings, she would sing her plaintive song.

Each day, when Norsha was busy, Necro told Arnold more that he needed to know about Klaptonia, being careful not to give away the pretence that this was indeed the Replic Dornal. As they journeyed Arnold's grasp of the language grew. He was inventive in making up new words, making the old magician smile. Sometimes when they quietly argued in Dirtyurb, he would catch a glimpse of

Norsha as though she were listening. Could she be? Was she a spy? He no longer thought too deeply about these things. He knew that as the river carried them along so all would be revealed.

Now and then he wondered about the real Dornal, soldiering away down there at Denfield Comprehensive. No doubt he was bored out of his skull, but at least he wasn't, like Arnold, in danger of life and limb...

But, of course, Arnold was quite wrong.

Chapter
34

DORNAL BLUNDERED ACROSS the yard, not looking where he was going. But every now and then he would look at his hands and arms to see whether the heat waves of shame, humiliation and growing anger which surged through his body had reached his skin. Was he reverting entirely to his natural orange colour? Would he have to face school in the morning, orange all over, the target of twelve hundred mocking pairs of eyes and a thousand brilliantly witty remarks? The Replic of Klaptonia was discovering what it was like to be scorned and derided like a comic grafton ordered to act the fool at a luxon banquet. He ground his teeth and walked on.

But he was not alone. He was followed. With the incredible speed that only rumour can reach, the girls of 3H who stood and cheered on the touch line while Dornal ploughed through the opposing team, had heard the news from the changing room. Little Arnold was on gas and it had turned him a funny colour.

"Where did you say, Nicola?" demanded one of the group as they sat on the wall and watched Dornal head for the bike sheds.

"You know, where it matters. You know, his public parts."

"You mean his private parts, dear."

"Well, they're public now."

"I don't believe you," said a third member of the group. "I've heard of all shapes and sizes but I've never heard of different colours."

"S'true. It's . . ." she lowered her voice, ". . . orange."

"Orange!" Shrieked four voices together. "What, like a tangerine?"

"No, more like a jaffa, they reckoned."

"Hey," said Nicola, "we've got to find out. I can't bear not knowing."

"Oh, I shall die," gasped another as she flounced over the wall.

"Shut up, he'll hear you."

The cheerleader lowered her voice: "There's only one way to put the mind at rest."

The others stared, suddenly silenced: "You mean . . ."

"Seeing's believing."

"Nicky, you're disgusting."

"No, I'm not. I've got an inquiring mind, that's all. Listen. All of you get behind the bike sheds and wait. Leave this to me."

The others slipped away and hid in the shadows behind the shed. It was nearly empty now, only a few machines stood in the racks. Nicky sidled up alongside Dornal. "Arnie," she coaxed.

Dornal looked at her. He vaguely knew this girl as a trouble stirrer in class, but she had never spoken, nor even looked at him before. He felt suspicious and made to move on, but she put a caressing hand on his arm.

"Some of the girls asked me to ask you for your autograph."

"Autograph?"

"Yeah, you were brill on the field today. You really saw 'em off. Cor, when you went down the centre, like Gary Lineker, only butcher, like."

"Why can't they ask themselves?"

"Well, you know," Nicky was walking alongside him now, arm in his. The sensation was not unpleasant, but he had an uneasy feeling. She was too friendly.

"Where are they?" he asked.

She leaned against him, steering him a little to the left. "Just over here, round this corner, come on," she wheedled as he hesitated.

The bulk of the bike sheds loomed over them. Dornal heard whispering and giggling on his left. He looked back. There was no one in sight and Nicky was hurrying him on. Her grip on his arm became firmer.

Suddenly, she said, triumphantly: "Here we go!"

In a trice, Dornal was on his back. His sports gear was thrown one way, his school bag another. Eager hands plucked at his clothes. One moment he was looking up at a circle of grinning, sly, eager girls' faces. The next moment, his shirt had been expertly plucked out of his pants and pulled over his face. Someone knelt heavily on his arms. Another body dropped across his legs pinning him down. Swift hands plucked at his belt buckle and zip.

"Come on lad," muttered Nicky, "show us your satsuma. Seeing's believing."

Chapter 35

IT WAS LATE evening and the waters of the Long River shone with the light of the sun setting amid the grey folds of the Prussy Peakers which drew nearer with every day's sailing. In another three or four days, reckoned Necro, the raft would carry them into the foothills of the Blue Mountains and from then on his power could neither predict nor avert any dangers.

The three of them lay quietly on the rough timbers of the raft as if the approaching mountains had sent each of them into their own thoughts. Arnold wondered what the other two were thinking. Both had their secrets. Necro had told him much about Klaptonia, but there was much, he knew, that the old fox was not telling him. And Norsha guarded her secrets with silence. Why had she helped him? Why did she seem to be spying on everyone? Was she an agent? Just now all he could do was let the raft carry him on. In the end he might find out all secrets — including why he had been shuffed for Replic Dornal.

A strange noise broke into his thoughts. He half sat up and saw that Norsha was braced, alert against the rudder bough, her keen eyes peering into the red line of the sunset. Behind and above them the darkness had raced forward to cover most of the sky. The sunset light formed a tunnel into which they were moving and the sound came from its depths.

"What ...?" began Arnold.

It came again, louder, more drawn out, throbbing, mournful. Like an animal in pain, he thought, a very large animal. He didn't like to think how large it might be. Norsha pointed to the right bank ahead. And again the mournful murmur arose. Arnold realised at last. Not an animal in pain but someone singing. Like Barry Manilowe doing "If I fall in love," but with cosmic amplification.

"Sumko's yurming," he gasped.

They nodded, eyes wide. The words were indistinct but they seemed to suggest the incredible unhappiness of some lost, large soul, someone in a lot of trouble. There followed a silence, as though a verse ended. The crew of the raft held their breath. Then they felt on their hands a breeze, a draught of air, blowing strongly up river. Necro shook his head.

"A wif. But there is no waf a-da."

Norsha chuckled. Arnold suddenly understood. Not a breeze, but a deep breath.

"Num," he said, "Sumko's breeling before he wonzes his yurm."

The breeze died and again came the sighing, dirge-like sound. The setting sun was like a finger nail rim on the distant horizon and nightfall now made the sound stranger and sadder.

"He atta have a vasto pang," said Arnold.

"Hm," grunted Necro disapprovingly as he listened. "Winzi garbers. Sentimental rubbish!"

The second verse was barely begun when their ears were shocked by a second rival sound.

Norsha pointed. It came from the other bank. Now the shape of the valley was lost in dusk and it was impossible to place it exactly. But there was no doubt the first singer had opposition.

"Eerol," said Necro, as if amazed.

The second song was so unlike the first it was incredible. It was tuneless, raucous, the words shouted out, rather than sung. It reminded Arnold of fifty blokes being turned out of a pub. The words were crude, and mocking the schmaltzy yearnings of the other, almost as though the second singer was trying to put the first off his stroke. For a few seconds the two songs rose and strove against each other in the night air, which was filled with the clash of tune and words, until the three of them put hands to ears and rolled around the raft full of laughter. The song broke off. There was silence for a moment, then from the right bank came a plaintive call, an affected voice, that of someone who is put out, but trying to maintain good manners.

"If you have to sing something different, at least try and sing in tune."

While from the right bank, came:

"You call that flork howling singing, you wally willy you. Why don't you drop dead and give us all a rest?"

"I have no wish to indulge in this kind of childish abuse. I have better things to do."

"You wimpy wallock basher. If you don't like your neighbours, why don't you move out? You think you're too good for this bank, with your poncy ways and ..."

"I absolutely decline to continue this discussion."

"Ah, get knotted, you poodle-doodle ..."

There came a terrific crump from the right bank, the sound of breaking glass and a loud cry of distress. Then a shout of glee from the other bank.

"Right, wait till it gets light."

Silence came abruptly, with total darkness as

though a curtain had been pulled down. The raft slid on through the night and after a few moments puzzled discussion, the three passengers lay down again and slept.

Chapter 36

HELPLESS IN THE gripping groping hands of the 3H girls, Dornal closed his eyes and waited for the second humiliation of the day as his shameful orange secret was revealed again. With a triumphant gleam in her eye Nicola reached for the zip. .

"Let's see your old satsuma, Arnie boy," she chortled.

But it was not to be.

Nicola said and did no more, for at that moment, her blond spikey hair was suddenly grasped from behind and she was lifted bodily from Dornal and hurled aside. Her body thudded against the wall of the bike shed. With the sound of ripping cloth a second tormentor was dragged off by her collar and vanished from Dornal's line of vision. In the open space he saw the furious dark face of Sharon, her teeth clenched as her hand came round to connect with agonising force on the side of the third of his attackers.

The rest did not wait their turn. They were up from his arms and legs in a flash and running away across the yard. Sharon helped Dornal up. As he restored the dignity of his clothing, Sharon walked towards the leader of the little episode who was leaning dazed over the wall and gave her a thoughtful kick on the backside.

"Clear off, you kinky little bitch before I scalp you," she said pleasantly.

Nicola saw she was on her own and wasted neither time nor words. Her heart full of anguish, she made tracks for the school gate. It was a bad end to a promising afternoon. Now Dornal and Sharon stood alone in the shelter of the bike shed. He leaned on the wall and felt his breath rate slow down. Sharon stood in front of him, hands on the wall on either side of his head and looked at him curiously.

"Are you OK, Arnie?"

He nodded. He could not speak. His head was full of Klaptonian.

"What's this garbage they're talking about you, about your skin being a funny colour?" She hesitated, then nodded downwards. "You know."

He was silent, while thoughts ran round and round his baffled brain. He looked at Sharon's face, the thoughtful, friendly eyes, and made a decision. He spoke slowly, trying to find the right words.

"I must tell you, Sharon, that I am not Arnold – your friend – I am really Himsir Dornal, Replic, er Prince of Klaptonia. I have been . . ."

He broke off in mid-sentence. A wave of anger went through him as her face broke up into laughter, which she just as swiftly stopped with her hand. For a second the two stared at each other then she touched his cheek.

"I'm sorry. I shouldn't laugh. Listen. If you like, I'll call you Dornal, I mean just between the two of us. But, mate, if you want the mob off your back, then you have got to be Arnold ninety-five per cent of the time."

He tried again: "This colour, this orange, is my own colour." He paused as he saw the gleam of laughter in her eyes, then pressed on. "In my own planet all people are like that – tanji, orange. I never realised people could be white until I came here."

Sharon burst out.

"What's all this about white? What's the big deal about white? I'm not white. Most of the people on this planet aren't white. You know that as well as I do, Arnie."

"But, you are different, anyway, Sharon," said Dornal. "And I – I like your colour."

"Thanks very much." Then she stared at him again. "You mean all this, don't you – Dornal – this trip is really for real. You *are* this Dornal feller. This is serious."

She leaned forward impulsively and put her mouth to his lips, drawing her hands down to press them to his cheeks. As she did this, Dornal felt a warm glow spread from the base of his spine and rise through his body. Sharon jerked away from him.

"Arn – Dornal. You *are* changing colour." She stood back and studied him.

"Hey, this is great. Really great. It beats dirty-pink any day of the week. Almost as good as black."

Dornal felt the warm glow vanish and a chill welled up in his stomach. In the hands of this girl he had no control over his colour.

"Aaah, it's going again now," she said. She stood closer until he could feel the lines of her body against his. She slid her arms behind his back and pressed more closely in. Her face and lips joined with his. Automatically Dornal responded. It was a totally new experience for him, quite unlike froobling, but it seemed natural. He put his arms round her back and he held her so tightly she gasped.

"The colour's coming back again, Dornie," she muttered. Then she chuckled: "And now its going again. Hey, maybe it just comes when we – like do this."

Do this. What was this? Dornal wondered. For the moment, he didn't care. Colour or no colour, he put his lips to hers. He was no brilliant thinker, but when he got an idea ... The clinch might have lasted for ever but they sprang apart as they heard from beyond the corner of the shed a savage call.

185

"Arnie boy. We know you're in there. Come out. It won't take long."

They both recognised the voice. Both formed the words at the same time.

"It's the Yobs."

Chapter 37

THE SUN CAME up with violent suddenness. It was Sizda and the air shimmered in heat. The raft had slowed and spun gently round. Arnold looked about him. They were in the middle of a lake, its water mirror calm. But that was not all...

On either side were gardens and lawns and beyond them houses. But they were enormous, walls as vast as tower blocks and over them rose, like gigantic haystacks, thatched roofs. Out of the chimneys welled smoke as thick as from the funnels of an old ocean liner. And in the gardens flowers and vegetables stood like trees. But there was more — on one side all was neatness, on the other bank the walls were grimy, hedges broken down, garden littered with rubbish. Windows were broken and stuffed with sacking pieces as big as ship's sails. The contrast was cosmic, and comic.

Necro was awake. He whispered in awe.

"Now I know where we are. This is told of in legends. We are in the land of Super-Wimp and

Mega-Wump. They are old neighbours and enemies. Their quarrels are part of ancient myth. But no one has ever seen them."

"Well you can start now," muttered Arnold as the right-hand cottage door swung open and a colossal, rake-like creature tall as a tree and dressed in a multi-coloured skin tight tunic strode into the garden, chains jangling round his neck. The shock-waves of his feet pulsed through the bed of the lake and set the raft dancing.

"Flatt!" whispered Necro. "Fonz he doesn't ibe us."

But it was too late. Super Wimp's shadow blocked out the sun as he bent over the lake. Arnold saw earrings in the ribbed and pointed ears as massive as tractor tyres. Then came the voice, musical and modulated as a bell in a church steeple — if you were trapped inside.

"Squizzers, abso squizzers. Breakfast. I'll get my net and scoop them up and Femuria can make them into a quiche."

He turned and vanished indoors, and Arnold said in an awed whisper:

"Breakfast means us."

"Jacco," Norsha leaned on the oar. "Let's dap to the yondo poz. We can lurc in the garber." Arnold turned to lend a hand with the sculling, when she stopped and pointed. He turned.

The opposite cottage door crashed open. It stuck, then with a rumbling curse and a splintering crunch it flew back cracking bricks and making the soil shake. In the doorway was another figure, as broad as Super Wimp was tall, like a walking mountain, his wrinkled hose held up by a belt in which studs glittered like traffic signals in the morning sun. The shirt stained with many a giant meal, hung open to show a chest hairy as a wooded hill.

"Mega Wump," whispered Necro, unnecessarily.

Crouched down, not daring to look, they felt him lumber to the lake border. The ripples made the raft shift. A tumultuous splashing followed, as hundreds of gallons of water were scooped up and flung over the massive face, head and shoulders.

"Disgusting, totally disgusting."

The reproachful voice boomed from the other shore. Super Wimp had come out again. Arnold squinted upwards and saw the tall elegant figure holding up a sort of shrimp net, if shrimps were like baby elephants. The mesh hung down striking the water like a shower of rain. The raft shifted again.

"Get lost, you pansy poop. If I want to wash here, I will. What I do on my side of the lake has nothing to do with you, interfering wally willy."

"I simply don't see why I should have to watch you. Why can't you wash in your bathroom like any civilised person?"

" 'Cause I've got my firewood in there, haven't I, you toffee-nosed git."

A pause followed. In the silence Norsha gently pushed on the stern bough. Arnond reached out and together they began to row the raft slowly forward.

The air shook. Mega Wump was laughing, a thunderous, jeering laugh.

"Look at him. After butterflies, again are we? Big ponce. Na,na,na,na,na."

"I absolutely refuse to continue this ridiculous discussion. I have far more important things to do."

Water surged behind the raft.

"Look out!" gasped Arnold. Super Wimp was trawling.

From the farther bank Mega Wump exploded: "You long streak. You dodgey whippet. Having a crafty fish in the lake. Thought I wouldn't notice. Those are

188

mine, my side of the lake, you bent beanpole."

"Don't be absurd. Anyone whose eyes aren't full of sleep can see they're my side of the water, and I'm having them."

"Oooh, aren't we talking big. Ooooh, I'm scared stiff. I'm shaking. Super Wimp's leaning on me, love. He's going to do me a mischief."

From the depths of the ramshackle mansion came a screaming laugh that made Arnold's ear drums quiver. The window shutters were flung back and a second voice rasped through the air.

"I'd like to see him try. I'd just like to see him try. Why don't you go and do your flower arrangements, you posy little creep?" howled Mrs Mega Wump. In his battered and confused mind, Arnold supposed it was Mrs.

Now shutter bolts were drawn on the other side. A voice fluting like a train whistle blasted out.

"I fail to see what all this has to do with you. In my opinion women who stir up trouble between men, are beneath contempt." Mrs Super Wimp, had made it a quartet. Her opposite number came back smartly.

"Get back to your macramé work, you stuck up tart, you."

Mrs Super Wimp yawned.

"Always the same. Totally inadequate people just fall back on abuse. A sure sign of a lower mental level. Ignore them darling. Just you fish up that breakfast. I'm quite hungry at the thought of it."

"If you think your poncy husband is going to steal our breakfast, you have another think coming. Mind you, a square meal would improve you. One quick fart and you'd take off."

"I'll treat that with the contempt it deserves," said

189

Mrs Super Wimp slowly and deliberately closing the shutters.

This act of contempt stirred Mega Wump into action. Before Super Wimp could stop him, he plunged into the water and snatched the net from his neighbour's hand. The tidal wave flung the raft up in the air, with the three sailors clinging on for dear life. It fell back into the turbulent waters with a deadly crack and the three felt the ropes snap and the timbers wrench away from one another. Arnold lost sight of the other two as he was flung sideways. He grabbed wildly, but could not hold on. He sank into the water made murky by the churning struggle of the two giants.

As he came up into the air, he felt the rough surface of a log. He clung to the underside and, hanging on like grim death he paddled with his feet, not seeing where he was going but hoping he was moving into the mid-lake current which would carry him away from the turmoil.

With a great snapping sound and a splash of falling timber and rope, Mega Wump broke up Super Wimp's fishing net and flung it over the lake.

"Right, you great Nance, see if you can fish with that!"

Back came the measured tones of Super Wimp. Arnold shook his head from his hiding place under the floating log. What self control!

"Typical. Absolutely typical. You can't have your own way, so you smash things up."

That touched a raw nerve.

"Who are you calling childish, you stringy squit you? Think you can talk your way out of anything, don't you? Well, talk your way out of that."

The air was split by a whistling sound, followed by a splintering smash. Some kind of projectile had found its way through the Super Wimps' cottage window. An outraged female voice, still just under control floated out.

"That is beyond a joke. I hope that you are going to claim compensation for that, dear."

"I shall do more than that, my angel. I have had enough. I have got my mad up. Unless he apologises and repairs the damage, I shall, I shall ..."

"Go on, let's hear it," jeered his opponent. "I'm trembling. I'm wetting my pants."

There was a pause. The lake surface calmed. Arnold, arms aching from the strain of holding on to the log sculled frantically with his feet and wondered where his companions were. He did not dare stick his neck out to look.

"I shall hit him with my flower arrangement."

The air rocked with coarse laughter.

"Did you – did you hear that, Lacra? Did you hear what posy boy said," Mega Wump wheezed. "Cor, he's going to hit me with his flower arrangement. Go on, I'm waiting. Which side do you fancy, you creep?"

A few seconds passed in silence, then Arnold heard a whistling sound followed by a cracking thud like a vast rock hitting a hillside. From the side of the lake came a cosmic wail of outrage from Mrs Mega Wump.

"Oooh, you swine. You hit him with the pot end. That wasn't fair. Are you all right, love?"

There was a rending creaking sound, as though a mighty tree were being uprooted. A great movement of the air and then an incredible thrashing splash as the body of Mega Wump toppled into the lake, sending water hurtling in tidal waves to either shore.

Arnold felt his log race forward, rise into the air and then crash to earth. The shock threw him from the log and his senses left him in darkness.

Chapter 38

"COME OUT, ARNIE boy. We know you're in there with your big sister. It's no good hiding."

The crunch of boots on the gravel near the wall came nearer. Then it halted a few yards from the bike sheds. Eenie's voice, gently menacing spoke more in sorrow than in anger.

"You've been striping us up, Arnie, haven't you. Making out you were nix on the pitch. Taking us for a ride. Having a giggle behind our backs. Come on out, Arnie, come and take your punishment, there's a good boy."

The footsteps came nearer still and there they were, all four of them, lined up across the path, barring the way out of the little corner where Sharon and Dornal were standing.

"Oooh," said Meanie, shrilly. "We got here in the nick of time, before they got going, didn't we? Was he going to show you his tangerine slice, eh? Little devil."

Eenie took over again.

"Arnie, we'll level with you. We'll give you a choice. You get your knees busted or you don't. Can't say fairer than that can we?"

Dornal stepped forward. The distance between him and the Yobs narrowed. Sharon moved with him.

"I don't know what you mean," said Dornal, with dignity. "I just played my best, to win right at the end of the match, according to the rules."

They stared.

"Hey," said Mynie, his forehead creasing. "You mean you waited till the last five minutes on purpose? All that possing about earlier on, you were making chimpies out of us, weren't you?"

He turned to Eenie, forgetting his place for a moment: "I told you we shouldn't trust him. I told you he was putting us on. But you wouldn't liste. . ."

Eenie's elbow moved sideways with casual grace and Mynie gasped for breath.

"We are wasting time. Listen, Lineker. The final, right?"

Dornal nodded.

"The final. We've got money on it."

Dornal shook his head, baffled.

"Yer," said Mo, "if the school loses we make fifty nicker apiece. If the school wins, we lose a lot more. We don't like that."

Dornal squared his shoulders: "Of course the school must win. That is what everyone wants."

Eenie tapped his right fist into his left palm.

"No, that is not what we want. That is the choice, Arnie boy. You lose the match, you stay in one piece. You even get a ten from each of us. You win the match, you don't stay in one piece."

"Of course I shall win the match, in the last minute," said Dornal. "For the sake of the school. Not to do so would be despicable."

He was pleased with the speech. He had remembered it from the last instalment Mum had read to him the night before.

"Right, that answers the question then," said Eenie. "We have to bust you now."

He turned to Sharon.

"Listen birdie, you get lost, eh? You haven't seen anything, right?"

Sharon eyed him with contempt.

"No, you get lost. Get back to the zoo."

"You're going to be sorry, baby. You won't want to look at your boyfriend when we've finished with him. And when we've finished with you, your Mother won't want to look at you."

Dornal stared.

"You'd attack a girl? You cad." He did not know what the word meant, but sensed it was a great insult.

Eenie grinned: "Yer, we're a pack of bounders. We're going to scrag you. We're going to do nasty things to you – first. Then we're going to do some other nasty things to her."

Eenie nodded to Mo. He didn't like getting marked and found it simpler to let Mo do the rough work. No sense, no feeling. Mo moved forward, then hesitated as Dornal turned to Sharon, put his arms round her and kissed her warmly. Before their incredulous eyes, a bright, orange flush rose up from the throat of his open shirt and spread like a tide over chin, mouth, nose and up to the roots of his hair. Then releasing Sharon he swung round and struck Mo with the force of a light tank.

He hit him in several places at once, according to the classic Klaptonian combat gambit in which the sources of appetite are simultaneously cut off. Mo sighed and sank down, head between knees, hands and arms vainly trying to restore circulation to the damaged parts. Meanie and Mynie saw two outstretched hands reaching for their jacket zips a second too late, then they were drawn together by magnetic force. Clonk went their heads like over-ripe coconuts and down they slid across the prayerful form of Mo. Eenie stationed like a seasoned general at some distance to the rear, about faced with the skill and speed which made him a superb centre half. His legs were working in perfect unison as Dornal plucked him off the ground by his collar, swung him round three times and allowed his circling face to connect with the other fist held out in the on guard position.

"Ooof," said Eenie, for once lost for words as he sank down to join his stricken troops.

Sharon looked at Dornal, awestruck. He took her hand and raised it to his forehead.

"Fracca yaccas," he said, then: "Is the colour going?"

She chuckled: "Yeah, you're almost back to dirty-pink again, Dornie."

Eenie tried to roll off the heap of bodies and struggle to his feet. Dornal replaced him with a slowly outstretched foot, then kissed Sharon gently. They both smiled foolishly at one another.

"I can see nothing to laugh at," said a severe voice behind them.

Sharon and Dornal leapt apart and turned round.

Standing a yard or two away, briefcase in one hand and the binoculars she had forgotten to put down, in the other, was the Head.

Chapter 39

ARNOLD CAME TO his senses. Not to sight or sound, but smell. Not smell but stink, stench odour more foul than he had ever smelt, or imagined he could smell. All around him, to right, left, above, below. He was in it, right in it. He was trapped to his waist in a swamp that stretched out in folds of chocolate brown around him, while from it rose giant shapes like rocks and boulders. Above was the distant, dazzling blue sky, and the sun's rays beating down drew from the swamp a dancing haze, a curtain of reeking gas.

He tried to move, but his legs felt as though he was wading through treacle. He tried to avoid falling, lest his hands, arms or face should slide into this indescribable filth. If only he could reach one of those rocks or logs or branches, which stood up in this mire which surrounded him as far as his eye could see. He braced his hips, held his hands high above his head, and surged forward, every muscle in his body going at the same time. One foot struck something solid, and urged him forward. The other hit liquid rottenness and he felt his leg dive down. Another wrench of his body brought his leg up again, forward and on to more solid ground. He drew in a breath, then wished he hadn't, but he had no choice. Either way he was suffocating. Now he was choking. Another lunge brought him within reach of a whitened bough that stood up in the foul waste like a skeleton limb. It wasn't a bough – it was a bone, a huge thigh bone. And in that moment he realised the other object near it was a huge, broken pot.

This wasn't a swamp, a marsh, it was a rubbish dump. His racing mind came up with the answer. They had been thrown from the lake into a rubbish dump – Mega Wump's. With painful effort he swung round. Yes, a hundred yards away was the derelict back porch of the Mega Wump mansion, and as he watched the door opened and a shower of food scraps flew out. But worse was to come. With hideous squeals, round the corner of the cottage ran three creatures, short fat snouts snuffling, monstrous haunches quivering. Arnold knew they were pogs, but the size to suit a Mega Wump cooking pot. And in that moment came another chilling thought. Pigs eat anything. So without a doubt, did pogs. He had to get out.

He waited, sweat running from his hair and down his chest, clinging to his bone, stock still while the terrible triplets gorged. Then grunting and snorting they backed round the corner, out of sight, and his heart beat went back to normal. Now he began to look around him. He could see trees in the distance, shimmering in the haze — woods on rising ground. Behind lay more hills. The Prussy Peakers, so near, it seemed, yet so far. How big was this dump? Did it spread right to the trees? His eyes swept the brown terrain and the outcrops of bone, pottery, timber, debris of the Mega Wumps' not so private life.

He could see what Super Wimp got so mad about. And, my, thought Arnold, didn't that nice chap have a vicious temper. Never trust people when they're too polite.

His eyes travelled from point to point, trying to pick up a trace of the others. But there was no sign. Had they been buried? He pushed the thought away. But if they had survived the break up of the raft, as he had, they could not be far off. He leaned on the bone he had gripped, and to his alarm it lurched to the side. But it came to rest flat on the gruesome surface, its far knuckle touching an old broken leather bottle. Magic! thought Arnold. He pressed down on both elbows and heaved himself from the morass on to the rough solid surface of the bone. As the rest of his body came clear he discovered that his sword had snapped off in the fall. Only the hilt still stuck out of the belt. He shrugged. Well, it might be a magic sword, but it hadn't done him much good.

He stood up, balanced on the end of the bone and

launched himself on to the leather bottle. With a squelch it keeled over and he made another few yards along this second bridge. A large shard of pottery came next, then the planks of an old box. Each time he made another yard or two, his eyes would look ahead, spotting his next staging post. He chose his direction with care, picking new objects which stood up well. So his progress was zig zag, but he persisted, keeping his eyes on the treeline ahead and his back to the Mega Wumps' mansion. He noticed that he was now breathing normally again. He paused a moment to rest. His clothes, now ragged and stained, were drenched in sweat and his head spun with the effort. How long could he keep this up before he was exhausted? But he had to get on, he couldn't stop for long.

It was then that he caught a movement from the corner of his eye. Something scuttling over to his left, a flash of dark and light. Cramp gripped his stomach, then he jerked back upright. Norsha the servant girl, legs bare to the hip, her ragged dress tied between them, was leaping from point to point, effortless jumps, balancing like a bird, heaving bones and planks before her, stepping along them, then hurling herself forward to land again bird-like on the next solid point.

"Norsha!"

She turned at his call, her teeth flashing a greeting, then she raced forward again leaving Arnold to his plodding progress. It was then that Arnold's feet missed their mark and slid into the foul mess. He realised beneath it was solid ground. He had gone in only up to his knees. Now he could wade through it. He moved forward, each step taking him on to higher ground. Soon he was clear of the marsh and on to light sandy soil with stunted pine trees close at hand. Norsha appeared again, to his right, untying and smoothing down her dress, rubbing the dirt from her face. Arnold raised his hand, felt the crusted filth on his own cheeks and clawed at them in a sudden fit of nausea. Then he caught her eye and laughed and for the first time her eyes met his steadily and she did not look down.

"Necro?" he asked.

She shook her head and waved him forward.

"We can't slep him," he said.

She shook her head more violently.

"Numda. Ma-da is Soggerda. If we ding in this grav, we will glug."

Suddenly her voice was commanding. But Arnold hesitated.

"Num, we can't slep the seeni kojer."

"The Nurbul Replic is magnolious," came a voice from behind them. There on the edge of the rubbish swamp, Necro stood upright as if he walked on the ooze. Arnold stared, then he noticed that the old man had tied short planks to his feet and walked as though on snow shoes.

"Wizzi, O Necro."

The old magician pointed forward and marched on into the trees kicking off the planks. As Arnold followed, he noticed how the sky had darkened and the air cooled. Evening was here and with it the clouds of the approaching rain day were gathering. Half walking, half running, weary now beyond pain, he struggled on after the others. He stumbled in the light soil, sprang up again, dodging among bushes and tree stumps. The clouds hung lower as the ground sloped upwards, the air grew colder and now the sun had vanished behind the hills. Soon they were in darkness and the way became more tortuous and uneven. Arnold tripped over roots and rocks,

199

slipped in sand pockets. Only the sound of the others' scrambling footsteps kept him going.

Then they were clear of the trees and sliding and clambering on a bare low slope. Arnold paused for breath and looked upwards. But — now the sky overhead was clear and full of stars. And now he could see the outline of the rocks ahead and the climbing figures of his companions. He put on speed and caught up with them. He grasped Necro's sleeve.

"The murg has shivanned," he said.

Necro stopped and looked up, in surprise.

"Zitto — a cristi looma. But, scan afto."

Behind them Arnold could see a distant bank of clouds on the night horizon.

"Over there it will be Soggerda," muttered Necro, "but *here* will be another Sizda."

Then he snapped his fingers: "I wonz to bonz. We are in a grav where there is no sogg, no murg, no bliz nor verd. Only sizla and sind."

"That's why the grav is starco."

"Yumda," said Necro, his voice hushed. "This is the Topwondom of the Yurbusa. Come," he added, "we atta lurc. We natta be ibed when da-spang meho."

They searched for a half hour before Norsha's keen eye spotted a narrow cleft in the rocks. They squeezed in, all three, and if Necro noticed Norsha was with them, he said nothing.

In the dark, dry crack in the rocks, they crouched and slept the sleep of the exhausted. It was the sun's eye glaring into the opening that woke them, heating the rock around until it baked like an oven.

The three struggled out into the blinding day, bright blue sky and flaming yellow sun above, wave upon wave of sandy ridges, rocks and jumbled stone on either side. It was a desert land that stretched from here right to the Prussy Peakers which stood out like a blue frown above the horizon.

"Right, where do we ...?" began Arnold.

But he said no more. All around them, in a wide circle were men of such brilliant orange skin that it seemed to flash back the sun. Long white cloaks hung from their shoulders, helmets of some green glass-like substance glinted on their heads. And gleaming wickedly were the four foot long blades of the curved and naked swords they held in their hands.

Chapter 40

AT THE SOUND of the Head's voice, severe, but concerned, the Yobs awoke and stirred in their heap on the school yard. While she gazed at them in amazement they unfolded one by one and stood in front of her. Eenie was first to react. Holding his hand to his battered face, he burst out in tones of injured indignation: "We were jumped Miss. Him and some other blokes. They got us in this corner and beat us up."

"That's right," mumbled Meanie through his split lip now swelling like a tomato. "There were about six of them."

The Head turned and looked at Dornal, but he was silent. He did not believe what he was hearing and could not think of an answer.

"You lying gits," exploded Sharon. "You were going to duff Dorn – Arnold."

The Head's eyebrows went up.

"She started it, Miss," Mynie put in. "She got us up here. We thought something was wrong and we were trying to help. Then him and his mob jumped us."

Enraged Sharon started at Mynie. The Head breathed in. It did not make much sound but it was enough to stop Sharon in her tracks.

"I think you had better go home, young lady," she said. "I'll see you tomorrow. You four," she surveyed the Yobs with a strange look in her eyes. "Go to the sick bay. I'll see if we can find someone to fix you all up." She paused. "I don't think the damage is serious."

Now she turned to Dornal. "You can come with me."

Still baffled, Dornal followed the Head into the school building and up the stairs to her study. He recalled the last time he had been in this room and wondered if the Head had any idea who the intruder had been that evening. The Head threw her bag on the desk and nodded to a chair nearby. She sat down then looked up in surprise to find Dornal standing not on the other side of the desk but close by her.

"Arnold," she said quietly, "is there anything you feel you ought to tell me?"

He said nothing. She went on: "I – er – watched this little fracas from my window. I saw you – on your own – render four of the hardest cases in the third year unconscious in five seconds flat. To say the least it seemed out of character. Put another way, it seemed impossible."

She paused: "Then I noticed something strange about your appearance. I noticed it before when I found you on the playing fields, doing press-ups for forty-five minutes. Your face was a strange colour. In fact it has only just now gone back to normal."

Dornal had a sudden impulse to challenge the Head's

idea of a 'normal' colour, but remembered in time and kept his mouth shut.

"It seemed to me that there could only be one explanation. Some sort of stimulant. Arnold?" Her voice became more emphatic and less friendly. "I think you had better tell me. Your parents should know. Have you – have you been using solvents?"

Solvents? Dornal looked bewildered.

"Have you – been sniffing, Arnold?"

His eyes opened wider.

"Gas, Arnold. Gas." The Head was beginning to get exasperated.

Dornal drew himself up firmly.

"I cannot explain. There are some secrets which I must keep."

The Head rose.

"Secrets?" Her voice was menacing.

Dornal stood his ground.

"There are some things I cannot tell you."

"You had better ..."

"But," he rushed on, "there are some things that I must tell you. There is a plot against the school. Some people would like to see the school closed down and you dismissed ..."

"Arnold, what are you talking about?"

Dornal gabbled: "Some people – the Slamboss – er the Games Master, think you are a quiche-eating wimp."

Now the Head's colour rose. Creases appeared round her eyes. Dornal pressed on.

"The Yobs are betting on the school losing the finals, but I will not permit it."

Dornal sank on one knee and to the Head's stupefaction, he took one of her hands and placed it reverently on top of his head.

"I will defend the school, and you, to the death."

The Head snatched back her hand.

"Arnold, get up."

She drew in a deep breath.

"Are you sure you can get home on your own?" she asked.

Dornal nodded energetically.

"Very well, then. Go straight home. I shall 'phone your parents. There will be no need for you to come to school tomorrow. After that we can decide what to do. Off you go."

Chapter 41

THE LEADER OF the swordsmen stepped up to Arnold, his long white robe swirling. Before Arnold could move, he had snatched the sword hilt from his scabbard. The whole band burst into hysterical laughter as he waved the short bent piece of metal in the air. Out of the corner of his eye, Arnold saw Norsha turn away to hide a smile. Necro stood quite still.

"We shanx in nosla," Necro said calmly, addressing the leader.

"Yumda," said Arnold, remembering he was supposed to be Replic Dornal. "We are on our todd dro the Prussy Peakers, to roob with the Gloami Kojers."

The swordsmen looked at him for a moment, then slowly circled round, fingers pointing to the side of their heads, and at one go, all fell into each others' arms and laughed until they wept. They then sprang apart and punched each other, repeating Arnold's words.

Now the leader put two fingers to his mouth and whistled. From over the nearest sand dune came a small procession of nedders, not the huge billowing creatures they had ridden through the Bashi Rangles, but small leathery creatures, with long necks and spidery legs. As the first nedder came close, Arnold was seized and placed on it, closely followed by Necro and Norsha on two of the other beasts. Another shrill whistle and in minutes the caravan was winding its way up the glittering stony slope under the burning blue sky. The nedders went at a ferocious pace, though they seemed only to be walking. What would it be like, Arnold wondered, if they cantered or galloped?

He gripped with knee and hand and tried with all his might to keep his seat while their captors, swords now stowed in their belts, rode or ran beside them, stopping every now and then to point at Arnold and let off great shouts of high pitched laughter. The heat rained down, sweat flooded over Arnold's body as his nedder swayed up and down the desert roller coaster, the surface ahead shimmering like water. And after half an hour's backbreaking ride, the troop raced up a last hill, and they looked down on a broad valley. The contrast was unbelievable. Green everywhere – clumps of trees and shrubs winding channels of water all leading from a circular pool set in white stones before a splendid long low domed palace.

Waving their swords, laughing and shouting the band rushed down the slope, the nedders scrabbling and bucking. They swerved round the curve of the lake to burst in through a court yard gate crowded with men, women and children, all dressed in the same white robes and green glass caps. The crowd fell in behind them as the horsemen burst through, rode up to the broad steps before the palace doors and leapt off their mounts. Without a word, they snatched Arnold and his companions down and hurried, almost hurled them up the steps. The doors swung open. From either side came a terrific blast from long bell-mouthed trumpets.

In front of them, a huge hall, pillared and shaded, stretched right up the farther end, where on a platform, richly curtained, sat half a dozen incredibly old men and women, their green caps flashing with blue, red and yellow stones. Feet barely touching the ground, the three were hurried along the floor and then flung on their knees at the foot of the dais. The swordsmen grovelled alongside them, in front of their rulers, who looked down and nodded gravely.

For several seconds no one moved. Then their escorts rose and stood at the back of the three travellers. Arnold wondered whether it was safe to stand up. He found grovelling on the floor highly unsuitable, but something told him to keep his head down. At length the oldest of the elders leaned forward, his green jewelled cap on the side of his head, and pointed to Necro.

"O, Shanxer," he said. "Yurb us a Talwon."

What? Tell us a story? Arnold could not believe his ears. All that trouble just for a story. But wait, what did Necro call these people? The Yurbusa. Maybe they were kinky that way. But what sort of story? He wondered. By the sound of those soldiers, it would have to be a funny one. They seemed to have a great sense of humour, though he felt rather uneasy at someone who laughed with a four foot carving knife in their hands.

As Necro hesitated, the old man frowned.

"A Talwon, O Shanxer."

He wasn't asking, he was telling.

Suddenly the guard captain flashed out his sword and placed the razor edge caressingly against Necro's throat. To prove the point he took a lock of Necro's white hair and gently touched it with the blade. The severed lock fell to the floor and Necro's wrinkled orange features turned pale.

"What Talwon would you have, O er — Zalti Topwon?"

Arnold heard a shuffling sound behind him and peered cautiously round. The great hall had filled. The crowd in the court yard had now pushed in and were standing, squatting, leaning around. Mothers with babes in arms stood next to bearded warriors, children clung to the robes of old men. All stood, mouths slightly open, eyes gleaming, waiting.

"Yurb us a Talwon, O Shanxer." The voice was uncompromising.

"Shall I scroll you the Talwon of the Misti Finner of Necoa?" asked Necro. Arnold shifted on his knees and tried to make himself comfortable. He loved stories and he had never heard this one — the Magic Fish of Necoa. But they had. Immediately from the crowd came a cry of annoyance. And the old man shook his head.

"Shall I scroll you, then, the Talwon of how the Bashi Rangles began?"

The noise grew deafening. Even the little children were shouting "Num, num." The rulers frowned. Necro breathed in deeply.

"Shall I scroll you the Talwon of the Sizla's Shanxon?"

The oldest elder tottered to his feet and flung out his arm. Necro was dragged to his feet and before Arnold or Norsha could move, he was hurtled from the hall, to disappear through a side door which closed behind him with a clang.

Now Norsha was hauled to her feet and the crowd called:

"A Talwon, a Talwon. Yur bus a zizzer."

For once, Arnold saw Norsha at a loss. Her face seemed blank. She shrugged her shoulders.

"The Talwons of Necro are my Talwons. I recc num yonco."

"Yondi, yondi!" chanted the crowd and to Arnold's horror the girl was snatched from his side and in a couple of seconds had vanished through the same door which had swallowed up Necro.

Now he was left alone. His mind began to go round in circles just as it always did at the start of an exam. He couldn't think of anything. He couldn't remember a story. Had they heard Snow White or Rumpelstiltskin? Could he translate them. Then he had a sneaking feeling he couldn't remember Snow White. At least he couldn't tell it from the Ice Queen or the Snow Maiden. Or was it the Snow Queen or the Ice Maiden, or the Snow Goose, or the Goose Girl? He felt his brains slowly scramble as he was seized and stood on his feet.

The old man sat down. The crowd was so quiet that when Arnold cleared his throat, it sounded like a gun going off. Even in the cool of the throne room he felt the sweat trickle down his neck. What had happened to Norsha and Necro? He didn't know what was the punishment for not telling the story, but he guessed it might be unpleasant.

"Yurb, O Juvi," commanded the ancient. "Yurb us a zizzer."

A zizzer? He hesitated. Now the crowd took up the chant.

"A zizzer, a zizzer. Yurb us a zizzer."

The Klaptonian was vanishing from his mind like water from a leaky bucket. Very soon he'd forget his own name. He got a grip on himself and did what he always did at exam time. He closed his eyes and started with the first thing that came into his head.

"There were this feller, like. He were in t'Army, tha knows. He went off t'war and what wi' one thing and another, he were away for getting on for four years. He were an' all."

After the few minutes he realised he was using Dirtyurb. No one in the hall could understand a word. But he couldn't stop. His tongue was on automatic pilot. He pressed on.

"While he were away, abroad like — he'd happen think on now and then about Mam and Dad, back wom. And it were a right laugh, but he couldn't stop thinking about the owd outside privy that stood at 'bottom of t'back yard. It were nobbut an old shack, and he used to hate it. He could not abide that outside privy."

Around Arnold, the hall was still. Those standing up, leaned on the wall or on their neighbours, or sank down to squat on the floor. He didn't dare look at them. He ploughed on.

"Thought of that owd privy turned him up. Any road, when t'time come for him to go wom, like, from demob, he thowt 'I'll fix that outside privy for good an'all'. So, what d'you reckon he did? I'll tell thee. He pinched a hand grenade. He did an' all. Tha wouldn't credit it. He fetched it wom wi' him. And when he got wom, well his Mam were out. Shopping or summat, like. But his Dad were in, so he said 'Now then, our Dad.' And his Dad said 'Now then, our son, 'art a blowing. Tha Mam'll be in any minute, oo'll mash up. We'll have a cup o'tea. So sit thysen down and put 'wood in t'ole.'

" 'Nay, Dad. I've to do summat fust.'

" 'Getaway, son. Can it not wait on?'

" 'Nay, Dad. It's that there outside privy. I'm going to blow it up.'

" 'Tha's not, lad?'

" 'I am an' all our Dad.'

"Well, his Dad shook his head.

" 'Ta' munna do that, our lad.'

" ''Am going to, our Dad. Don't thee try and stop me.'

" 'Nay, lad, be told. Don't do it.'

"Well, t'lad got in a right temper. 'I'm a man now. I'll do as I see fit. I'll do this, if it's t'last thing I do.'

" 'Suit thysen, lad, but . . .'

"T'lad weren't listening. He marched out, pulled pin out of t'grenade and blew that outside privy to bits. Then he marched back in t'kitchen for his tea, like. And his Dad looked at him.

" 'Ah telt thee tha munna do that, son.'

" 'Why not, our Dad?'

" 'Thy mother were in there, that's why.' "

All around him, Arnold now began to hear gentle buzzing sounds. He was puzzled but pressed on. So far his head was still on his shoulders.

"Just at that moment, t'back door opened and in come his Mother. She looked in a right state, dress in rags, her face dirty. She looked terrible.

"Lad rushed to her and he said:

" 'Eh, our Mam. Are 't'a all reet?'

" 'Eh, son,' said his Mam. 'It must have been summat I ate.' "

The buzzing grew louder and at last Arnold ventured a look around him. He looked to left and to right. He was flabbergasted to see that every person in the hall, young and old, the rulers on the thrones and the soldiers on guard, were snoring gently. They were snoring in time. They were all sound asleep.

He gently stepped over the nearest soldier, then the next. No one moved. The snoring rose and fell like waves on a distant shore. He headed for the side door.

He stepped as though he walked on hot coals fearing to make a single noise. Breath held painfully tight in his chest, he reached the edge of the hall. The door opened slowly and beyond was a long arched passage leading to the outside air. In the distance across the huge court yard, a small group of nedders was tethered to a post. He set off at a run, his feet slithering in the light sand that covered the stones.

As he came up the nearest nedder turned its head slowly. He snatched the bridle and pulled it away from the others. He did not know what he should do next, except that he wanted to get out of the palace court yard. How he was going to rescue his friends he could not say. But for the moment, he was moving.

But even as he climbed on the nedder's back, he heard shouts and the sound of running feet. From out of the palace, the white robed guards were pouring and racing in two directions, one lot towards him, the other towards the court yard gate.

He jerked on the bridle, dug in with his heel and slapped the broad rump, but the beast would not move. And now the fierce warriors, sword in hand were all around him.

He was trapped again.

Chapter
42

THERE WAS A reception committee waiting for Dornal, at home. One member of it wanted him to have his tea. The other wanted to have a word with him – and it was clearly going to be more than one word. In the end Mum got her way and Dornal sat down at the table. He was hungry and Dad watched with a massive frown as the meat pies vanished one by one.

Abruptly he got up: "Come on," he said brusquely to Dornal, "I want a word with you."

He looked at Mum.

"We'll go in his room. I want a word with him on his own."

Mum looked concerned.

"You're not going to ...?"

"No, I'm not. I ought to skin him alive, but I won't," muttered Dad.

Dornal followed Dad into his room. Dad looked round briefly, then swept a pile of clothes off the only chair and sat down. Dornal sat on the bed and faced Dad. After two seconds, it was Dad who looked away. He was uneasy. But he recovered himself and spoke aggressively.

"Look, lad. I've had the Head on the 'phone. I don't believe it. Never mind about you scoring three goals in five minutes, which I don't believe anyway. Or beating up four blokes, which I don't believe, either. There's something funny and I'm going to get to the bottom of it. You and I have got to get one or two things straightened out, starting with you."

Dornal rose and spoke with dignity.

"I have done nothing to be ashamed of. And you have no right to speak to me in the way you are doing."

Dad's face turned purple.

"What do you mean, no right? Who do you think you are? It's your father speaking to you."

Dornal's lips tightened.

"You are not my father."

"What are you raving about?" Now Dad was on his feet, menacingly.

"I am not your son. I am Replic Dornal of Klaptonia. I have been exchanged for your son."

Dad sat down again. His colour paled slowly. Then he shrugged and said resignedly:

"You think you're the Replic of the Topwon of Klaptonia, do you?"

Now it was Dornal's turn to stare.

"Ye—es, I do."

Dad hesitated a moment, then said:

"Son, er Dornal, my old wipper. I think we'd better have a bitti roob together. There are some things you ought to know."

Chapter 43

THE CAPTAIN OF the guard reached out and took the bridle of the nedder. The other guards fell in on either side. With one movement all drew their swords. Arnold, chilled inside, waited for the simultaneous blow of eight razor edges on his tender skin. But nothing came. Instead they raised their blades above their heads and marched with him towards the palace steps. As they advanced with Arnold's mount between them the palace doors swung wide open and at the top of the steps appeared the elders and behind them a great crowd of the people, young and old, all wiping their eyes as if rubbing sleep from them.

As Arnold and his escort reached the foot of the steps all raised their arms and cried out with a loud voice.

"Yay to the Yurberkoj. Freeber of Zizz!"

And in that moment, Arnold knew the secret of the Yurbusa. They were the original people who could not go to sleep without a story. And over the centuries they had heard all the stories there were until none could put them to sleep. And he realised with a shock that they hadn't understood a word he had said and it did not matter. Just the sound of the old shaggy dog story droning on had worked the magic.

With sudden idiotic pride he guessed that he was the first storyteller to put an entire nation to sleep with an old joke.

The oldest elder descended the steps, followed by the others. As he came near he bowed low and beckoned Arnold down from the nedder.

"The Yurbusa griv that you atta plog bego so jacco. Nocca have we eeroled so froobli a Talwon."

"Mumble, mumble," murmured the crowd as they grovelled. It was the lowest grovel and the biggest that Arnold had seen in Klaptonia. Then the eldest rose and with him the people, and a host of delighted faces each under their green glass caps, unfolded as they stood up and shouted again.

"Yay to the Freeber of Zizz. Ding with us for occa."

Stay with us forever? That was a long time. He had better speak quickly.

"My compers," he called. "Numdoo would lux me stacc than to ding with you for occa, and yurb Talwons dooli looma to tring you to zizz." In that moment he remembered an incredible amount of boring stuff from school which he could recite in story form, guaranteeing eight hours zizz for anybody: The square on the angle of a right angled triangle is together . . . no that wasn't it. Never mind. What was he raving about. He wasn't staying here.

"I atta bego. I atta todd dro the Prussy Peakers to roob with the Gloami Kojers."

At the sound of these words, the Yurbusa turned and looked at one another until the vast crowd boiled like a porridge pot. They tapped their heads and then, looking at him again, they burst into laughter.

"Num, num, num," they chortled. "Numpo!"

The eldest elder grasped Arnold by the shoulders. "Numpo! Numko mehos from yond the Prussy

Peakers. Numko rigs the Groobi Choob. Numko brees to ibe the Choob of the Sizla."

Arnold braced himself: "I grovel. But I atta todd."

The ancient ruler snapped his fingers. People pushed through the crowd, bearing huge leather bags which they emptied on the ground at Arnold's feet with the flash and gleam of coins.

"Scan, Yurberkoj. We will freeb you toowumper yoggles a monz and as many wallocks as you can chumble."

Arnold swallowed. Two thousand was a lot of yoggles. But how did the yoggle stand on the international money market these days? And he had a feeling that after the first half ton, wallocks tended to taste the same. He bowed and said:

"Num num. I atta todd."

"Trewumper," cried the old man.

"Num num." Arnold tried to make it final.

"Wonti wumper."

"Num," he shouted.

There was a hush in the sun drenched square. The old ruler looked sick. All the people turned to one another and then without a word, they burst into tears. They threw themselves on the ground again, beat with hands and feet on the dusty square and howled. Even the guards threw down their swords and wailed. The old man who still seemed to have control of himself, said:

"We cannot freeb you stacca. If you will not yurb 'yum' we can singo freeb you the Topwondom. You atta be our dooler and you atta chip my bonce." He put a hand to his neck and gestured towards one of the long razor sharp swords.

"Oh, num," said Arnold, deeply shocked. He couldn't behead the old boy.

"You'll yurb 'yum', then," put in the old ruler, with

a cunning look. Arnold breathed in deeply. If he said 'num' they'd all start howling again and he couldn't stand that.

"I will ding a bitti, but in tree daj I atta todd with my compers."

At once the elders and the escort burst into delighted laughter.

"Oh, don't fratch about them. They are tentoo."

"What do you mean, taken care of?"

Without thinking, Arnold burst into Dirtyurb and stepped forward. The old man and his followers stepped backwards. They fell against one another and soon the entire population was falling like ninepins.

From his prone position, the ancient said.

"Those yondo too, they are garbers. We chumbed them to the Vasto Flork."

"You did WHAT?" yelled Arnold.

"You must be out of your bonces. Fed them to the Giant Shork. No way am I going to tell you any more stories. Not even a punch line, if you've done that."

They knew what he meant all right. The Guard Commander said hastily:

"They are zupped out on the zalter. The Vasto Flork has nocca flapped in."

As he spoke, those around him looked up in the clear blue sky. A young boy on the edge of the crowd, cried out:

"I can eerol the dong of its flappers."

"Jacco, then," shouted Arnold. "Jacc and slep them and I'll yurb you as many Talwons as you lux."

The hollow space beneath the palace walls filled with a deafening sound of cheering. Arnold was pushed back on to his nedder. The guards, swords drawn, ran in front. The elders grouped themselves behind and the whole rout set forward with gongs

beating and trumpets blasting. They flooded out
through the great gateway and into the open space
beyond, where the crowd divided and marched in
two columns, on either side of the lake. Now they
were heading away from the trees and gardens and
across a stony plateau. His nedder broke into a trot,
the guards shouted and the entire Yurbusa population began to run over the hard flat surface.

Ahead of them, the hard blue sky met the hard
brown earth like a knife edge. This must be the cliff
top they spoke of. But what lay beneath? As they
pressed forward, Arnold suddenly heard above the
noise of the scuffle and patter of a thousand feet, the
sound of an enormous carpet being rhythmically
beaten. Others heard it too, and the children cried:

"Vasto Flork. Vasto Flork."

The noise swelled and drove the crowd forward at
greater speed. Now they were close to the cliff top
and a third noise forced itself into Arnold's confused
ears, that of rushing water. Now he knew. They were
on a crag above the Drago Soggon, the Long River.
The sound of wings drew nearer, clearly heard above
the music and shouting. And soon, they were silenced as the beat of wings was joined by a rush of
wind and a dark cloud seemed to pass between them
and the sun.

There they were — two bodies stretched out on the
rock. Their faces looked towards him in amazement.
He flung himself from the nedder and ran towards
him. But the guards ran faster and barred his way.

"Let me through, you maniacs. Untie them," he
screamed.

They shook their heads and pointed behind him.
The elders were solemnly advancing on them, the
crowd following silently behind as the sky above
them grew darker and a great shadow swept the

plateau. Arnold forced himself to look up. There it was, about half a mile up in the sky. As big as an airship but shaped like a pig with enormous snout and flapping ears and wings like Concorde. This was the Giant Flork, legendary beast, largest of the uncaught flying pigs. And its E.T.A., he guessed was no more than thirty seconds.

"Slep 'em," he commanded.

The eldest elder, puffing a little but with that mixture of dignity and cunning shook his head.

"Premi! Acco to be our Yurberkoj. Frywumper yoggles a monz, and ..."

The old swine, he was beating him down from ten to five thousand. Arnold clenched his fist.

"Acco. But slep 'em before it's too dilli."

The old man hesitated.

"What's blunt?" Arnold felt his voice break in excitement.

"Premi. We atta slam a seeni Yurbusa chimper on you."

Play an old joke on him? Was he out of his mind?

"A chimper, a chimper," roared the crowd.

"Acco, acco," he said. "But jacco, jacco."

Before he knew what was happening, three soldiers had seized him and amid the cheers and laughter of the Yurbusa, they carried him to the edge of the cliff like a sack of potatoes, and heaved him over.

Chapter 44

DAD SIGNALLED DORNAL to wait. He left the room and came back in a few minutes with three bottles of Guinness. He poured himself a glass, drank deeply and thoughtfully.

"Want one, Dornie?"

Dornal slowly took the glass. The dark liquid was rich and smooth. Like wallock root beer, perhaps. Clearly a grafton drink. But that didn't matter now. He drank.

"Not bad eh? Beats yoot wine any daj of the weeg."

Dad grinned at the baffled look on Dornal's face. Then he leaned forward.

"I had finkles about you for some time. Certain things you did and the way you did them. Then when you wouldn't read and got Mum to do it for you I guessed you weren't Arnie. He reads yellow pages for fun. Then Mum mentioned that when you got excited, you started to show the old tanji tinjer. That said only one thing, this wipper's come down the Slypa from Klaptonia. Hey – go easy on that mate, I'll give you another, but drink it more slowly."

He half filled Dornal's glass, then went on:

"When we went to the soccer match, you knew no more about football than fly in the air, but you knew all about slamming. A real Hodbung Crusher, I'll bet."

"Shredder," said Dornal automatically. "But – I don't under. . ."

"Look, son. You think you are Himsir Dornal, Replic of the Topwon, don't you?"

Dornal nodded, still mystified.

"Well, mate, you're not."

Dornal put down the glass and bounded to his feet, face glowing. Dad waved his hand.

"Fold, there's a slecc Replic," he grinned. "Look, it's a wise won that knows his own father. That wally who's Topwon now. He may be your father Klaptonian style, but his real name's Joe Radleigh, and he belongs here in this house."

Dornal frowned: "Who, then is the Topwon?"

Dad pointed a broad finger at his own curving belly.

"Me, son, me. Listen. Before Arnold was born and you were picked up around Necoa, I was the Nurbul Replic. I married Hermiss Motpa, very glinti, but a bit snobbot and always fratching about gora on the bricca danglers."

Dornal smiled in spite of himself. That was Topma.

"Time was coming for the old Topwon to auto-snuff and for Motpa and me to go to the Twinki Timm for our Replic. I was set to take over. And I was getting a bit uneasy about the way Slamboss seemed to be running everything, together with that snake-loving, spell-banger Necro."

Dad sipped his Guinness.

"Did you ever wonder why there were two Perms on Klaptonia, two kojers who go on living regardless, no auto-snuff at fifty for them. One is Necro, he's as old as yoot roots, and Slamboss, who's older than he looks. I don't know how he does it, maybe something he sprinkles on his flork. Anyway, it seemed to me that the Topwon ought to be the ruler and the Slamboss should look after the Dongon and the Slams."

Dornal's eyes gleamed. He nodded and drank deeply. Dad put a restraining finger on his wrist.

"Go easy on that stuff. Mum'll flake me if you get legless. Anyway, just before I took over, we got warning of this assassination plot by the Gloami Kojers. So I was beamed down here and Joe Radleigh was beamed up there. You are his Replic, and our Arnold is mine."

Dornal burst out: "You mean that Compo Gormer up there is really the Nurbul Replic?"

Dad nodded: "If you go by who your father is, then he is. But you're the Replic of Topma all right, so if you go by your mother, then you are the Replic."

Dad opened the last bottle and topped up Dornal's glass.

"But, since you're down here, it doesn't matter. Who'd be a Himsir? All they do down here is open fetes and frooble off duty with film stars. Dead boring."

Dornal gritted his teeth.

"You mean stay down here, give up my life and rank on Klaptonia? Never be recalled, while someone else takes my place?"

Dad chuckled at the sight of Dornal's face.

"I used to wait for the call. But in the end I knew it wasn't coming. And it's amazing how little yonc it makes to the loyal subjects. They'll do a humble mumble and a civil grovel for a pog in a chooner provided they think he's the Topwon. The fact is, son, they didn't miss me and they won't miss you."

"But — but, that gormer, I mean, your Arnold, he'll get morbed. Doesn't that worry you, Da..." Dornal's voice trailed away.

Dad shook his head and carefully divided the rest of the Guinness between the two glasses.

"Yes, go on, call me Dad. I'll call you Dornie on the quiet. We'll get along. Believe me, life with Mum down here, is good. I'd rather live in this dump with her, than in that shotto up there."

He grinned.

"And don't worry too much about Arnold. He may look like a wally but he wasn't born yesterday."

Chapter 45

FLUNG BY THE joking Yurbusa, Arnold fell like a stone from the cliff, with the blue sky, the massive brown cliffs and the dark depths of the gorge below wheeling around him. The cliff shot away, the sky shrank, the green trees and dark waters of the valley grew larger as the seconds of his life whipped by. His mind was clear. His thoughts raced. But it wasn't like drowning. He didn't see all his past life. Oh no, he was much more interested in his future life — all four seconds of it.

But into his mind like a bell, sounded the word of Necro, that Soggerda in the Bashi Rangles, when he threw coloured stones on the white cloth and tried to forecast whether Arnold would die that day.

"On Klaptonia, O Replic, you do not die unless you are intended to, and then only if you let someone kill you."

Unless you are intended to. But it was a joke. The old ruler said it was a traditional joke. Was he lying? But why should he be? You don't offer a good Yurberkoj every yoggle in the treasury, then throw him away, do you? And if they didn't mean to kill him, they wouldn't mean him to smash on the rocks at the bottom, would they? Arnold thought fast on his feet. He thought even faster flying through the air.

Flying? That was the word. As he thought it, his arms opened out as though he were playing bombers in the infant school yard. He leaned to one side and felt the wind whistle past him. Without thinking he opened his mouth and...

"Brrrrroooooom," he howled.

He wasn't going down any more. He was banking and zooming. Something loomed dark in his eye corner. He was heading full tilt for the cliff. Where was the joystick? Breathing in deeply, he braced back his shoulders, straightened back and legs and felt himself shoot up the cliff face, almost scraping it with his undercarriage. His neck went back and he began to go into a roll. Leaning to one side, he folded his wings and reduced power. Now he was gliding along the river valley and he had the machine under control. Another deep breath and he began to climb steeply out of the gorge and into the wide blue yonder.

"Wooowwwoooowwwwooww," he sang as he soared clear of the gorge, banked and circled. There below him lay the plateau, burning brown in the sun, the oasis, the white palace. And more directly below, running in all directions, the great white and green clad crowd. And within their widening circle, the vast brown bulk of the Giant Flork, folding its wings and settling like a grisly mammoth on its prey. The figures of Norsha and Necro, staked out helpless on the rock were cut off by the horrible folding mass.

Arnold swung out, seeking more height. A desperate plan had come into his mind. Time to stop thinking and to start thumping. As he drew away he saw, at an angle the figures on the rock, as small as toys.

The ghastly creature settled, wings half folded on

the cliff edge, its great jaws reaching out, like some cosmic alligator. From its throat came an obscene grunt of appetite which reached up to Arnold as he came into position to dive. He swung over lazily and came down on the Giant Flork out of the sun, just as it took off, the two limp bodies held in its jaws.

"Rooorrrooorrraaaeeeiii," the deadly whine rose to a crescendo as he came down on the left ear of the Flork. Timing his dive perfectly he zoomed up so close that the foul smell of the beast almost choked him.

"Reeeaaaaaggghhhh!"

He looped over the Flork's skull effortlessly and came back into positon for a second attack. But his opponent had had enough. The mighty jaws opened wide, the zigzag teeth gleamed in the sun. Something flew from the gaping mouth and fell into the depths of the gorge. But the other had vanished, inside. Arnold had been too late. One of his companions had plunged to their death, the other had been swallowed.

He choked with anger. Revenge, the need for revenge, filled him savagely. But the Giant Flork was not waiting. On beating wings, it headed up and away towards the gloomy heights of the Prussy Peakers.

In this instant, he realised something, as he poised over the river valley.

"I'm not Klaptonian."

And with that, he dropped like a stone.

Chapter
46

THE HEAD DROVE to school in a thoughtful mood, brooding about yesterday's bizarre events, and what they might mean for her future, or her sanity. A quiet shy boy in the Third Year, studious, dreamy, bullied, incompetent at sports, had undergone a character change. As she drove slowly along with the traffic streaming through the shopping centre, she ticked off the points in her mind.

In one day he had: scored three goals in as many minutes, to put the school in the junior league final; put five of the opposing team in for repair, along with two sets of goal-nets; put four of the toughest nuts in the Third Year in for repair; turned a bright orange colour and talked a lot of nonsense; warned her of a plot to get rid of her, and close the school, and promised to defend her to the death.

The strangest thing was, thought the Head, as the car came to a halt by the zebra crossing, the nonsense wasn't nonsense at all. The Council mafia were plotting to get rid of her, flog the school grounds to Tesco or whoever, or at least merge it with the old grammar school down the road and appoint a macho dimwit Headmaster over her head. But how much could Arnold know of this?

She knew the question was ridiculous. The kids always knew. If she decided to quit, it would be all over the school before she'd put the 'phone down. She looked in the driving mirror. Her lips were moving. She was talking to herself again. Maybe she should resign. Maybe she should walk into the Education Committee, look at 'Oily' Oliver – Councillor Edwards, the chairman and say:

"Councillor Edwards. You may take this job and stuff . . ."

She could do it, too. Goodbye to 'Oily' and his mates would be dead easy. Goodbye to the staff, well some of them like that Neanderthal Man, the Games Master, would be easy too. What she would miss, she thought as she saw a surge of first years streaming across the road twenty yards away from the crossing, would be the kids. What would she do without them, bless their cotton socks? She vaguely heard cars behind her, hooting to her to roll forward, but her eyes were suddenly on the pavement leading to School Lane.

There was Arnold, walking arm in arm with dynamic Sharon. That was a remarkable couple for you. Around them were a crowd of groupies from the second year. The Head, released the handbrake and moved her car on, and then quickly rolled down the window. She heard the shrill voices in the morning air.

"Tanji Arnie. Tanji Arnie," came the chorus.

"Yeah, like a jaffa slice. Nicky said."

"Come on Arnie, show us your Satsuma."

Every now and then Sharon would turn menacingly and the crowd would scatter. But that was not all. Behind them walked the Yobs. Eenie was carrying Arnold's bag, Meanie was carrying his sports gear. Mynie and Mo had to make do with a plimsoll each.

Cars hooted again. The Head recovered herself, and drove on. Yes, the kids certainly made life interesting.

Two hours later, the Head sipped her coffee and looked out at the crowds roving around the school yard. She had just finished a very strange discussion with Mr Radleigh. He had been rather evasive about his son and his strange condition, but he seemed completely unworried. He was sure, he said slyly that it was just something he was going through, just something a growing lad has to put up with, like puberty. He had even started to say, why I was the same, and then he had looked very strangely at the Head and changed the subject. But no, he was quite certain Arnold was not on drugs, or gas. Arnold might be disorganised, he was not stupid. It was funny he was doing well at sports and badly in his English, but you can't win 'em all.

After half an hour, Mr Radleigh got up to go. At the door he turned and said: "I wouldn't want him to leave. He's much better off here than anywhere else he might go ..."

Anywhere else? The Head was baffled. But she decided to put Arnold and his behaviour on one side and get on with her memo to the Education Committee about the future of the school. As she worked, she found herself chuckling.

Come on Arnie, show us your satsuma, indeed!

The lads from 3H came off the fields in a great rush, pushing and shoving their way into the changing rooms. In the middle of the crowd was Dornal.

"Come on Arnold, let's be having you," shouted someone. "Let's see. Don't be shy."

Eenie turned on them.

"Knock it off. You get his amber up and you'll get your legs broken."

That silenced them. Dornal's savage attack on the Yobs had been reported all round the school.

But Dornal had come to a decision. He sprang up on to a bench.

"Eerol, you dimmos. I'm tanji and I lux it. Its nacho ..."

They stared at him, and he realised what he was saying. He switched to Dirtyurb.

"I was born like it — orange. That is the way we are where I come from. And we're as good as you lot, your dirty-pink mob, and no better. We're as good as Gloami Kojers and no better. We're kojers. We're people. So you can stuff it.''

And with that he whipped off his shorts and threw them into the air.

There was a strange silence. They looked at him. Then one lad pointed and said, in an awestruck voice.

"Arnie, it's gone. You've lost your tangerine bit. You're dirty-pink all over."

Chapter 47

ARNOLD HIT THE water, arms and legs going like a windmill and plunged into its green depths. The chill shock gripped his limbs and carried him down, while his chest muscles clamped on his lungs in a desperate effort to keep out the water. He felt his feet hit sandy bottom, his knees bent like a spring and with every part of his body fighting separately for life, he shot up towards the air with the sunlight bursting like a yellow explosion in the water above him. Then he was out in the air, foam and spray around him, brown rocks and blue sky above, gasping like a fish and lashing out to get clear of the remorseless current drawing him downstream. At first the tug seemed too strong but he battled away, using bits of every stroke he ever half learned at the baths. He felt the tug grow weaker and he drew panting and wallowing into the shallows to land on hands and knees, exhausted, but safe.

He crawled out and lay on the rocks. His mind shut out the crazy battle in the air and the sight of his companions in the jaws of the Giant Flork. They had been through so many adventures together, but now he was truly on his own in a strange part of a strange planet, among even stranger people. Who cared whether he was Himsir Dornal or not? Anyone who met him would find out he wasn't even Klaptonian. His real life fantasy was over. He was Arnold, lost and alone.

He began to clamber up the rocks. At first the slope was easy, but as he drew away from the river, so the rocks stood up more steeply and the going got harder. The air grew warmer. He started to sweat. He pulled off his ragged cloak, slung it over his shoulder and tucked the ends in his belt. The sun beat on his neck, his mouth grew dry. His mind wandered but he kept on climbing, not daring to look down. He scrambled from foothold to foothold, crevice to crack, stone to stone, moving upwards all the time.

He was moving downstream too, away from the plateau where the Yurbusa lived. Did that make sense? Was he out of his mind? If he climbed straight up and went back to them he would have a job for life, telling boring stories. But no, something stuck in his gullet about the idea of working for a bunch of jokers who staked out two people as bait for a flying pig, then threw you off a cliff. You could do too much for a regular wage packet. Then, what would happen when he ran out of boring stories? Pig food? No doubt. No thanks, mate. He scrambled on.

Towards dusk he struck what looked like a pog path just below the top of the cliff. It was no more than a couple of feet wide, but it was like a high road after his mountaineering. He pulled himself upright and one hand on the rock face, he walked on, into the gathering floom, steadily westwards, following the vanishing sun, on towards the looming blue folds of the Prussy Peakers.

Just when he could no longer see an inch in front of him, his hand slipped on the rough stone. His body lurched into space, but he was falling not towards the water, but into the mountain side. He landed on hard ground and lay there winded for several seconds. As his eyes got used to the deeper darkness he saw a circle of faint half light. He had fallen into a kind of cave.

He was too exhausted now even to stand up. He crawled away until he found a corner in the cave wall, found what seemed to be a pile of dead leaves and collapsed upon it. He heard the rustle of tiny feet moving away from him, but he was too far gone to care. He was soon asleep.

He woke to find the cave filled with light. His clothes were still damp from his near drowning and stiff with dirt. His limbs were bruised and creaked as he moved. But he was alive, and hungry to prove it. Outside the sun was shining. He stripped off his chooner and hose and scrambled to the edge of the cave mouth, where he spread them out to dry and sat warming his body. He glanced over his orange skin, with that white patch down there, a bit, he thought, like you get when you sunbathe in trunks. No point in hiding it any more. If he sat in the Klaptonian sun, would it go orange, he wondered? Then he suddenly remembered Dornal. Was he hiding his orange bit down there?

His stomach rumbled. Sooner or later he'd have to look for food. What would he eat? Could he catch a pog? How would he cook it? Or wild wallocks? What *did* wallocks taste like? They sounded like parsnip. Or potato perhaps. He was a luxon, well a pretend luxon, so he wasn't supposed to eat wallocks. Still who cared? He heard a rustling noise in the cave, like the rustling last night. What was it, a detachment of feetles looking for someone to amuse? He shuddered. Could be a small creature on its own. Should he go and bonk it one, and have it for breakfast? His stomach turned. Fantasy adventures don't include eating raw meat and insects. The picture of a bowl of Crunchy Snibbles floated in front of his eyes. He was hungry.

He couldn't stay here. But where should he go? On to the land of the Gloami Kojers to force them singlehanded to yield up Hermiss Roshan? Well, to be honest, no. As he sat in the growing warmth of the morning sun, he realised that any heroic ambitions he might have had, were draining away fast. Now that Necro and Norsha were gone, what was the point? Maybe it was the hunger or the loneliness. He started to talk to himself.

"Why go on pretending. I'm not Replic Dornal, Hodbung Slammer, I'm Arnold Radleigh and I wouldn't be Dornal if they paid me. Anyway, by all accounts he's a bit of a noddy."

The scratching sound seemed closer, but Arnold ignored it now.

"I know he's got more bottle than I have. Who hasn't? But do I have to be a headcase just to stand up for myself? I'm Arnold, I'm a Dirtwon. I'm all rosi-dirt deep down. Why should I be ashamed of it?

"And why trundle off trying to rescue a Princess whom I've never seen, and anyway, if she's anything like Dornal, she's probably a toffee nosed prune and if she met me she wouldn't even wipe her feet on me."

What was that rustling sound?

"Let's face it. If it was Norsha and I could save her life, I would, whoever she is, even if she's a Gloami Kojer agent. I'd do anything. Yes, I would. I did try. I tried that night in the forest. I tried with the Giant Flork. I did, didn't I Norsha? You know that."

As Arnold finished his speech, the sounds in the cave suddenly changed into a breathless gasp. That changed into a snort, and then into a chuckle, and then burst out into laughter that filled the cave and echoed into its depths. Someone scurried across the rock and slid into place beside him, bare legs touching his. In a panic he grabbed his tattered tunic and slapped it over his lap.

"Norsha. How did you ...?"

She raised a hand and held it in front of his face. It was full of purple berries. Laughing she pressed them into his mouth. He gulped them down, the sweet juice sliding down his throat. While he choked and gasped she grinned slyly and said:

"Norsha? Who is she? She's just a dirty flunker-dima. Who cares about her?"

She paused.

"I am Hermiss Roshan — the prune nosed toffee ..."

"Give over," he said without thinking, "you mean toffee nosed prune."

His voice trailed away. He stared at the orange face, the mischievous laughing green eyes.

"That's Dirtyurb. How ...?"

She pushed back the dark hair with her hand, stained purple with the juice of the berries.

"All the time while you and old Necro whispered, I listened to the yonco words you were yurbing."

"You were listening?"

"I was. I crept closer and listened. I have discovered that no one really sees servants. So they can find out secrets."

She licked her fingers.

"When they told me I should be ringed with Himsir Dornal, I thought why should I spend my life with someone I do not know? So I disguised myself as a grafton dima and came to the palace to see what he was really like. At first I did not care for him. Brave, but arrogant and rude, even to his mother. Then," she looked sideways at Arnold, "he changed. Cowardly, thoughtful, indecisive, crafty, but kind, even to graftonas. So I wondered: two Dornals, is that possible?

"Then, I thought: if there are two Dornals, which one should I choose?"

Arnold forced himself to look at her.

"Well, which have you chosen?"

She looked down at the rags across his thighs.

"That was my problem. I had chosen. But then this morning I learned the one I thought was a Replic was just a Dirtwon from another planet with a dirty-pink stripe."

"Oh," said Arnold and looked down in dismay.

"Then I thought. Hermiss Roshan has to marry Dornal."

"Oh!"

"But Norsha is only a graftona, and she can choose her froober if she wants. Who cares what graftonas do?"

She looked out at the river and hummed the yoot froot song. Arnold cleared his throat.

"Norsha?"

"Yes — Arnie." Her face was serious again.

"What is froobling?"

She chuckled: "Something only for Klaptonians, but ..."

She reached out her elbow and touched his. An electric shock ran right through him.

"No one will know, if I tell you, will they?"

Chapter 48

"THANK YOU, THANK you, I must go." Councillor Edwards, chairman of the Education Committee, smiled the smile which had earned him the name of 'Oily' Oliver, and got up from his chair at the Headmistress's desk.

"Are you sure you won't have another cup of coffee?" asked the Head, sweetly, praying to herself that he'd say "no".

"No, thank you, must be off. Another meeting, duty calls."

He leaned across the desk and clutched her hand, holding on to it for several seconds. Then, to the Head's despair, he sat down again.

"I always enjoy looking round your school Hilary."

The Head wondered to herself when she had invited him to use her first name.

"Marvellous atmosphere, so free and easy."

He leaned back in the chair.

"Of course, some parents don't approve, I know, but then, they don't appreciate modern methods, do they?"

He showed his teeth. The Head nodded and said nothing. She knew he was going to be really nasty in a few seconds.

"Of course some would say the sports results ought to be better when you consider all the facilities you have here. But then, Hilary, you've never been keen on competitive sports, have you?"

The Head put on her reading glasses. She wasn't going to read, but the lenses made him look like something out of Spitting Images, and that helped.

"All these things count for some people, you know when we're agonising over which schools are going to go and which to stay."

The Head put down her glasses on the desk. She did it more forcefully than she meant and startled Councillor Edwards.

"You've seen what our parents think?" she said sharply.

"Have I not? I have to hand it to you, Hilary. You have done a good job on the public opinion side. You know I'm with you all the way, but," he lowered his voice, "you know what the Committee is like. There are some – er – backwoods-persons. Between you and I and the old goal post, winning the Junior League Finals would do more in their eyes than two million letters from parents."

He got up again, moved to the door, then stopped. Now for it thought the Head.

"I've just had rather a good idea."

Liar, thought the Head. You planned this from the start.

"Why not, on the day of the finals, have a sports event, sort of Mini Olympics, involving other schools? Invite 'em here. I'll bring the Committee. We're due to have a certain important meeting at that time."

The Head clenched her fists under the desk and imagined them meeting round Edwards' neck.

"We'll have our decision meeting then. The Mayor can come along and I'll find some cash for prizes. And we can announce what is going to happen about the school mergers, etc. How about that?"

The Head gritted her teeth: "It isn't long to prepare for a

sports event, you know. Earlier than we would normally have it."

"Oh, I'm sure the school could rise to the occasion. From your point of view, a marvellous opportunity to show how you use all the facilities – playing fields etc. Sort of Open Day with your school at the centre."

He smirked once more.

"Don't get up, Hilary. See myself out."

The door closed behind him and the Head who had half risen sank down again, chin on hands. 'Oily' Edwards was setting her up. He was closing the school down and this sports day lark was just a way of convincing doubters that her way of running things was not up to scratch.

She walked to the window. It was near the end of the day. The school yard was empty, but a small group of third years lingered by the bike sheds. She recognised them – the Yobs, Nicola and her Iron Maidens, but there was Sharon – that was an unusual mixture. And right in the middle, holding forth was Arnold, somewhat excited, but, she noticed with relief, his colour was normal. Still they shouldn't be hanging about at this time, though there was nothing disorderly going on.

A sudden impulse struck her. She left the room and made her way in long strides down the stairs and out across the school yard. She took the group by surprise. They all looked sheepish. But Dornal who had been in full flood, turned and smiled.

"Good evening, Ma'am. We were just talking about the school being closed down."

"Oh, really, and why do you think this is going to happen?"

" 'Course," said Eenie, lip curling. "We just saw 'Oily' Ollie. He's been nosing round school all day, casing it."

"Yer," said Mo, "right oiler. When he was magistrate he gave our kid – ooh," he broke off and rubbed his ankle.

"He wants to flog the place off as a commercial sports centre," said Nicola.

"We shouldn't listen to rumours," said the Head.

Not much, she thought to herself.

"About the school, though, I wonder if I might have a word with you people."

"With us?" Dornal leapt off the wall and stood close by. He bowed. "A civil grovel, O Magnolious . . ." he began.

The Head stared.

"I mean, we're all ears," said Dornal, going slightly orange at the tips of them.

Chapter 49

DAYS PASSED. NORSHA and Arnold stayed near their cave home. When the sun shone they hunted for berries. Now and then they caught a wild pog and roasted it. They climbed down to the river and bathed in the deep green pools. When the mists came, the rain, the snow and the winds, they climbed back into their cave and waited for fair weather.

They learnt more of each other's language and amused themselves by mixing the words in nonsense talk. And talked about everything under the sun. But in all their talk they could not decide whether to move on or return. Now that Norsha had revealed she was really Hermiss Roshan, there was no kidnap plot and no rescue to attempt. But what did it all mean? And could they make the long journey back without Necro's guidance? Poor old Necro, swallowed by the Giant Flork. It was a terrible end, even for a tough old chap like him.

They searched the ravine downstream to the point where it vanished into the massive rock wall of the Prussy Peakers. They searched the wooded slopes above. But in the end they had to give up. And still they could not make up their minds what to do. Partly it was because their lives were easy with no one to bother them. Partly it was they felt no urgency to go back to their former lives. They had dropped the idea of being Hermiss Roshan and Himsir Dornal and were just Norsha and Arnie, and that was enough.

There came a day though, when they had bathed in the green pool, then clambered out to sit on the rocks. Norsha stared at Arnold.

"Arnie, you are total rosi-dirt."

Arnold looked down. Norsha was right. He had reverted completely. He was dirty-pink all over. Every trace of tanji had gone. He was back to normal, whatever that means.

"That settles it," he said, "I can't be Replic Dornal any more. So we can't go back."

Norsha laughed: "Well, Hermiss Roshan would never be ringed with a rosi Dirtwon. She has her position to think of."

"Be like that," said Arnold grumpily.

She rubbed his elbow with her own.

"She could marry Replic Dornal when he comes back ..." she said slyly.

"If he can rescue her from the Gloami Kojers," she added quickly at the look of alarm on Arnold's face. Arnold laughed and turned to her.

"Never mind the old wallocks, Norsha. We can't

stay here all our lives can we?"

She pushed out her lip. "Why not?"

"Well — er — we're going to get bored in the end."

She nodded. "Let's go on then ... I mean go on go on. Go down the Drago Soggon and under the Prussy Peakers. Find out what the Gloamis are really like."

He hesitated: "A bit risky, isn't it?"

She glared at him, then pushed him so violently that he fell over. She jumped astride his chest, pushed back his arms and looked down at him.

"You are a — a — cowardy pudding."

"You dimmo, you mean custard," he gasped. "Get off, you're squashing my breakfast."

She rose and fell down heavily on his stomach.

"Custard," she shouted till the rocks rang. "Custard."

Heaving up, he jerked with his arms. She flew backwards, rolled on the rocks and vanished over the edge. Arnold leapt up and peered over. Below the water eddies where she had fallen were spreading out. But there was no sign of her.

"Norsha! Norsha!" he shouted. Back came the echo. But there was no sign of her long hair and orange face breaking the green surface of the water. In a panic, he stood up and dived in. The depths opened and took him in. Above the yellow spot of the sun showed and around were quick flashing points of light where small fishes swam to and fro. But below was gloom. He raked with his hands on the sandy bed, but only made the dark waters murkier. He trawled around but could feel nothing. His breath gave out and he shot up to the surface. Out in the open air he glared round wildly, his vision blurred by water.

There was a strange noise. He placed it. Someone was laughing. Seated on a rock like a mermaid, was

Norsha, throwing back her long wet hair.

"You ..." he lashed out to the side. Grinning she reached out a hand as if to help him out, then at the last moment, pushed him back and dived in beside him. As they bobbed up and down, she said, her voice serious.

"There's nothing to wait for, nothing to go back for. Let's make a raft and go on down the Long River."

Chapter 50

THREE DAYS LATER, Norsha and Arnold launched their raft made of driftwood bound with knotted creepers, on to the pool. They paddled it around for an hour. It wandered here and there as they paddled and turned in half circles. But it did not sink. There was room to sit or lie. And so, before the sun was high, they set off, their supplies of berries, yoot roots and bits of roast pog wrapped in what was left of Arnold's cloak, its rich fabric now ragged and dark.

As they weaved their way downstream, drawn on by the mysterious current that ran towards the blue mountains, the rock wall rose up before them. And as it came nearer the sound grew louder from the heart of the towering stone, first a whisper, then a mumbling and as the day moved on to sunset, to a rumbling. Their eyes met but neither said anything.

Both knew that minute by minute they were approaching the great cleft where the river finally vanished under the Prussy Peakers. Somewhere within that huge mass, if the Legend was true, the water plunged into the centre of the planet. How far, how deep, they did not know, for no one had returned to tell. Gathering dusk and the gloom of the ravine depths merged as the undertow pulled on the raft more urgently. Arnold pointed to a narrow strip of shore at the foot of the rock wall.

"That's our last chance for a camp and rest," he yelled above the roar of the water. "Shall we pull in?"

But Norsha shook her head: "No, tomorrow's Soggerda. The water will flood that strip in the small hours. Better drown with our eyes open."

Arnold gulped and nodded. Both leaned on their branch oars and held the little craft in the centre of the current as they drove on, faster and faster as the river narrowed. Now the mountain stood up like night above them. Behind them the light of the sun vanished and like a mill race the sluicing water carried them under the arch of a greater darkness, into the pitch night of the world below the Prussy Peakers.

Nothing but dark above them, on either side from the curved tunnel walls, nothing but dark in the depths below. The raft rushed on and now the noise of plunging water ahead rose to a thunder that beat their ears into deafness. They could not speak, nor shout, nor hear. Pain shot through their heads and breath died in their lungs. Together they crouched down, then lay on the timbers of the raft, flung their arms across each others' bodies and laced fingers and toes into the creeper knots that held the raft together. Arnold felt Norsha's body pressed close to his, her arm gripping his waist as he clung to hers.

He closed eyes, ears, mind to everything else but her as the raft slid on into an explosion of blind noise.

The water let them go. They flew into space and the air rushed past them, down and down.

Arnold felt his fingers burn as the creepers cut into them. Norsha, he and the raft were as one creature holding on desperately to life in a void of lightless thunder. Then they hit water, foam and spray overwhelmed them. The shock of the crash drove all feeling from Arnold's body, all sense from his mind. He was unconscious as the raft sank like a stone, twisted, turned, and sprang up like a cork on to the surface again.

And it was over. The raft floated on flat water, sliding along as the current took up its flow beyond the huge cataract. Arnold opened his eyes. Darkness still cloaked them round, but the brutal noise of the falls had given way to the faint chuckle of small waves around the prow. He struggled for breath and heard Norsha gasp as they untwined their grip on each other and carefully sat up again.

"We got through," he said marvelling.

"Yes, we got through."

Their voices echoed away. The cavern of the river was growing. The roof of the rock rose away from them. Arnold took his bough oar from its loop and stretched out to right and left. He could touch nothing. The river was widening. There was no means of knowing how wide. And they could not stop. He breathed in again and now was conscious of a strange odour, like the sea, like fish, like depths away from fresh air and sun. As the raft slid on it grew more pungent.

"This tunnel needs ventilating," he said.

Norsha took his arm. There was a tremor in her fingers.

"That is not the tunnel. There is something living, some creature in here."

"You're joking," said Arnold in a low voice. But he knew she wasn't.

"Listen," Norsha spoke again.

Out of the still of the cavern above the faint rippling of the waves pushed ahead by the raft, a new sound was forming from the long reaches ahead. It came in pulses, rose, grew louder then faded. It was a rumbling, thought Arnold.

"It's another fall," he half-laughed.

"No, no," muttered Norsha. Her hand gripped his arm again. Now he gripped hers, as the rumble rose to a moan, like a vast cow with bursting udders, and then spiralled up to a hellish shriek. The silence that followed was more menacing than the sound, as they waited, second by second for it to come again. When it came, it seemed to change position, veering to the right.

"It's moving off, whatever it is," whispered Arnold hopefully. Why was he whispering?

But it wasn't. He felt the water swirl beneath the raft as though the current changed direction. And suddenly, mysteriously ahead, on their right, was lighter air, a misty whiteness. But they were not coming out in the open air. They were swinging into a cross current in another cavern.

As the current spun them round, the faint light, like early dawn, that streamed from the distance, lit up the roof and walls of the cavern which rose in towering white columns, like some enormous temple to meet high over their heads. Below the water spread like a black marble floor. The sight took the words from their mouths as they stared at the reaches of this underworld cathedral. The light now came from behind them, and they were heading for the gloom again.

And with every second the smell, the stench of sharp decay grew stronger. Arnold held his fingers to his nose, but had to release it as he choked for lack of air, then choked again as his lungs filled with the foulness.

"The cave's narrowing," he muttered. But almost as he said the words he knew somehow that he was wrong. They were drifting helplessly towards a great gap, a huge cave within a cave, a dark void with jagged edges out of which came that rumble, which grew to a moan, which rose to a maddened shriek.

They knew that they were sailing towards the open, howling mouth of an enormous creature that lay afloat on the surface in the half dark before them. The jagged edges were its teeth and the mouth opened so wide that the bulk of the creature crouching behind was hidden.

Norsha took an oar and tried to swing the raft aside. Arnold joined her, but the current was too strong. They could not escape, they were being drawn helplessly into the gaping throat.

"The Vasto Shork," breathed Norsha, as the raft swept on past the harrowing teeth and into new darkness in the noisome, stinking hole of the monster's throat.

Chapter
51

A VIOLENT SHUDDER seized the raft. Arnold and Norsha were thrown to either side. Arnold felt himself turn top tail to land like a stranded fish, half stunned, choking on the fetid air, limbs recoiling as he felt the slimy softness of the Shork's inside rise around him. A spasm that threatened to swallow him, passed and he found himself half seated on what might have been a mud bank — but he knew it was no mud bank, but the stomach wall of a monstrous creature, the like of which he knew could not exist — an aquatic pig the size of the House of Commons. The Talwon of the Vasto Shork was true and he had the inside story.

"Norsha," he whispered. Why was he whispering?

"Norsha," he shouted.

"Here!" her voice blasted in his ear. She was next to him. He grabbed her in relief and her elbow rubbed his.

"We're alive so far," she said.

"Till he starts digesting us," he said. Why didn't he keep his mouth shut?

"How do you know it's a he?" Norsha was being mischievous — or hysterical.

"The Giant Shork is neither he nor she."

"What are you talking about Arnie?"

"I said nothing."

"Yes you did. You said 'The Giant Shork is neither he nor she'."

"No, I didn't, you said that."

There was a silence while both touched each other uncertainly.

"It was I who spoke," the voice came again. Norsha and Arnold both shouted aloud in astonishment.

"NECRO! How did you get here."

A small light glowed in front of them. It spread a little circle of illumination — just enough to show the seamed orange features, the sharp black eyes and the straggly white hair of the old magician.

He smiled: "How lux to ibe you, Nurbul Replic," he said, ignoring Norsha. Arnold felt a sudden rush of irritation. But he put it on one side.

"We thought," he stressed the 'we', "we thought the Giant Flork had eaten you."

"Ah yes," murmured the old man. "Indeed after your valiant attempt to rescue me from the Flork, I was indeed swallowed. The beast flew with me to its nest high up in the mountains, where it cast me up for its brood to eat."

"Yecch," said Arnold, "what a ghastly fate."

"Indeed," said Necro, "but I have not lived for — er — as long as I have, to end up as baby food. I was too tough, too sour for their tender digestion. The anxious parent tried to chew me into smaller fragments, but to no avail."

"Aaargh," said Arnold.

"It was uncomfortable," admitted Necro. "But in the end the Giant Flork gave up and cast me out of the nest. I rolled down the mountain side for a mile or more before I came to rest. After a few days to recover, I descended to the Drago Soggon, hoping to find at least the remains of the Nurbul Replic."

"Thanks, mate," said Arnold.

"But, alas, I found nothing. So I set about making a raft to travel on. I dared not go back to the Yurbusa. Nor did I dare return to Tipacal and admit that I had lost Himsir Dornal. So, against my will, I set off down the Groobi Choob, only to be swallowed by the Vasto Shork."

"Cor, so there are two rafts in here, now."

"I have counted some twenty pieces of wreckage, O Replic. We are not the first to venture here."

"Where are they all?" asked Arnold. Silly question.

"The Vasto Shork digests slowly, but eventually all travellers go the same way. Others have," Necro paused delicately, "departed."

"Well, I'm not waiting for Porky's digestive juices to start working."

"Alas, Nurbul Replic, what can we do?"

Arnold lost patience: "Will you give over with this Nurbul Replic business. You know, I know, Norsha knows, I'm not Himsir Dornal, I'm Arnold Radleigh, from Dirt — I mean Earth."

Necro was shocked: "You have told your secret to this graftona?"

"That's another thing," said Arnold aggressively. "She's no more a graftona than you are. She is Hermiss Roshan in disguise."

"How do you know that?"

"Because — well, she told me."

"And you believed her, Arnold. If she is a spy she might tell you anything knowing that you are — ahem — rather well disposed towards her."

"Well, if she's a spy, why are you talking like this in front of her."

"I suppose, Arnold, that nothing matters now that we are trapped where even my magic will not help. We may say and believe what we like ..." His next words were cut off as the three were thrown against each other by a great convulsion. The soft-walled chamber in which they stood had suddenly tipped over.

"What's that?" gasped Arnold.

As the shaking and the lurching stopped and the beast lay at rest again, Necro said:

"The Vasto Shork has dived to avoid the Sun."

"Now you really can pull the other," said Arnold rudely. He heard Norsha laugh and felt her gently rub her elbow against his.

"No, no, O Arnold. I speak only what is so. The sun on its journey from west to east travels through the Groobi Choob, the Cavern of Doom. As it passes through the sind is so great that it cracks open the walls. The water at the surface boils and the Giant Shork must dive deep down to avoid being charced alive."

"Necro, I know you are a wise man. But I just don't believe you."

"Oh, Arnold," said Norsha, "I fear it is true."

"Aha," said Necro, his voice full of suspicion. "If she is the Hermiss Roshan, how does she come to yurble Dirt-way?"

"Oh, because she ..."

Arnold's voice faded as the Shork's stomach walls suddenly squeezed together and then expanded once more. Thrown to one side, Arnold felt the slime clutch at him. He reached out until he found Norsha.

"Right," he said. "I am not staying here any longer. I am not waiting for melt down. I am getting out, and I am taking Norsha with me, whether she's a princess, a maid-of-all-work or a Gloami Kojer mole. And you, Necro can do the other."

"But how can we get out?" Both spoke together.

"Dead easy. I read in this book about a bloke called

Sinbad. He was trapped inside a whale. And he made a fire out of his raft. So what we do is collect all the wreckage. So shine a light Necro."

As the circle of light gleamed in the darkness, the three began the teeth gritting task of salvage, throwing the branches and lumps of wood on to the stomach floor. Gradually the pile built up until it was waist high.

"OK," called Arnold. "Do the old boy scout trick, Necro. Set it alight."

Chapter 52

THE RAFT WRECKAGE soaked in the gastric juices of the Giant Shork was slow to take fire, but after some minutes of struggling in the noisome dark, Necro grunted with satisfaction as a small red glow appeared at their feet. Norsha and Arnold let out shouts of triumph as the first wood lump ignited and the flames shot upwards. But these changed in the instant to cries of disgust as the flames vanished in thick clouds of acrid smoke.

"Yaaargh," spluttered Arnold. "Which way is the mouth?"

Necro waved the small light above his head, then pointed past the cloud of smoke. Holding their noses, eyes closed, the three stumbled round the bonfire and made their way, hands linked, over the ridged ooze of the stomach. As they cleared the fire area there came the first quiver as the Shork felt the heat in its guts. Another shake, more violent, threw them to the side. Yet another and then a terrible spasm and a huge bellow of pain.

The dark in front gave way to a circle of half light as the great throat and jaws gaped wide, the jagged teeth silhouetted against it. They darted forward. The mouth crashed shut and they were tangled in the coils of the monster's tongue. Again a violent shudder, a yet more terrible cry of agony and a combined hiccup, belch and sneeze tore the jaws apart again.

All three were lifted up by overwhelming force and shot forward out of the Shork's mouth and hurled into space to fall in the water several yards ahead of the rearing snout. As he passed, Arnold felt one of the teeth rake his chest. A sharp pain, the flow of blood was followed by the quick, clean shock of water, as he plunged into the depths. He came up to find Norsha at his side, shaking long hair out of her eyes. She jerked a thumb and he turned in the water to see waves rushing towards them as the Shork struggled desperately to rid itself of the agony in its belly.

"The side," shouted Norsha and set off with a tremendous overarm stroke. He followed. It was not far and the faint cavern light showed up the curving side. Norsha was scrambliing out on to a narrow ledge just above the water line. As Arnold followed she pointed back. To his horror Arnold saw the old man floundering in the water. Behind him, bow waves shooting back like an arrow came the Shork, eyes gleaming in the monstrous fat of its huge cheeks.

Without a word, Norsha and Arnold plunged back

into the water, yelling and splashing to confuse the Shork. The old man was sinking fast as they grabbed him under the arms and struck out again for the side. Behind them a spasm of pain stopped the monster in the water. Then it surged forward again just as they dragged the old magician on to the ledge.

With a shriek and a cloud of unspeakable breath from its nostrils the Shork crashed against the rock face, its jaws biting home on the ledge as the three split up and ran for their lives. Enraged it sank back, and the water boiled around it.

"Down here," called Norsha, doubling back and grabbing the old man. Arnold followed them as the Shork surfaced again and stormed at the side of the cavern like a colossal torpedo. They ran for dear life, the Shork followed. On came the saw-edged snout, the foul cloud of breath, the shrieking onslaught. And at the last moment, they found a split in the rock, no wider than a body and crammed themselves into it, thrusting Necro before them, just as the rock edge behind them crumbled in the Shork's teeth.

Again and again it struck, and each time as it drew back in fury and pain, they dodged out of hiding and tried to put distance between them. But each time, the deep set eyes, the quivering nostrils found them out and again came the thunderous rush of flesh and bone. Hour by hour they dodged and ran and hid and tirelessly the Shork hunted them down the Cavern of Doom. As the fire inside it died down, it hunted in silence, only the rush of waves in front of its snout, warned them of attack.

And it was getting lighter. The half light in the cave was growing from dawn to something near full day. The cavern arch above showed in more detail. They could see the rock wall stretch away in front, with the rock ledge clinging to its face.

Necro looked out from behind a sheltering rock fold.

"We must move on."

"It's too risky. There's no shelter just ahead," said Arnold.

"We cannot stay," groaned the old man. "We shall be caught by the Sun."

"The Sun?" Arnold was stunned.

Norsha nodded vigorously. "It is true, Arnold."

He began to protest but even as he did, he realised that the air was growing warmer. Beads of sweat formed in his hair. As the light grew, the temperature rose. And across the water, the great animal surfaced a moment, then ducked its head. Warmth and light grew and in the background rose a faint hissing, like escaping steam.

"He's diving," said Arnold. "Let's go."

They ran, pulling Necro behind them, while at their backs, the light grew, the waves of heat rolled towards them, searing their backs and from the water waves of steam wafted forward, overtaking them.

Their voices or their scent aroused the Shork. Suddenly the two great pointed ears broke surface, then the massive head and jagged jaws. Hunger, vengeance triumphed over its instinctive fear and it stormed through the near boiling water after them.

"There's a crack in the rocks, a little way ahead."

Necro groaned: "I am gravved. I shall morb. Slep me."

"Leave you? Don't be stupid," shouted Arnold. "Listen, Norsha you get Necro in there. I'll try and hold it off. Go on," he insisted.

He halted, facing outwards towards the water. Leaping up and down he screamed and flapped his arms. The Shork changed course and hurled itself at him rearing up out of the water. He hung on until the last moment then leapt aside, as the great snout smashed into the wall, the bristles rasping his legs. As the Shork slid back into the water, he repeated his war dance.

But in that moment he lost sight of his pursuer as a great crimson yellow burst of light bloomed like a flower in the cave. He was overwhelmed by a pulse of heat, staggered and blundered against the wall. He heard, not saw the Shork's next furious leap from the water. It seemed his body would melt and shrivel in the world of boiling heat that wrapped him round.

He felt rather than saw Norsha's hands grip him and pull him along the rock face. He fell, but still her hands held him. His body scraped along stone, head, knees, elbows bruising, scraping, as he was dragged like a sack finally into the safety of the rock crevice. The air grew hotter by the second as the three crouched, arms round each other. Dark vanished even in their shelter, giving way to white light and heat. Pain was unbearable. Arnold felt his lips swell and burst.

And at the moment of their greatest torment, they heard a mighty burst of sound, and a scream at the end of the scale. Their noses filled with an incredible smell of burning flesh. The light and heat passed in that moment and with the dark there fell into their hiding place a shower of hot lumps that burned their skin and made it run with juice. As they scrambled to brush this off, Necro put fingers to mouth and murmured:

"Ah, Shork chops."

Giggling, they ate as only those who have been hungry for a long time can eat. Then in the dark they slept. They woke at last to find their hiding place was filling with light. Arnold tried to rise, but

Norsha and Necro pulled him back.

"Wait O Arnold, till the Sun passes."

As the heat and light wave rolled over them, he heard Norsha speak in wondering tones.

"Arnold! It must have happened as you stayed behind to save Necro. You stayed too long in the heat of the sun."

"What is it?" Arnold was bewildered.

"You have turned orange, crozmi tanji."

"It is true, O Nurbul," said Necro. "Now you are completely Klaptonian."

Arnold looked down at himself. It was true. But as he raised his eyes again, he stared at Norsha. And he saw that Necro was staring, too.

"You have changed, Norsha."

Norsha looked at her arms and legs in wonder. The orange colour had gone, overlaid with a hue as dark as night.

Necro breathed one word: "Gloami!"

Chapter 53

THE HEAD'S OFFICE was crowded with people, some seated round the table she used for urgent meetings, some standing and arguing or looking sideways through the window. The window was slightly open, letting in the light breeze of an early summer day and the sounds of shouting, clapping, cheering from the playing fields. At the table,

Councillor Edwards beamed round at the others.

"Perhaps we should make a start, ladies and gentlemen. We're ten minutes late and it is rather important business — the final decision about the future of this school and six others in the area."

"Perhaps another five minutes, eh Oliver?" urged a portly man in a bright yellow waistcoat and check suit from the other side of the table. "After all Messrs. Brown and Arkwright should be here." He looked at his watch. "I can't think what is keeping them."

"And I," said a thin lady in glasses, "cannot imagine why we should wait any longer for them. It is grossly impolite to ..."

"Hear, hear," echoed a grey-haired, stocky man who stood at the window. "What is more," he said, moving to the table to stand beside Councillor Edwards, "since they are both members of your Party, and you have a majority anyway, I can't think why you're hanging about."

"Because, Arthur," said Edwards pompously, "I like these things to be done properly."

"Get away," retorted the other. "You know perfectly bloody well — pardon my Spanish — that your lot met at the Club last week and worked it all out. We're just here to make it legal."

"Right," put in a plump woman in dress and cardigan at the table. "You've made up your mind. You're closing this school and flogging the buildings and ground off and all this is window dressing."

"That's it," said the short man, pulling back a chair and sitting down. "While we are hanging about here, we could be out there in the sun watching the games. I'll tell you what, mate," he leaned forward, "you'd better make sure we get out of here in time for the district final. My boy's in goal today. I might miss the sports. I'm not missing the match."

"Huh," said the plump woman. "He reckons that's all a

foregone conclusion, as well." She paused to glare at Edwards. "We all know why you've arranged it here today. You're sure this school's going to be bottom of the heap in the sports and probably lose the soccer final – and that'll justify what you're doing."

"Well, Mrs Thomas," said the yellow waistcoat man soothingly, "you have to admit that this school, with all these facilities ought to do better. Perhaps the problem is lack of motivation. It seems a pity if all this public money should be spent on facilities that are – er – not appreciated."

"Some of us," replied Mrs Thomas, "think there are other things in life than sports results."

Councillor Edwards tapped the table: "We seem to be starting our discussion already." He shrugged. "Very well, I suggest we go ahead and hope that our friends will arrive."

The door swung open, hitting the wall. Two men, faces red with excitement and the effort of rushing upstairs, came to a halt by the table. Everyone's eyes turned to them.

"Well, gentlemen," said Councillor Edwards, "better late than never."

"Hey, Oliver," burst out the first of the late arrivals, too worked up to remember his manners. "You've cost me twenty quid, you have."

Councillor Edwards drew in a breath, while the grey-haired man chuckled sardonically.

"I'm sure we can discuss our private business afterwards, Gerald," said Edwards smoothly.

"Get off with your bother," came the reply. "You reckoned the school here was going to lose this afternoon, didn't you. I mean, that's why I'm voting for closing it."

"Ay, ay," said the plump woman. "Here we go. Spit it out, lad."

"I put twenty quid on the result with Barry Macmillan, Chairman of the School Parents," ran on Gerald, ignoring Edwards' frown.

"I'm sure this is a side issue," said the yellow waistcoat man.

"That's what you think," said Gerald. "Listen. This school is leading by fifty points in every event. They won the relay, boys and girls – by nearly a hundred yards. I've never seen running like it."

"So that's where you were, Gerald," Edwards exploded in exasperation.

"That's it," said the second man. "We got here early. thought we'd watch for a few minutes. Then we saw this little bloke, third year. D'you know what he did?"

"I'm not sure we need ..." began Councillor Edwards.

"Ah, but we do though," put in Arthur, "let's be having you."

Gerald gasped: "He's beaten the European Record in the high jump, long jump and pole vault. He's knocked the Olympic Record off in the javelin."

Those at the table were on their feet, ignoring Councillor Edwards. Their eyes were on the window. One was sneaking to the door.

"And now," said Gerald, "in five minutes, he's having a crack at Sebastian Coe's record in the 1500 ..."

"I'm not missing this," said Arthur pushing back his chair.

Two minutes later, Councillor Edwards and the man in the yellow waistcoat were alone, staring at one another: "Well Oliver," said he, "I think I'll join them. We can have the discussion afterwards can't we?"

"Er – yes," said Edwards, uncertainly, "I suppose we can."

Chapter 54

DAY FOLLOWED DAY in the Groobi Choob. The three travellers made their way, now scrambling along the rock ledges, now swimming where the rocks plunged sheer into the water. They moved on as the light grew dimmer in the wake of the swirling sun, and took shelter as the light and heat swelled, warning of the approaching ball of fire. They rested in the deep fissures of the rock wall, ate the charred remains of the unfortunate Giant Shork, and slept in the hot dark.

They talked little, only the necessary words. Arnold saw the old magician's eyes turn now to him and now to Norsha. There was a touch of malice as he eyed her now darkened colour. He said nothing, but Arnold knew what his glance meant. This proved she was what he had suspected all along, a Gloami Agent in disguise.

Arnold said nothing and avoided Necro's glance. For him, she was Norsha, and that was the end of it. And if that were not enough, the three of them were bound together by danger and the threat of death. This girl — princess, servant or spy — had saved their lives and was their companion in adversity. And they had to go on, whatever lay before them, and in the future.

Arnold tried to ask the old man what they might do, but he would not talk, though his eyes flickered in Norsha's direction. Arnold grew impatient. And a time came when they rested in a rock cleft, and it seemed the girl was sleeping. He turned to the old man.

"Look, we can't go on with this lark much longer — dodging the Sun. Sooner or later, we'll be caught out in the open. Or the meat'll run out and we'll just starve. Isn't there some way, through one of these crevices, we can get away from this Cavern?"

The old man shrugged: "Somewhere beyond these rocks, I am sure, lies the land of the Gloami Kojers. How to reach it, I cannot say. Nor what will happen to us when we get there. That I dare not imagine."

"But how do you know they'll be hostile?" asked Arnold.

"Because — because," the old man said slowly, "we know our feelings to them. We have always hated and feared them. Why should they not hate us? Besides, with their cold way of life and dark colour, they must envy us our warm ways and glinti tanji skins. It stands to reason, does it not? Only the great gods can love everyone," he added as though that were final.

"I say we ought to take our chance," said Arnold. "What can the Gloamis do to us that's worse than being fried alive?"

But the old man was already snoring.

Next day they wrapped up the few remaining lumps of meat and set off. They marched for an hour or so, while the light and heat grew behind them. They passed rock fissures which were too narrow to enter, and had to press on. The more they hurried, the more the sun came on behind them. Their bodies ran with sweat and their skin began to tighten on their heads.

On came the sun. Their scrambling footsteps sounded in the emptiness of the cave. But soon that sound was overwhelmed by the hissing of the steam.

"Run!" commanded Norsha. "I see an opening."

They ran, slipped, staggered, pulled themselves up and at last reached the dark crack in the rock.

"It's too narrow," said Necro and moved to pass by. But Norsha seized him and pushed him violently in.

"Will you charc, you seeni gormer?" she yelled. Behind Necro, she and Arnold pressed in. The walls closed in on either side, and the rock scraped skin and tore at their clothes. Bones struck painfully on curves and edges of stone. It seemed there was no room to pass. But Norsha roughly pushed Necro on.

"There must be a way through," she grunted. Then in the dark, Arnold heard her singing.

"When the yoot froot is in blosser ..."

He joined in as he strained to force his body through the cleft. Only the old man was silent, as they pushed him ahead. And then they heard him gasp.

"We are through."

The cleft had opened out and they were into a cavern. It was pitch dark but dry underfoot. Arnold noticed that the rock floor sloped gently upwards. Necro halted, held up his arm and the small light glowed. The dark tunnel, high and wide enough for all of them to walk along, stretched ahead.

"Well, what now?"

"I say we go on," said Norsha, firmly.

"You know where it leads?" said the old man, accusation in his voice.

"Of course," she answered, her voice faintly sarcastic. "To the grav of the Gloami Kojers."

Necro's eyes turned to Arnold's in the faint light, then he put it out and the three marched on.

The tunnel twisted and turned, but led upwards all the time. They came to a cross tunnel, chose a right turn and marched on. Soon they rested again, and by common agreement, they ate the last lumps of meat they carried.

"Well," joked Arnold, "our next meal comes from the Gloamis."

No one answered. On they went. More turnings, more crossroads. They swung to left and right and always they moved upwards.

"Soon we must come out of the rock," said Norsha.

Half an hour later, Necro said: "I see light ahead."

A faint mist of lighter air showed far ahead and they hurried forward. As they reached it, they ran into blank rock, but high above them light streamed as though from a small port hole. Norsha seized Arnold's arm.

"See, steps in the rock."

Steps like a stone ladder led upwards and they began their climb, heaving the old magician up between them like a sack of potatoes. Time and again they had to rest, clinging with fingers and toes to their holds. And at last, at the very top where the light streamed through, they found their way blocked again.

Necro peered at the wall.

"These are shaped stones, without mortar," he said.

"Come," said Norsha. Arnold and she put their hands on the nearest stone and heaved. At first it would not move. But then all three pushed with all their might and with a scraping clatter the stone fell away from them. Other stones slid down.

Arnold was first through the gap. Now they were

in a narrow, curved passage which led away to the left. For a moment they hesitated. Then they moved forward on tiptoe. The air was heavy, the walls damp.

"We are beneath a castle," said Norsha.

The passage ended abruptly in steps winding upwards in a spiral. They climbed more slowly and carefully. Norsha stopped and raised her hand.

"I hear voices," she said.

Now they crouched under the stone ceiling at the head of the steps. Her finger came to her lips as Arnold and Necro pressed close. Arnold could hear the murmur of voices above. Men were arguing, their voices rising and falling.

Necro listened closely. "It is a war council," he said, and his dark eyes fixed sharply on Norsha.

Silence fell above them and spread through the stones. And in the silence they heard a voice, commanding and brutal.

"We atta inslam, nimmo, seppo dilli."

Necro turned to the others. "I was right. They are plotting invasion. We are in the heart of the Gloami Kojer power."

He turned to Norsha and spoke bitterly.

"You have done your job well."

Chapter 55

NORSHA TURNED AT Necro's harsh words and glared at him, her face only inches away from his in the confined space beneath the stone floor.

"You are an old fool, or worse," she said. "I know no more of this place than you."

"But," she turned now to Arnold, "I am going to find out more. If someone is planning to invade, we must know who, and where and when."

"How?"

For an answer Norsha hunched up her shoulders beneath the stone block and began to heave. Arnold shrugged, then pushed up alongside her and they strained together. The stone squealed. They stopped in alarm. But the voices above went on. The stone grated and shifted upwards. Dust and dirt drifted downwards on their faces. A small draught tickled their necks. One inch, two inches, the stone lifted and pushed back.

Now they could see across the floor above, grey stone and brown rushes. A huge chest or screen in carved wood blocked the rest of the view. Now one last heave and the block they were lifting swung up to rest on the wall behind. Swiftly they clambered up and pressed into the narrow space between the trap and the wooden barrier. To the right was a stone wall, no hangings. To the left Arnold could see the shape of a table leg.

The voices had stopped. There was an eerie silence in the room. Arnold held his breath as Necro pulled his old bones through the trap door behind him. Surely the people in this secret council would hear them? But no, they had paused to drink. There was the scuffle of a leather bottle, the gurgle of wine, the smacking of lips. Then the voice they had heard before through the stone, spoke again, this time clearly, distinctly, and the meaning was unmistakeable.

"We atta inslam — yamp dro the Prussy Peakers and flomp on them. Dong before they are triggo."

Behind their hiding place, all three stared at one another, mouths open. But the look of shock was greatest in Necro's old eyes.

There was no mistaking that brutal commanding voice.

It was Slamboss.

And then came the Topwon's voice, weaker, indecisive, but still protesting.

"But there's no sigger of any inslam from them."

"All the more derfer to inslam premi, to trim their groovi scim to inslam us."

"But ..."

"No tocca to slep. Our Dongon, bladers, crushers, skullers, shredders, are all triggo."

"But I nocca freebed the eerwego dooso," said the Topwon, peeved.

"I freebed the dooso. All you atta doo is put your brand on the Yoohoo."

"You have no doos ..." Topwon protested.

"No doos?" The Slamboss's voice rose to a roar. "Who do you wing doolis this topwondom, you slurder?"

"Er — you, Slamboss," came the feeble response.

"Where would you be seppo me?"

"I ..."

"You know *where* you'd be seppo me. Would you lux to meho there?"

"Er — num."

"Num. I bonzed it. You lux the slecc bree up here don't you, you bulko bitti pog."

Despite themselves, Norsha and Arnold had to suppress a chuckle in their hiding place. The Topwon spoke again, his voice worried:

"What about Himsir Dornal? Will the Dongon yamp seppo Dornal?"

"Ha. I am slyping bladers down to fring him back from Dirt. He can string the Dongon as soon as he mehos. But I hank them in yampo-compo nimmo."

"But what about the shuff Dornal — the Dirtwon."

"Him," the Slamboss's voice was full of contempt. "The Dirtwon. That diddli, crimpi bitti pog. He's shivanned dro the Bashi Rangles with that Gloami Kojer nebber Norsha, and that," Slamboss ground his teeth, "that goovi coiler, Necro."

He slammed his fist on the table.

"We shall yamp on the Gloami Kojers and shredd them to slep Hermiss Roshan."

The wooden screen went over with a crash. The two men at the table leapt to their feet upsetting the flagons of yoot wine across the maps spread out before them, as Norsha and Arnold sprang out, both shouting.

"You dredji shork!"

The Topwon collapsed in his chair, orange face draining to a dirty-pink. The Slamboss, however, flushed a deeper orange until the top of his bald head glowed like a beacon through his three green tinted strands of hair.

"I am the Hermiss Roshan. I was nocca snaffed," said Norsha.

"Garbers," bellowed the Slamboss. "You are a graftona, a nebber for the Gloami Kojers." He pointed a sausage-like finger at her features burned dark in the Cavern of the Sun. "Ibe her blusher — the crozmi Gloami tinjer."

"Pull the other, Slamboss," sneered Arnold, advancing to the table. "There are no Gloami Kojers. The Purple People don't exist. They are numdoo but a Talwon for twinkis. You hoked Replic Dornal to slyp to Dirt and you doosed your Lurci Flunkaj to morb me — out in the Bashi Rangles."

The Topwon looked at Necro, he eyes round. Now that his face had paled, Arnold thought how familiar it looked. The Topwon stuttered:

"Is all this crozmi, Necro? About the Gloami Kojers?"

The old magician had hobbled across the room and now sat on a stool in the corner. He looked at the ground and said nothing.

Slamboss bellowed. "He is too timpi to yurb. This Gloami Kojer nebber has him in her shredd, too."

Norsha leaned over the table towards the Topwon. She held out her hand. Something flashed in the light. It was her little jewelled mirror.

"Ibe this crist, O Topwon. It is the ringing freeb I had from Himsir Dornal. Do you recc it?"

The Topwon looked at the mirror. He nodded, but his face was still baffled.

"You are crozmi Hermiss Roshan?" he asked.

"Num," Slamboss's fist crashed on the table again. "She is a Gloami Kojer wanging to be Hermiss Roshan."

Necro rose wearily and stood at the table. But his voice was firm.

"Staccot, O Slamboss. Topwon, it is crozmi. We have shanxed dro the Prussy Peakers, we have dragged the Bashi Rangles, we have ibed the slam of Super Wimp and Mega Wump, we have rigged the morbi chimper of the Yurbusa, rigged the chomp of the Vasto Flork and ibed the grooso morb of the Vasto Shork. We have shanxed the Groobi Choob and dragged the sind of the Sizla, sef toccas sef dajs. We meho to scroll you — there are no Gloami Kojers. It is numdoo but a Talwon."

Slamboss was silent, but his face still glowed with fire, his teeth were clenched.

Necro went on: "And you Topwon are not crozmi Topwon. You are a Dirtwon shuffed for the crozmi Topwon who nimmo brees on Dirt."

"Hey, you mean my Dad is the real Topwon," gasped Arnold, as the pieces of the jigsaw fell into place in his mind.

"Ha," laughed Norsha. "So you are the crozmi Himsir — Replic Arnold."

"Yumda," said Necro, straightening his shoulders and staring down at the Slamboss. "Numdoo is what it wings. Topwon is not Topwon, Norsha the graftona is crozmi Hermiss Roshan."

He paused: "And Arnold is not crimpi, though he is diddli. He divved our brees, in the Groobi Choob. He rixed his bree to div my dredji skellers. If Dornal wigs not to meho to Klaptonia, we shall have a merri Replic in Arnold. Himsir Arnold can secc Dornal's loc."

As Necro spoke, Topwon shook his head and sat down shakily in his chair. Slamboss moved sideways to stand between Necro and the door. Necro went on.

"The crimpi, goovi won is me. For yexes I have liffed Slamboss with his hokes. Slamboss is the vasto hoke. He is not a luxon, but a grafton, his fawon was a plodder copping poor clodders. And he has passed his tocc for auto-snuff, but I have secced him in bree with the shreddi dosers I have freebed him."

Slamboss took a threatening step towards Necro, hand on knife, but Necro was unmoved.

"I have wigged. It is tremmed. No more dosers for you. In won yex you will auto-snuff, zinto."

Slamboss stretched out his hands as if to strangle Necro, then changed his mind.

"Gormers, all of you. You credd I will slep a wipper and a dima and a seeni coiler chimp me? Ha, my bladers have slyped to Dirt to cop Himsir Dornal. But Himsir Dornal will nocca doos this mondo. His morb in an umbro dib to div Hermiss Roshan will be grivved by all Klaptonia. I shall dool in his loc."

"You'll never get away with this," shouted Arnold.

"Huh, you shuff Replic. You and this shuff Hermiss. You shall morb too, along with this seeni slurder, Necro."

He raised his voice.

"Esco!"

The door burst open. Heavily armed crushers rushed in.

Arnold and Norsha swung round to the trap door. But as they did, two figures appeared on the steps below, grinning evilly. They were Hitman and Nobbin.

"Oh, sinters, Dadwon," said Nobbin. "Do I get to graf with the Diji Nan iron?"

Chapter 56

THE SCHOOL HALL was filling with teachers and parents, crowding round the table loaded with glasses of wine and plates of cheese. The celebration after the sports day and soccer final was getting underway. The Head, wine glass in hand, smiled sweetly at Councillor Edwards.

"Well, Oliver, that was a surprise, adjourning the Committee meeting. Shall we have to wait another week for a decision?"

"Don't you worry, Headmistress," said the grey-haired Councillor grinning at her from behind Edwards' back. "He can postpone the meeting as long as he likes, he'll never get a majority for closing the school now, not after his mates lost all that money."

"Money?" asked the Head innocently looking at the Committee Chairman who was busy in his mind sticking pins into a wax image of Arthur Stott.

"Her, her," he said, "just a private joke."

"Nothing private about it, Olly," said Arthur, "eh Nicky?" And he turned to the Councillor with the rimless glasses who was standing nearby. "Councillor Edwards's friends had laid anything up to fifty quid on your school coming bottom of the heap today."

He patted his pocket.

"Some of us, who backed the school, have been well rewarded. There's some justice left in the world. Heh, heh,"

Arthur chuckled. "Not bad eh, for one school. Won the final six-one, broke fourteen Olympic and World records in one afternoon."

"They'll have to be confirmed, of course, Arthur, you know," put in the Councillor with the yellow waistcoat. "They may be a bit of a fluke."

"A fluke," roared Arthur, making every head in the room turn. "The England team could do with a few flukes like that, I can tell you. Hey, there's Mr Radleigh. Come over here Joe."

Arnold's Dad made his way through the crowd. Funny, thought the Head, just now his face has the same faint orange flush. Must be something to do with excitement.

"You must be very proud of your son, Mr Radleigh," she said. "Don't you think so, Councillor Edwards?"

'Oily' Edwards smiled a sickly smile and decided to circulate amid the crowd and talk to other people. The circle round the Head began to exchange jokes and mutual congratulations. The Head looked again at Arnold's father. She hoped nothing was wrong. Arnold's sports successes were over the top. Was he taking something? She pushed the thought from her. Instead she thought of more pleasant things. Thanks to the kids, the blessed kids, the flash plan to flog the school had run out of steam. She was sure 'Oily' Edwards would think of something else, but for a while the school was safe and she had time to think.

She smiled at the people round her and began to make her way through the crowd, but she had gone only a few paces when there was a tremendous disturbance over by the door. There was shouting, people were turning with shock on their faces. She made her way there, quickly. Struggling in the doorway were a boy and girl still in their sports gear. Their faces were white with shock.

"Miss, Miss!"

"What is it Nicola?" demanded the Head.

"It's terrible. It just happened, out of the blue. We didn't believe it."

"What happened? Tell us, please."

The two gasped out their story.

"There were twenty of them. They came out of nowhere. They had weapons. Swords, daggers and things, like that."

"Swords?"

"Yeah, and they had green tunics, yeah and orange faces."

"And they came running over the playing fields and they . . ."

Nicola hesitated.

"Go on, what did they do."

"They cut the Games Master up outside the gym — and they dragged Arnold off. They've taken him somewhere."

"We must call the police," said Councillor Edwards, looking round wildly. But the Head was already running through the doorway, followed closely by Arthur and Arnold's Dad. As they ran across the yard, Mr Radleigh called:

"We need to be careful, these men are dangerous. I know."

The Head shot him a puzzled glance, but ran on. By the playing fields a crowd of third years was milling round.

"Dangerous or not, they're not doing things like that in this school," shouted the Head.

"Right on," answered Eenie, who fell smartly in behind her, followed by the Yobs. As the crowd of parents and pupils streamed up to the gym they saw in the distance the retreating figures of the attackers clambering over a wall, Dornal in their midst. From inside the gym came the sounds of groaning.

"Mr Boardman," called the Head, firmly. "Pull yourself together."

All at once the slithering slurping sound stopped and at the door appeared the battered figure of the Games

Master, completely reconstituted. He wobbled over to the Head.

"Oh, I feel terrible. They were diabolical. Horrible men with orange faces. I thought it was a crowd of jokers from another school, at first."

The Head looked the Games Master over briefly then turned to the crowd: "The question is, who are they? Where did they come from?"

Arnold's Dad stepped forward.

"I can explain, Headmistress, but I'm afraid you won't believe me."

The Head looked at him.

"After today, Mr Radleigh, I will believe anything."

He took a deep breath: "That was a raiding party of warriors from Klaptonia – yes I knew you wouldn't believe me – but it is true. They came to take back Dornal."

"Dornal?" The Head's eyes opened wide.

"Yeah, that's right." Sharon pushed her way through the crowd. "He was exchanged for Arnold. They must both be up there now."

The Head controlled herself: "But – how?"

"They beamed down from the other planet. They must be beaming up again now," said Arnold's Dad. "That raiding party makes me fear the worst."

"Can we stop them? Is there time?" asked the Head.

Mr Radleigh scratched his head. "If I remember . . . yes remember . . . I'll explain another time, the Beam, it stays open for ten or fifteen minutes – long enough to count to a thousand. The trouble is," he said hopelessly, "it's so long now I can't remember where the Beam comes down."

"I can, though," put in Sharon.

"You can?"

"Yeah, I was there, when Dornal landed and Arnold was taken off, though I didn't understand it at the time."

"Right on," said Eenie. "That telephone kiosk in the Arndale. That explains everything . . . well sort of."

"Let's get there and kill 'em," shouted Nicola.

"Right on," shouted the others.

"Too late, they'll be on their way up, now," said Arnold's Dad in despair.

"We need," said the Head decisively, "a 'punitive expedition'."

"I know," said Councillor Edwards, who had just arrived, "let's contact the SAS."

"No time for that," snapped the Head, "there's only one thing to do. Send 3H."

Chapter 57

THE GUARDS CHAINED Necro, Norsha and Arnold to the wall of the torture chamber and marched out. Hitman slowly stirred the coals in the brazier. As he worked the bellows, they glowed red, then white.

"Dadwon," slavered little Nobbin. "Can I have a dib. You yurbed I could have when I was wonti-too."

"You're not wonti-too. Not till the hando monz. Doolis are doolis, sonwon. I'm not won of your soggot Dadwons. I secc my yurb. I may be a bit obsi. But I credd in grafting dooli. You're not dulti enough to barbic kojers. It's wizzi graf."

"Ding a nimmot," said Arnold, "what's all this garber about barbic. There's no doob to barbic us. Slamboss reccs all he has to recc about us."

"That's staccot from you, Dirtwon," said Hitman. "Barbic is wizzi. You don't have to have a reason for it. A crozmi wizzer grafs sleccest when he's wingo. He can't graf to doosos."

He pulled out the glowing iron and blew on it, sending off a shower of sparks.

"Ooh, that's froobli and sindi. Yumda. I'm wingo now.
I've been wingo since yorni brecc, a-da. I recced there was sumdo wonzo about a-da, and nimmo I recc what it is. I'm going to make sumko pang for no derfer at all."

"Oh, Dadwon," breathed Nobbin reverently. "That was a crozmi dredji bonzer."

"Yum, sonwon," said Hitman, lumbering towards Arnold. "I was going to wonz with the Dirtwon, wasn't I? Or umpo Norsha. Num, she's Hermiss Roshan now. Well she atta be premi. I'll barbic her, then the Dirtwon, and secc streeki Necro till last." He hummed as he pushed the iron deeper into the brazier.

"You bonz, dimmo," said Norsha, "what occos to graftons who even yurb yarbi to a Replic, never mind barbic? There are wonti-fry yonco wiccas. Just bonz about that."

Hitman frowned.

"Did you yurb wonti-fry?" he asked. "I've got wonti-too in my Scroll."

"Nimmo, there are wonti-fry," said Norsha contemptuously. "I've hacked up tree zotti wons, while I've been eeroling you. So before you wonz, bonz. As you freeb, so shall you be freebed, but stacca, stacca."

"Don't eerol her, Dadwon. She's only dibbing to pang you. She knows how winzi you are. How a bitti doofer can aj your tem."

"Nibbic, sonwon, I'll just fold a nimmot, till I'm slecca."

Behind Hitman there was a battering at the door and little Nobbin ran to open it. Two guards marched in. Between them, half walking, half dragged was the Topwon. He had a black eye and his tunic was torn.

"Hey, what's happened to you?" asked Arnold.

Topwon shrugged: "I need my bumps feeling. I told the Slamboss what to do with his eerwego dooso, and he got annoyed."

"Good for you – er ..." began Arnold.

Topwon laughed shakily: "You could call me Dad, if you like Arnold. I mean I nearly was your Dad. You see, I was married to your Mum when it happened, but that was before you were born."

The guards pushed Topwon to the end of the wall, chained him next to Necro and marched out. The door clanged shut.

"Funny thing, son. I can call you son, can I in spite of everything?" said Topwon. "I'm not very proud of it, actually."

"Sure, go on," said Arnold encouragingly.

"You see, I was always mad on reading. Used to read any adventure, Tarzan, Superman, Batman and Robin, that bloke on Mars. Couldn't get enough of it. Well, when I was short of cash for books, I used to make up these adventures to entertain myself."

"Don't tell me. You invented this place called Klaptonia, where ..."

"That's it. Anyway, one day, not long after I got married, I was walking in the old shopping centre, where they had the Market. Do they still have the old Market, son? It was smashing, all sorts of stalls, second hand books, and all."

"Nah Dad, it's all gone. They bulldozed the lot, put an Arndale in. It's not the same at all."

"No respect for anything, have they, lad?"

Topwon turned to Norsha.

"Grovli Hermiss Roshan. Do excuse us. I haven't yurbled Dirt-way for yexes."

"You're not homesick, are you?" asked Arnold wonderingly.

"Not on your nelly, lad," said Topwon. "Why, compared with what I was pulling down on the railways, this is a doddle and all found. I do get a bit fed up with flork, though. I mean Topma's got 137 recipes but there are 364 dajs in a yex. Still I mustn't grumble. You make your bed, you lie on it."

"Hey, Dadwon," said Nobbin indignantly, "They're morbing tocca. They're doing it on waffer."

"No, ding a bitti," said Hitman. "I can bonz what they yurb. You wing you get narco with flork, Topwon. Well you atta dib wallocks — wallock soup, boiled wallocks, wallock salad, wallocks au gratin. You can go narco on wallocks. You luxons don't bonz at all."

"I've never bonzed," said Arnold, "why you don't have a mixed diet on Klaptonia, you know flork and wallocks for everyone."

"Why, that's sacrilege," put in Necro, who had been listening keenly. "that would change our way of life totally."

"I don't believe it," said Arnold, "do you Norsha?"

She smiled. "I'll try anything new. Like the Dirtwon's way of froobling. Though it seems quite fantastic, as though someone's made it up."

"Right on. Try something new," said Arnold, "and how about giving up this habit of cutting people up because they upset you. That's a rank turn off."

"Ding a nimmot, ding a nimmot," said Hitman. "You are a real juvi coiler. I can ibe what you're dibbing. You hank to morb our Klaptonia Breeli Tod. All this roobing about wallocks and flork, it was all stringing up to snuffing our Breeli Tod — nojo doofers like morbing and panging and — yum, I wyped — barbic."

He picked up the torturing iron and advanced on Arnold.

"I will wonz with you. I've wigged."

The white hot point was a foot away from Arnold's

chest and he felt the little hairs curl. He braced himself
to do something heroic, like spitting in Hitman's eye
when he realised that spitting was something he'd
never been very good at. He formed his lips into the
rudest word he could think of, when he saw that
Hitman's mind was on other things.

"What was that son?"

Nobbin put his head on one side. And now everyone
in the chamber was listening to the strange sounds
that floated down the stairway outside. From up above
came the sounds of battle, ferocious fighting. Shouts,
cries of pain, the clash of steel filled the air.

"Go and scan what it is son, while I todd on with
this."

Nobbin started for the door, but before he could
reach it the massive timbers shook and burst open.
The door flew back and hung drunkenly on its hinges.
Through the doorway fell half a dozen Klaptonian
crushers, sprawling among the rushes. Behind them
entered a huge scrum, a motley crew of boys, girls and
adults.

First came Dornal, face glowing orange over his
track suit, javelin in hand, fencing foil in the other,
Sharon wielding a hockey stick, Eenie with a length of
bicycle chain, Mo with a spear (or was it part of the
school railings?). Dad swept in with a vault pole
carried like a lance and this by accident or design
struck Hitman in his most private aspect.

"Oof" he cried and folded gently to the ground.

"Aaah, Dadwon," howled Nobbin as Nicola lifted him
by the ears.

The invaders snatched up keys and freed the
prisoners and they had gathered round rubbing
wrists and ankles, when there was a fresh commotion.
Topma in full crown and robes marched in
imperiously.

"What is this? Topwon and Replic shaccot. I clim a scroller."

She stopped, looked at Dornal, then Arnold, at Topwon, then Dad, and lastly at Sharon, then Norsha.

Then gracefully, she passed out.

Chapter 58

"NOW," SAID DORNAL, as Hitman, Nobbin and the crushers were shackled to the wall, "now for the real cause of the trouble."

"Right on," said Arnold, snatching up a sword from the floor.

"Slamboss," they all yelled and poured through the shattered door and up into the passages above. There they found detachments of 3H driving disarmed skullers, crushers and shredders before them, their wrists bound with sticky tape.

"Take them all to the City Square," called Dornal. "Harm no one who surrenders. Follow me you others."

A picked detachment, hurried down the network of stone corridors towards Necro's spell chamber, where reports said Slamboss and his bodyguard were making a stand. Back in the torture chamber, Topwon with Topma seated on his knee was gently fanning her back into consciousness and trying to explain to her what had happened.

As the assault team arrived at the open door of the

Spell Chamber Necro gave a cry of distress. The window was open and between door and window all was chaos, smashed retorts, ripped documents, broken casks. The room was empty save for two of Slamboss's men who lay on the floor.

"Poor old Clarence," cried Necro.

The faithful snake had taken toll of the attackers, but now lay still under the Magic Table, the top of which was cracked and splintered. The snake slowly raised its bruised head, and Necro smiled in relief then turned to the shattered Mirror.

"No means of seeing where they have gone," he said.

"We can stop them at the city gates," said Dornal.

The old magician shook his head.

"There are too many escape routes, I know. I arranged them."

He looked shamefaced at Dornal.

"Forgive me, Nurbul Replic. I thought I knew best. That was why I had the Breeli Doser, so that I could live on and preserve wisdom from one generation to another. But you young people know better than I do. Men like Slamboss should not be trusted. Those who want to take charge of everything should not be allowed in charge of anything. And those who help them are just as guilty."

"Where will he go?" asked Norsha.

"Into the wastes of the Bashi Rangles."

"We shall hunt him down, then," declared Dornal.

Necro shook his head.

"Why trouble? Within a year, he will auto-snuff. The damage he has done here is for one purpose — to find the secret potion of Life.

"He thought I kept it hidden here. But the fool does not know that the secret potion can be brewed from wallock roots. All that is needed is the formula, and that," he tapped his head, "is here."

"If that's so, why not give it to everyone?" asked Arnold.

"Ha," said Necro. "I would not wish immortality on a pog!"

"OK," said Sharon, "what happens next, when things are cleared up? What are you going to do, Dornie boy?"

"The first thing," said Dornal, "is to disband the bladers. Thanks to Norsha and Arnold, we know there is no Gloami Kojer menace and there is no need for the Dongon, now."

"Be careful, O Replic," said Necro, "what will so many bladers do with their time, in future, with no useful occupation."

"Ah, poor little bladers," said Mo sympathetically.

"I know what," said Sharon, "we've got a spare Games Master. I somehow think he may be looking for a job. He can look after them."

She deepened her voice.

"Come on you lot, let's be having you. Out in the Bashi Rangles."

All laughed and streamed out of the Spell Chamber and headed through the Shotto to the City Square. Sharon and Dornal, Arnold and Norsha walked arm in arm. As they entered the Square, a thunderous cheer went up from the waiting crowds.

Dornal turned to Arnold.

"There's a thought now," he said. "Would anybody notice, if you stayed here, and I beamed back to Dirt?"

Arnold grinned.

"Not now."

Now you are triggo to bonz your Klaptonian

YURB LIST

A

Abno	Unhealthy
acco	agree, OK
a-da	today
affi	nice
afto	behind, after-ward
aj	upset, arouse
aji	nervous
arble	persuade
arbi	arrogant
argle	scream
atta	must, should
auto-snuff	self-destruct

B

barbic	torture
bego	go, depart
bingi	lucky
bitti	small
blinki	tearful
blinki-twinki	cry-baby
bliz	snow
blosser	flower, blossom
blunt	wrong, incor-rect
blusher	face
bonce	head
bonzer	mind, thought
bonzot	school
compo-bonzot	comprehensive school
yoggo-bonzot	private school
boot	manage
brand	name
brecc	morning
bree	life, breath, air
Breeli Tod	Way of Life
breeli	alive
breez	miss
bricca	wall
bulko	fat

C

carbi	black
cham	room
champ	win, beat
champed	beaten
champi	victorious
charc/ charcer	burn/fire
charco	burned
chex	test, proof, clue
chib	cave
chimper	joke
chimpi	mischievous
chimple	snigger
chooner	coat, jacket
chossy	confused, chaotic
Choob	Tunnel
chumble	eat
chumb	meal
chumber	food
clim	demand
cloot	clothes
coiler	snake
cop	take, arrest
compo	together, com-prehensive
comper	friend
credd	believe, trust
crimpi	cringing
crisper	salt
crist	mirror
cristi	clear
cristing	clearing
crozmi	true, truly
cubber	bucket

D

dap	row(boat)
daj	day
dajis	days
dang	hang
danglers	hangings
darlo	dear, darling
derfo	because
derfer	reason
dib	attempt
diddli	cunning, devious
didjer	number
dilli	late
dima	girl, maid
ding	wait, stay
div	rescue
doddo	slowly
dong	strike, blow
donger	soldier
dongon	army
doo	perform, performance
doob	need
doobic	urgent
doocum	invitation
doolis	rules, instructions
dooler	ruler
dooli	every
dooliwon	everyone
doolus	advice
doople	ask, request
doos	give order
dooso	order, command
dopa	emergency
doser	dose, potion
dosh	bath
drag	long, last
Drago Soggon	Long River
dredji	despicable
dro	through
dulti	mature, grown up
dumper	chest, box
dunn	doubt, not believe
duplic	twin

E

eelie	evasive
eerwego	mobilise
eerwego-dooso	mobilisation order
eezer	chair
esco	guard
exo	get out!
expo	outside

F

fanz	fancy, wish for
finkle	suspect, suspicion
finner	fish
finni	suspicious
flake	skin
flatt	lie down
fliccot	sudden suddenly
flocc	plains
flomp	fall
flump	fail
flunker	servant
flunker-dima	maid-of-all-work
flunkaj	service
flutt	twitch
fold	sit down
fonz	hope
fonti	optimistic
foss	cross
frang	brought
fratch	worry, bother
freeb	give, gift
freebon	sacrifice
fresci	loose, free
frij	freeze, cold

fring	fetch, bring	hando	near, next
frooble	make love	hank	want
froober	sweetheart	heel	follow
froobli	lovely	Hermiss	Princess
froota	orchard	Himsir	Prince
fylo	dismiss	hinkle	suggest, insinuate

G

		hissers	shame
		hoke	trick, deception
ganner	greed	Hoker	Magician
garber	rubbish	hoki	deceptive
gid	mount (horse)	hoko	rigged, fixed
glib	drip	hokot	disguised
glinti	fine, beautiful	hosto	enemy
gloami	purple	hulko	huge
glob	drop		
glom	warm		
glug	drown	**I**	
gora	blood, bloody		
goral	heart	iball, ibe	see
goron	family	inco	come in
gormer	wally	incwi	nosey
gormi	stupid	impo	inside
gorner	fist	immo	soon
goover	traitor	inslam	invade, invasion
goovi	treacherous		
graf	work, task	**J**	
grafton	worker		
graftona	woman worker	jabber	dagger
grav	ground	jacc	hurry, run
gravved	floored	jacco	quickly
grid	get rid of	jenko	know all
griv	mourn	jotto	simply
grooso	horrible, horribly	juvi	young
grov	respect	**K**	
grovel	submission, apology		
		kojer	being, person
grovli	please		
gru	monster	**L**	
gruj	hate		
		liff	help
		lobber	ball
H		loc	place, find
		looma	night
hack	invent	loomi	dark
hander	nearer		

284

loop	surround
lurc	hide
lurco, lurci	secret
Lurci Flunkaj	Secret Service
lux	like, enjoy, please
luxon	aristocrat

M

ma-da	tomorrow
magnolious	generous
meds	fields
meho	return
merri	worthy
miggi	mean, stingy
ming	mix, involve
misti	magic, mysterious
Misti-Crist	Magic Mirror
Misti-Sticcer	Magic Sword
mondo	planet
moblot	division
mol	search
morb	kill, die, murder
murg	mist

N

nacc	faint
nacho	normal
narco	boring, bored
nebber	spy
nibbed	pegged, tied
nibbic	exactly
nicc	point
nid	nod
nimmo	now
nimmot	minute
nocca	never, not
nojo	important
nosla	peace
nuffle	humour
nuffi	funny, ridiculous

num	no
Numda	Oh no!
numdo	doubtless
numdoo	nothing
numko	no one
numpo	impossible
numti	careless
numyur	refuse, refusal
nurbul	noble
nybi	invisible

O

oba	revenge
obsi	old-fashioned
occ	chance
occa	ever
occo	happen, happening
occi	magic, spell
occul	wise
oko	admit
oodo	unable
ooti	empty

P

pallog, plog	gallop
pat	kick
pats	feet
patters	stairs
piccers	hands
piccle	handle
pinn	choose, choice
pitso	below
pog	K1, pig
poggi	foul
pogser	mess
porc	lie
poz	side
pozzi	spot on
prussy	blue
Prussy Peakers	Blue Mountains
puzzler	question

R

raji	brave, daring
rangle	swampland
raspo	harsh, tough
recc	know, knew
reechers	arms
reggo	always
Replic	son
Replica	daughter
reppi	famous
rev	turn
rig	escape
ringed	married
rix	risk, danger
rol	round, around
roob	chat, talk
rooble	discuss
roobing	meeting

S

sa-looma	tonight
scan	look, study, watch
scim	plan, plot
scroll	explain, tell, show
scroller	answer
secc	hold
seeni	old
seppo	without, except
shacc	lock
shaccot	locked, imprisoned
shanx	march, travel, journey
shanxer	traveller
sharp	right, correct
shelto	safe, secure
shim	climb
shivann	vanish
shotto	palace
shuff	exchange, change
shredd	power

shreddi	powerful
Shrefful	Mighty One
shuff	exchange
sicco	nasty
siccers	fury, furious
sigger	signal
sindi	hot
sind	heat
singo	alone
sinters	brilliant
Sizdo	West
sizla	sun
Sizzup	East
skellers	bones
skimp	jump
slaff	absurd
slam	fight, attack
slammer	warrior
slamber	ambush
Slamboss	Games, Battle-Master
slecc	good
slecca	better
slep	set free, let go
sluff	calm
slume	twilight
slurd	slime
slurder	toad
slurg	creep, crawl
slyp	transport
Slypa	Magic Beam
snobbot	conceited
snaff	kidnap
snuff	die
socca	sometimes
sogger	rain, shower
soggon	river
soggot	lax, sloppy
spang	light
spango	shining
spangs	shines
spanger	window
stacc	more
stacca	plenty, many
staccot	enough
starco	bare

286

sticcer	sword
stitcher	needle
streeki	thin
string	lead
sumdo	something
sumko	someone
sumloc	somewhere
swib	sweep

T

taccas	thanks
Talwon	Tale, Legend
tanji	orange
tanjer	sky
tem	mood
tentoo	careful, cared for
timm	tree, door
timmon	forest
timp	fear
timpi	afraid
tinjer	colour
toccas	times
toppo	official
Topwon	King
Topma	Queen
Topwondom	Kingdom
todd	go, walk
todder	road
toosers	twice
tosh	throw
tranc	quiet, be quiet
tremm	end
triggo	ready
trinkers	toys
tring	take, send
twinki	baby, child

U

umbro	helpless
umpo	maybe
umdoo	anything

V

vasto	huge
vaster	giant
verd	grass, green

W

waf	wind
waffer	purpose
wallock	KI parsnip
wang	fantasy, pretend
wangi	crazy
wango	fantastic
werfo	why
wicca	punishment
wicci	bad, naughty
wif	breeze
wig	judge, decide
wilber	forecast
wingo	inspired
wing	imagine
winkle	insinuate
winzi	sensitive
wipper	boy
wizzi	skilful, clever
wizz	skill, craft
wonz	begin
wonzo	first, special
wumpa	mile
wyp	forget

Y

yacca	greeting
ya-da	yesterday
yarbon	curse, sworn
yarbi	rude
yay	cheer, hail
yex	year
yogg	pay
yoggle	KI coin
yamp	march (army)
yampo-compo	marching order

yoggler	ransom	yurm	sing
yondi	away	yurmer	song
yondo	distant		
yonc	difference	**Z**	
yonco	different, strange		
		zalter	cliff
Yoohoo	Proclamation	zalto	serious
yorni	early	zalti	lofty
yum	yes	Zalti Yurbon	Great Council
Yumda	Oh yes	zinto	at once
yurb	word	zitto	of course
yurble	speak	zizz	sleep
Yurbi Cham	Council Chamber	zizzer	bedtime story
		zizzot	sleeping
Yurbon	Council	zoff!	get out!
yurbot	request	zotti	new, unusual
yurbul	language	zupp	tie up